THE LAST WORDS OF
MADELEINE ANDERSON

THE LAST WORDS OF MADELEINE ANDERSON

Helen Kitson

2019
Louise Walters Books

The Last Words of Madeleine Anderson
by Helen Kitson

Produced and published in 2019
by Louise Walters Books
Reprinted 2020

ISBN 978 1 999 7809 5 1
eISBN 978 1 999 7809 6 8

Typeset in PTSerif 11pt by Blot Publishing

Printed and bound in Great Britain by Clays Ltd, Elcograf S.p.A.

louisewaltersbooks.co.uk

info@louisewaltersbooks.co.uk

Louise Walters Books
PO Box 755
Banbury
OX16 6PJ

This book is dedicated to Allister, who might read it.
Also to Jane and Josef, who probably won't.

CHAPTER ONE

The sender of the letter I held in my hands had signed herself Madeleine, and how could she possibly have known how deeply that name would affect me? I felt the world around me cease to spin, a jumble of memories tumbling out from a cupboard stuffed with junk: balding teddy bears, cassette tapes with handwritten labels, pens with shattered nibs, yellowed birthday cards, dice from board games long since binned, luggage labels, school ties, smooth pebbles, broken jewellery, pictures torn from magazines. Reminders of people loved, admired, lusted over, despised. Names that no longer meant a thing, others that were invisibly tattooed on the fragile skin on the insides of my wrists.

Not difficult to imagine the grief, the tears, the unctuous if heartfelt outbursts of emotion along the "taken from us too young" lines Madeleine's death occasioned. My best friend since our first day at school. Dead at twenty-two. Her light snuffed out, at peace with the angels, *et cetera*. Mutely I accepted the commiserations, the clasping hands, the condolence cards littered with silver crosses and embossed lilies. Worse for her parents, of course. Like me, Madeleine had been an only child; unlike me, brilliant, brimming with that vague quality called potential.

1

Grief fades, but bombs leave black craters that can never entirely be filled. Weeks, months went by when I didn't give Madeleine more than a passing thought, though she was never entirely absent from my mind. But the letter, signed Madeleine, was enough to invoke that well-remembered face, and for too long I remained in my armchair, unable to summon up the will to move, to switch on a light, to eat.

The letter was similar to others I'd received in dribs and drabs over the past twenty-odd years:

Dear Ms Price,

I'm sure you must get letters like this all the time, and I apologise for adding to their number. I first read your novel when I was 17. I was a typically intense, literary teenager, in love with Sylvia Plath, Virginia Woolf, and green-spined Virago Modern Classics. I came across your book quite by accident in the library – I couldn't even tell you what drew me to it, and I can't explain what it means to me without gushing like a crazy fangirl!

I've never written a fan letter before (I'm sure every-one makes that claim) and I'm not sure why I felt compelled to do so now, except that I came across your book when I was packing up my stuff (first home of my own – can't really afford it, but I've got to move out sometime and it's about time my parents had the place to themselves!). I picked it up and found myself rereading it straight through, unable to tear myself away.

Once again I was blown away by the sheer power of the story, the beauty of the language, and I fell in love with literature all over again. I just wanted you to know that the power of your novel reverberates and will never stop.

With very best wishes,

Madeleine

Generally my correspondents were PhD students, or would-be writers asking if they could send me their manuscripts. This one asked for nothing, not even an autograph; nor did she expect a reply, though a return address label had been sloppily affixed to the back of the envelope. I was intrigued, and not just because of her name. The letter arrived at a point in my life when my early literary fame was not even a hazy memory for most people. One novel to my name – one, and one only.

Unable to repeat the trick, I'd long since been written off as a one-hit wonder, albeit that one hit had been enough, at the time, for reviewers to declare it a "master-piece" of "extraordinary vision".

'One might almost,' one reviewer speculated, 'be tempted to pronounce it a work of genius.'

Naturally they clamoured for more, and I dined out quite comfortably on this early success for a couple of years until the novelty wore off and I was dismissed as another literary fluke: a thrilling one night stand, but clearly not a stayer. A tease, in fact. The fairy dust settled and I retreated, the heavy gilded doors to the literary world closing on me until such time as I could present it with another glorious offering.

One gets over every disappointment eventually, or learns to live with it. Unable to settle to regular employment, I took a succession of part-time jobs, more or less unsatisfactory, before I found what I must think of as my niche. My current job – housekeeper, cleaner and cook for a vicar – was a good fit and I was tolerably content in a minor-key sort of way.

Madeleine's letter arrived on the doormat like a flare from another world.

Dear Madeleine,

Thank you for your letter. I receive so few "proper" letters these days. It's heartening to know my solitary novel is still being read and enjoyed. Literature has always been, for me, a solace and a source of wonder, but I sometimes think I would have retained my sense of wonder rather better had I not felt compelled to make my own contribution. The weight of expectation – publishers and readers too eager for a second novel – did rather crush me, the result being my well-documented literary constipation.

People tell me I've secured a kind of immortality and that some of the greatest writers are remembered primarily for a single book (one thinks of Lolita, Vanity Fair, The Great Gatsby) that soars above the rest; not to mention the number of writers who only ever produced one novel (you can supply the titles as well as I).

Still, I would feel a fraud to describe myself as a writer and I rarely give the book much thought, so it's nice to discover that it has a life of its own, independent of me.

I broke off, unsure how to continue, conscious of speaking too much of myself, yet what else could I write about? "Madeleine" had told me hardly anything about

4

herself, and to ask questions would be to invite a correspondence she didn't necessarily want. (Did *I*? Hard to say. I had a few acquaintances, a job; even, until six months ago, a lover; but since the death of Madeleine – *my* Madeleine – I'd always felt a sort of spiritual loneliness.)

If I didn't finish the letter now, I knew I never would. It would remain on my writing desk, one of those little jobs one means to get round to but never quite manages. The longer I left it, the harder it would be to complete, the less urgent it would become, until eventually it would be swept into the waste bin along with ancient cheque stubs, dentist reminder letters, bus tickets and all the other administrative detritus one hangs on to for no good reason.

Perhaps what I'd written thus far would suffice. I had, indeed, written far more – and rather more candidly – than I had in response to the first flurry of letters I'd received when the book was published.

Back in those golden days I treated unsolicited correspondents with a kind of patronising tolerance, accepting praise, the gushing insistence that my book had "spoken to them personally" as my right, responding with a few scribbled lines of thanks and, in the case of would-be writers, advice on how to find a literary agent. I cringe now – of course I do! – at how little thought I gave to those people who'd been moved enough to put pen to paper. How had I dared to dismiss them so readily? Yet it wouldn't do to attempt to atone for the scant interest I'd shown in the lives of my admirers by writing an inappropriately lengthy letter to Madeleine.

Therefore I added a couple of lines wishing her all the best and thanking her for taking the time to write. Trite, commonplace words. I added a PS: *Hope you've settled into your new home*, which struck a false note. It would have to do. I'd post it when I went to work.

My employer was not one of those modern, enthusiastic clergymen. He would have been ill at ease in an urban landscape and once frankly admitted he had more in common with Trollope's gentle Septimus Harding than with the type of priest who wants to change the world or, at the very least, get his face on *Songs of Praise*. He hired me, I believe, because of a shared fondness for the books of Barbara Pym. When I turned up for the interview, he excused himself to take a phone call and I occupied myself in browsing his bookshelves. He returned to find me with his copy of *Some Tame Gazelle* in my hands. Once he knew I was a fan, references and relevant prior experience no longer seemed to matter. He would be my timid curate and I his excellent woman. Not, I hasten to add, that there was so much as an atom of romantic, let alone sexual, frisson in our relationship. We suited each other, that's all. I poached eggs the way he liked them, didn't pester him to update his soft furnishings, and never, ever gossiped. I wasn't even a member of his congregation, or any other.

The vicarage was spot-on Barbara Pym. A rustic kitchen, lots of chintz, everything with the faded patina of upper-middle-class shabbiness that can't be faked. It was a family home, far too big for the unmarried vicar.

My duties were to cook his lunch and prepare evening meals for him to heat up later; he would delve into the freezer for one of the labelled plastic tubs of Bolognese sauce or stew I cooked in big batches. I saw to his washing, gave everything a dust and a vacuum, and generally looked after him. Not a demanding job, but it suited me. I could imagine pottering around that kitchen when I was well into my seventies, for my vicar wasn't the ambitious type and would likely remain there until he ended up on the wrong side of a funeral.

It was one of those glorious September days that provide the backdrop for every pretty costume drama, every gauzily imagined Edwardian picnic. The lazy drone of bees; the sense of outwitting autumn for a few weeks more.

When I took his lunch in to the study, the vicar removed his specs and smiled. 'Ah, the redoubtable Miss Price.' The same actions and words every day. 'And how are you today?'

'Fine, thank you, Mr Latham.' Neither of us had ever suggested we ditch the formalities and address each other by our Christian names. While I was Miss and he was Mr, the proper boundary was maintained: our relationship friendly, but rarely confidential. Today I rather regretted this, thinking it might have been nice to discuss my letter with someone. But, after all, what was there to say? Another reminder of how my star had burned out; cause, at most, for a few wistful reminiscences.

In my sensible shoes and striped cotton tabard, I looked more like a school dinner lady than a feted novelist.

Mr Latham sat in a leather chair of the substantial type that put me in mind of headmasters and private doctors. The window next to him stood ajar. A breeze tickled the net curtain, the leaves of a Japanese bean tree gently bumping against the glass. His long, bony fingers replaced the lid on a fountain pen.

I'd laid the tray with a lace-edged cloth, just as he liked it, the cutlery wrapped in a linen napkin. There was always a dessert course, fresh fruit salad in summer and fruit pie the rest of the year. Absurd, perhaps, but I was pleased he wasn't the type of man who was content with cheese and pickle sandwiches and paper towels. Standards must be maintained.

Occasionally he chatted to me on neutral topics, rarely evincing much interest in my life. I didn't mind; I'd had enough of people expressing concern for my welfare. From time to time Mr Latham and I talked about books; he was aware of mine, but we rarely spoke of it. I didn't even know if he'd read it. Ultimately, though, he was my employer, and friendship would have complicated a relationship that was satisfactory as it was. If he showed little concern for my general happiness and well-being, neither did he attempt to pry into a life that was, from choice, as buttoned-up as a winter coat.

'Such splendid weather!' he was moved to exclaim when I brought in his slice of apple and blackberry pie.

'Yes, indeed. I'm always a little sad when all the flowers die off, so a bit of sun makes up for the lack of colour.' This wasn't me speaking, it was "Miss Price": the part I played; an analgesic against the world outside, by which I mean the past and the uncertain future and all the knotted threads of my life. If I often found it hard to tear myself away from the vicarage, this was simply because it represented a calmer, more ordered world, where I briefly felt secure.

Back at home I made a desultory attempt on my own housework. I lived in a cottage, but not a roses round the door job; a more mundane ex-council affair. I daresay it was originally built as a family home, in days when families were large and toilets were outside. It had been modernised (fitted kitchen, indoor toilet and bathroom suite) and given the romantic name of Honeysuckle Cottage. Like my job, it suited me, its fey charm not quite eradicated by twentieth century builders.

Madeleine and I had often talked about sharing a house; our tastes were so alike, and we shared an appreciation of beautiful objects. Ah, Madeleine, how you would have wrinkled your nose at my avocado bathroom suite, my MDF bookcases, my easy-iron sheets! But you would have approved, I think, of my careless housekeeping, my mismatched crockery, the stray cat who'd become a permanent fixture on the sofa. Never fond of cats, I'd allowed Pushkin to wheedle her way into my home and my affections to the point where I'd become almost oblivious to the fans of black fur on the carpet, and provided her with expensive pouches of cat food. It seemed I was destined to become that modern cliché, the crazy cat lady.

Six author copies of my novel sat in a box under my bed and I kept a reading copy in the kitchen, next to the cookery books. Months passed without me giving it a second glance. It was considerably less dog-eared than the cookbooks.

I made a pot of tea, buttered a scone and sat at the kitchen table with the book open in front of me. Dedicated to Madeleine, it was, from a purely aesthetic point of view, a lovely object. The publishers gave the first thousand copies a cloth binding, gold lettering in an old-fashioned gothic script, and all editions featured pen-and-ink illustrations by a well-known artist. Even the paper was special – thick, creamy, with a raised rib. An object to be handled as well as read.

Reading random paragraphs, I stumbled across lines I'd forgotten, images that still struck me as fresh and surprising. A second book, surely, would have been an anti-climax after this fluke, this freak of literature! No matter. There would be no second book. I was the mayfly with gaudy wings who lived beautifully for a matter of days; the brief double rainbow; the fleeting moment of grace. But I hadn't died or disappeared. To have melted into nothing-ness... As far as the world was concerned I'd done precisely that, or as good as. Still here, but living in shadows.

A second letter from Madeleine arrived two weeks after the first.

What a treat to receive your letter! she wrote. *I never really expected a reply, to be honest. I felt a fool as soon as I'd posted it. Would have written back sooner, but am now in my new place, still getting everything straight, letters forwarded to me by my parents, when they remember!*

It's kind of weird in a way to think of writers – I mean great writers – having ordinary lives. I suppose many of them didn't (Genet, Wilde, etc), but I just can't imagine how you can tear yourself away from the lives you've created in beautiful prose to return to the mundane world. Same with reading, I suppose – being torn away from fictional worlds that often feel more realised than so-called real life.

Sorry, I'm rambling, and my prose is horrible! Writing this in a bit of a hurry! You probably won't believe it, or won't care, but I have literary ambitions myself – very modest ones, and I promise I'm not one of those rude, ungracious people who pesters authors to read their precious manuscript or anything like that!

It would just be good, if you could bear it, if I could talk to you now and then about literature. I'll be honest and say that I'd like to learn from you, but obviously I totally understand if you think what I'm asking is a huge imposition. Anyway, return address at the top of the page, and it would be really lovely to hear from you again sometime.

All best wishes,

Madeleine

P.S. Okay, this is crazy, but I always felt like your book was meant for me, because it's dedicated to a Madeleine. Your sister? One day, maybe you'll tell me about her.

CHAPTER TWO

Thus began a correspondence that lasted from September until December, when Madeleine made a tentative suggestion that we might meet up. A friendly overture after a series of letters in which she'd expressed some sharp observations about the state of modern literature that made me feel her intellectual inferior.

Letters weren't too bad; I had time to ponder my responses, even research the books and critics she mentioned. Meeting me in person could only be a disappointment. Denied the necessary time to structure my sentences, I feared I would panic, saying the first thing that popped into my head, however ridiculous. Better for Madeleine to hang on to her illusions, for if we met she would surely expect a "personality": a Virginia Woolf or a Dorothy Parker. Thus I put her off with pretend commitments, until a point was reached where I had exhausted every possible exit route, and to continue to fob her off would have looked like rudeness.

Then, where would we meet? She lived some fifty miles east of me – not an insurmountable distance, but was the correct thing to suggest we meet up at some convenient midpoint, or would she expect me to travel to her? And if she travelled to me, I would feel even more compelled to be the person she wanted me to be; and if

I let her down, she would rightly feel her time and money had been wasted.

Madeleine anticipated my reservations; some of them, at least. She wrote to say she was planning to visit Shropshire to research the writer Mary Webb with a view to post-grad study.

All very up in the air at the moment, she wrote, *but as I'll be in your neck of the woods anyway, it would be a shame if we couldn't get together. I don't want to sound like a mad stalker, but my PhD subject (if I get that far!! You know what funding's like these days) is long dead, and it'd be great to meet a living writer!*

So we agreed on a date, time and venue, and exchanged phone numbers in case of last-minute emergencies or weather-related delays.

For once the forecasters were correct. They predicted snow and it fell steadily during the evening before the day on which I was due to meet Madeleine. Several times I tried to phone her, but each time the phone kept ringing and didn't even go through to voicemail. Surely she would never risk travelling in such uncertain weather. If the reports were accurate, the snow would continue to fall for another twenty-four hours. No one quite believed it; it was a good ten years since a disruptive amount of snow had fallen in our part of the world. Nevertheless, I felt it prudent to warn her that she ran a real risk of getting snowed in. I told myself she'd check the weather before setting off.

Hearing nothing back from her, I had to assume she was still intending to visit. I slung my green Kånken over my shoulder, Pushkin watching me with the level of disinterest only a cat can muster.

'Shan't be long,' I assured her, having never been able to kick the habit of speaking to her as if she understood every word.

I was to meet Madeleine in a café – the quaint "Ye Olde Tea Shoppe" kind I hoped she'd find amusing. The sort of place where you can also purchase expensive silver-and-turquoise art jewellery made by a local craftsperson, and packets of every type of fruit and herbal tea imaginable. It wasn't a place I frequented often, though whenever I did I always felt an urge to join the Women's Institute or take up knitting. These urges tended to fade immediately I left the café.

I trudged through snow already several inches deep. I couldn't believe Madeleine would turn up, but no one needed to know I was waiting for someone, nor would they assume I'd been stood up when my companion failed to arrive. I'd have a coffee, read the paper, then leave.

A couple of tables were occupied, but my favoured seat nearest the window was free. If the conversation dragged, we could pretend to be transfixed by the view of the steadily falling snow. I wasn't sure why I'd arranged to meet her here. I could have invited her to my house, but I would have felt uncomfortable; I was so little used to visitors.

I'd deliberately arrived ten minutes early to give myself time to settle, to prepare myself for what had come to seem like a big deal. And yes, ridiculous as it sounds, the fact that Madeleine shared her name with my one great friend – the platonic love of my life, if you will

– was a significant factor in the state of my nerves. It wasn't, after all, a particularly common name.

The inevitable cappuccino ordered, I sat back and took a deep breath, telling myself she was probably as nervous as I, but hoping not, for the conversation would flow more easily if at least one of us felt relaxed.

The hands of the clock on the wall hit twelve. Any moment now... As if everyone's watch were synchronised! As if she were really going to come.

I tried to avoid looking again at the clock, and when I finally sneaked a glance I saw it was nearly ten past. Surely, by now... I'd give it another ten minutes then assume the weather had defeated her.

And then a lone person entered the café, but not a young woman. A stupidly handsome man of twenty-three or so with a rucksack walked over to my table, hands stuffed in the pockets of his faded jeans, a diffident smile on the prettiest male face I'd ever seen.

'You wouldn't by any chance be Gabrielle Price?' A deep voice, pleasing to the ear.

My heart literally skipped a beat. 'I am,' I admitted.

He bit his lower lip with enviably even white teeth. 'I think you might be waiting for me.'

Confused as much by his clear blue eyes and male-model cheekbones as by what he said, I shook my head.

He slid on to the chair opposite me, dropped the rucksack next to his feet, and sat with his hands clasped on the table.

'This is awkward,' he said. 'I mean, obviously I knew this would happen, but...'

I continued to gape at him, wondering what twilight zone I'd fallen in to.

He gave a low, tentative laugh. 'Thing is, I'm Madeleine. I mean, I pretended to be. Your book's dedicated to a Madeleine, and I thought maybe you'd be less likely to dismiss me as some kind of—' Palms turned up, a helpless gesture that couldn't fail to appeal. 'And I thought if you knew I was a bloke, you'd be suspicious – you know – not want to meet me.'

It was an explanation of sorts, but I remained confused. Why go to so much trouble? It seemed bizarre at best and I was glad I hadn't arranged to meet "Madeleine" at my house. And I will admit, had he been an unattractive man in his fifties, I'd probably have walked straight out. I did no such thing because this young man's beauty left me stunned.

He held out his hand and grinned. 'I'm Simon.'

I stared at the hand, afraid the simple act of touching his skin across the café table would propel me into the merciless pit of unrequited love (lust, if you prefer, but the end result is much the same).

He cocked his head to one side, tossing his blond fringe away from his eyes. 'Shake hands? Please?'

I could have laughed the matter off, told him to think nothing of it. Instead, I put my hand in his, feeling as if I'd handed over my life to him.

Another soft, diffident laugh. 'Guess I'd better order something.'

'Guess you had.'

Hands cradling my cooling cup, I watched the waitress take his order, her manner very different from when she'd taken mine. Unfair, of course, that youthful beauty should be so bewitching, the rest of us invisible courtiers to these princelings and princesses. We're programmed

16

to admire things and people that please our eyes, so I didn't resent the attention the waitress paid to my companion, irritated only by the fact that she probably assumed I was his mother. I was about the right age. The thought depressed me beyond reason. Simon was here only because I'd written a novel he admired, but I was vain enough to mind being written off as an unthreatening middle-aged woman by a slip of a girl with a ladder in her tights and wrinkles in her tiny black skirt.

I'm sure I didn't imagine the extra wiggle she put into her walk when she finally consented to leave our table. I gazed at Simon evenly.

'She fancies you. I expect you're used to that.'

A quick shrug. 'Not my type.'

'Look, Simon, this is a most peculiar situation we find ourselves in and I still don't understand your need for subterfuge. Or, indeed, what it is you want from me.'

'Exactly what I said in my letters. I really *am* thinking about studying for a PhD in literature, but I decided to take a year out to write a novel – or try to.'

'Oh. I *see*.'

He shook his head. 'I'm not being romantic about it, honestly. I'll give it a year. If it doesn't happen, I'll draw a line under the idea and settle down to being an academic, or get a proper job if the funding doesn't work out.'

'That's very... single-minded of you.'

'If I'm to be a writer, it's got to be now or never. I'm not the type to spend the whole of my life writing unpublishable novels and getting more and more depressed about it. All or nothing.'

'And you want my advice, I suppose? My pearls of literary wisdom?'

Again that endearing gesture of biting down on his lower lip. Finally, 'That would be presumptuous. If, in any way, I could assist you in resuming your writing career—'

'Oh, please! My day has been and gone.'

He frowned. 'No, really.'

Was he offering himself as inspiration, amanuensis, writing partner? I pushed my cup away.

'There are already far too many books on the market.'

'Yeah, and most of them are rubbish, if you want my opinion.'

I wasn't sure I did.

'This is a nice village,' he said, taking a sugar cube from the bowl on the table and crunching it in his mouth. 'It's oldy-worldy, but not chocolate box. Is it a large village or a small town? Either way, it feels real.'

'What would *you* know about chocolate boxes with pictures on them?' The only one I'd ever seen was the one my grandmother had used to store her jewellery.

He looked at me blankly. 'It's just an expression. The sort of pictures you get on greetings cards for old people.'

I sensed he was playing a role, although to what purpose I couldn't guess.

'It's not only the elderly who are seduced by the twee and the sentimental,' I said. 'Go around any stately home and eventually you'll hit the gift shop – pictures of the house printed on everything from erasers to chocolate wrappers, and very nasty and expensive they are too.'

'Oh, well.' A surly shrug. 'Heritage is big business, isn't it? God knows why, though. Most of the people buying gift shop tat would have been boot boys and kitchen maids if they'd been around two hundred years ago.'

He had some intelligence – he was a graduate, after

all – and I had the awed respect for intellectual endeavour shared by many intelligent people who've missed out on a university education. But was he a *good* person, at heart? I was finding it hard to see beyond his angelic face, the casually-rumpled blond hair, his smooth skin and elegant fingers. I would have been more open with him if he'd looked ordinary. If I weren't careful, I would say something regrettable and make a fool of myself. I'd known where I was with Russell, my ex. This was different territory entirely.

I caught the attention of the waitress and asked for another coffee. She took my order promptly, but her smile was for Simon. Credit where it's due, he paid her little heed beyond a cursory glance, his eyes on my face, not hers. A silly little victory.

'I wish I could start again,' he said, taking another cube of sugar from the bowl and rolling it between his fingers. 'I feel like I've made a bad impression – that you think I'm a bit of an idiot.'

I gave him a kindly smile, but didn't disagree.

'It's nerves, that's all,' he said. 'I never expected you'd agree to meet me, and by then it was too late to admit I was a bloke, and now I feel stupid.'

The waitress brought over my coffee. A little milky froth spilled into the saucer. 'Sorry,' she said, but didn't wipe it up. Simon folded a paper napkin and inserted it between my cup and saucer to blot up the liquid.

'Thank you,' I said, oddly touched, but also feeling it was the sort of thing an attentive young man might do for his grandmother.

'Whoever owns this place should tell their waitresses to treat every customer with equal courtesy.'

Was this thoughtful young man the real Simon, or was this part of his act?

'I would have been the same at her age,' I admitted.

'Really?' A smile dimpled his cheeks. 'I sort of imagined you were the type to shut yourself away with books and pens, learning your craft.'

I snorted. 'I was no Emily Brontë! Yes, I wanted to be a writer, but I was a very normal teenager.' Had I been? And what was "normal" anyway? I hadn't been a swot; equally I'd not been the wild type, too eager to grow up. A plodder in most respects. Dreamy, weepy, surly, resentful. The usual mix. Not clever or beautiful, both of which Madeleine had been.

'You never married? I mean, none of my business, but... well, a lot of women do, don't they?'

'So do a lot of men, but it's not compulsory.'

He blushed and looked down at the sugar cube dissolving in his saucer. 'Sorry. It's just... Well.' He looked up. His hesitant smile and fading blush put me in mind of Millais's paintings of children; the same suggestion of charming vulnerability. 'Sorry.'

'I never married because no one asked me.' Now he would imagine me to be a dried-up virgin and so, my better judgement overruled by vanity, I added, 'My last lover was married. The sort who'd never leave his wife.' I hoped I didn't sound bitter. If you take up with a married man, you can be almost certain it will end in defeat. Foolish to expect otherwise.

'I hate men like that,' Simon said with surprising vehemence. Had his father run off with another woman? Or was he just old-fashioned? I couldn't be bothered to bring out the tired old line about it taking two to tango. Instead,

20

I hauled on stage the other old chestnut: 'When you get to my age, men are either married, or sour divorcees. Or just plain sour.'

'You should choose younger lovers.' His tone was matter of fact, though I tried my hardest to pick up any hint of flirtation. I told myself to stop thinking along those lines; that path led only to crushing disappointment, didn't it?

'I think none at all is the wiser course.' I had little taste for going through the same old courtship rituals yet again. All that getting to know someone, deciding whether or not their little quirks and political opinions were those one could live with. Yet here I was, face to face with someone I hardly knew, wanting only to be the person he wanted me to be, hardly caring if his company would prove tedious in the long run. 'And what about you, Simon? Do you have someone?'

He shrugged. 'No one special. No one at all, really.' The statement seemed to make him miserable and I wasn't the sort to offer consoling platitudes.

This mulling over of our respective romantic situations put a damper on the conversation. He was probably keen to leave after what he must have found to be a dreary meeting. We would pay the bill and awkwardly go our separate ways and I would curse myself as I brooded over all the things I should have said; all the things I would have said if I'd been a braver woman.

'There's a lot of snow,' he said. 'I wasn't sure I'd get here in time.'

'You did, though.' But how? This was England. A few flakes of snow and all the buses and trains stopped running. To have got here on time – to get here at all – seemed impossible for him to have managed.

'Yes. But I'm not sure how I'll get back.'

I walked with him to the station, dreading the moment when we must say goodbye, the pain I'd feel if he shook my hand again.

Please let him give me a kiss on the cheek, at least. His hands on my shoulders...

We learned that all trains in and out had been suspended from our little station since the previous afternoon. I gaped at Simon. He laughed.

'I didn't come on the train,' he said. 'When I saw it was impossible, I persuaded a taxi to bring me.'

'From where, for God's sake?'

'Only from Shrewsbury.' Eight miles. I didn't believe him. The roads were so treacherous it was unlikely any taxi driver would have risked making such a journey. I didn't want to interrogate him – no harm had been done, after all – but I knew he wasn't being straight.

'I'll have to put up at a B&B,' he said.

'As you must have known you would.'

'It's fine,' he said. 'It's not the first time I've been stuck somewhere.'

It wasn't fine. There were only two B&Bs within walking distance and one was closed for refurbishment. The other claimed to be fully booked due to a party of Welsh people visiting our annual Christmas fair. We did no better at the one small hotel, which was full to bursting with two wedding parties, the first lot having been unable to leave due to travel issues.

'What about pubs?' Simon suggested. 'They some-times have rooms.'

After enquiring at all three of the village pubs without success, I was too cold, wet and fed up to persist.

'You'll have to stay at my house,' I said. 'I have a spare room.' I wasn't given to making rash decisions, and as soon as the words were spoken I regretted them. What was I letting myself in for? Yet I couldn't deny the relief I'd felt when it became clear there was literally no room at the inn.

'Could I really?' he said, all eagerness.

Had he planned this all along? But that made no sense. He couldn't have made it snow on this particular day. Nevertheless, I couldn't shake the feeling that I'd been set up. If it hadn't been the snow, it would have been something else. Was I being paranoid? I couldn't ignore the feeling that something about the situation was very wrong. If I'd had any sense at all, I would have made him explain himself to me before I let him anywhere near my front door.

But wasn't there a slim chance he was being entirely honest? A bit of snow was nothing to him. I would never have risked travelling on such a day, but he was young, probably saw it as a bit of an adventure, a lark, something to tell his mates about over a few pints. And I'm ashamed to admit that his beautiful smile did much to stifle my suspicions. No fool like a lonely middle-aged woman.

Run, run, said my head.

Stay, stay, said my heart.

'It would only be for a night, two at most,' he added. 'I mean, it can't snow for ever, can it?'

'No; I suppose not.' I sensed right there that inviting Simon into my home – into my life – constituted a grave error of judgement.

CHAPTER THREE

Our lives are composed of stories. Memories are stories and there are also the inherited stories, true or not, which add colour to our lives. My grandmother always insisted that her mother had been seduced and left pregnant by Lord Such-and-Such and that we were, therefore, possessors of blue blood. Doubtless such things happened in big houses filled with randy young (and not so young) men and a constant supply of domestics – ignorant, often far from home, economically and socially powerless.

The man who'd been my last lover, Russell Poole, had been unable to understand my attachment to family stories. I expected – wanted – some expression of sympathy when I told him I'd unearthed a document that proved my great grand-aunt had been sent to prison for concealing the birth and subsequent death of an illegitimate baby, born (aptly enough) in a stable. Russell had laughed, perplexed, holding up splayed hands.

'But it was all so long ago! You never even knew this woman.' He poured two glasses of rosé, offering one to me. Perversely I shook my head, though I'd been looking forward to the wine. From necessity we always met at my place, but Russell provided the drink.

'Oh, well,' he muttered, 'if you're going to be silly about it—' He placed my glass on a coaster, assuming I'd soon change my mind.

He was a science teacher. We'd met when I took a temporary clerical job at the local secondary school. The evening to which I just referred was the one, I subsequently realised, which marked the unravelling of our relationship. Shortly afterwards he took me to Paris for a long weekend. Only later did I realise he'd intended the trip to be a sort of parting gift – a final happy memory of our affair, one I was meant to treasure.

A woman is in no position to complain when her married lover decides to end it. "Making another go of his marriage" is the correct thing to do, and the abandoned lover must, if she has any decency, grudgingly accept this and let go. I refused to abide by the rules. I made scenes, threatened to tell his wife about us, deleted every one of the photographs I'd taken in Paris; pleaded, begged, threatened to kill myself...

The stupid, embarrassing nightmare ended only when he and his family moved away to Devon. Russell had tried to be kind to me, tried to make allowances, and I had no excuse for having behaved like a tiresome adolescent. At no point had he ever intimated that he intended to leave his wife for me.

'Be reasonable,' he told me. 'I made you no promises.'

And he hadn't. I'd clung to him because he was there, because he offered companionship and some measure of affection. Finally I understood why the last line of the Fleetwood Mac song "Man of the World" always made me feel so bleak. I had never been in love. Lovers, yes, but only the simulacrum of love.

Madeleine had been the one with the boyfriends, I the friend ready with a tissue to mop up the tears when it all went wrong. I was there to listen to outpourings of grief, offering chocolate and comfort, never daring to tell her I could have wept for joy every time she split up with someone, because then she was mine again.

Russell hadn't understood what I'd felt for Madeleine. 'A bit unhealthy, this obsession you have with her,' he'd said.

'I'm not obsessed!'

'It sounds very much like it to me.'

His training – scientific, everything to be tested, nothing taken on trust – had given him, or so it seemed to me, an inhuman disregard for emotions, intuition, the more "feminine" virtues. He said he was calm; I accused him of being cold.

'I'm a reasonable man,' he'd said, 'not an unfeeling one.'

We were too different, too driven by different desires. If I no longer missed him, I did occasionally wish I had more of his ability to consider logically any difficult situation.

Russell's distaste for Paris ensured our trip there would never have been a success. The city's associations with romance made it anathema to him, and he frankly admitted he never felt at ease in any place where he didn't speak the prevailing language. Our itinerary, too, was an unsatisfactory compromise. He was interested in buildings I scorned as bombastic – the Pantheon, the Palaces of Justice, the Arc de Triomphe. With bad grace he trailed after me through the cemeteries of Montmartre, Père Lachaise and Montparnasse, stubbornly refusing to understand why I found them so appealing.

It rained on the morning we were due to fly back to England – heavy, crashing rain falling from a school-uniform-grey sky. We sat in the breakfast room of the hotel, transfixed by the rain lashing against the glass; depressed by the weather, the stale croissants and tepid hot chocolate.

Russell was too rational to interpret these disappointments as omens or pathetic fallacy. 'Just as well we're leaving; the forecast suggests the rain's set to last.'

'It will be worse in England,' I said. 'I don't want to go home.'

'Everything must come to an end,' he said in that insufferable schoolmaster's tone of his.

'That's not the point!'

And so began one of those pointless tiffs about nothing that leave both parties enervated, injured and resentful.

My spare bedroom would become Simon's until he could leave. It was decorated neutrally, walls a conventional magnolia, the carpet beige, the furniture basic: bed, dressing table, chest of drawers, chair. No ornaments or pictures on the walls, the lampshade a purely functional one from Ikea.

No one had ever slept in this room. I'd deliberately decorated it in budget-hotel-room fashion to avoid indulging a sentimental urge to decorate it for Madeleine, she who had never seen my home or slept under my roof. This room no shrine, then, except to the gods of blandness. Simon would temporarily bring his personality to bear and I would welcome the change, for the room was studiously dreary.

Would he expect us to eat together, or would he trip in and out of the kitchen as it suited him, heating up a plastic tray of chicken korma in the microwave or pouring boiling water on to a Pot Noodle? And would he then slouch in front of the TV watching repeats of *Top Gear* while he refuelled? I wasn't used to sharing my home. I'd lived with my parents and then I lived alone.

'You'll hardly notice I'm here,' he'd assured me, but of course I would. It didn't matter how quiet, tidy and considerate he was, I would feel his presence eating into the space that was mine alone.

'I think I've become very selfish,' I told him. 'I never was good at sharing. It's because I'm an only child.' Glib, probably not true, but how else to account for the patho-logical fear I experienced at the prospect of someone else taking charge of the remote, possibly filling the house with unpleasant food smells, and all those other trivial things that now seemed more weighty than whether or not he was a psychopathic stalker?

'It'll be fine.'

'I don't want to make a big deal of this, it's just that I'm so unused to having anyone else in the house. I don't like staying in other people's houses, either. It's nothing personal.'

What if we were snowed in for days, even weeks? Perhaps he'd want to have intense literary discussions long into the night. He'd ask what I thought of the current thinking in post-colonial theory and I would be forced to admit I had no clue what he was on about. He would make me feel like some wretched Jean Rhys heroine, for ever out of kilter with the people around her. I would be another sad-eyed woman listening patiently while her male companion tells her she's stupid. Too sad, too lonely, too patient to object.

That wasn't me, surely. But neither were Jean Rhys's women stupid or even pathetic. Beaten by life, that's all. By circumstances.

To him it was a game. Playing house. I wished I knew for certain what my role was to be. I needed a script. I wasn't particularly house-proud, belonging to the Quentin Crisp school of dust management, but I would have wept unreasonable tears if he'd broken anything I treasured. Everything I owned meant something; everything mattered.

'I'll stay out of your way entirely, if you like,' he said. 'Okay?'

Of course he wouldn't break anything or steal the silver, and of course that had never really been the issue any more than I'd seriously worried about him cooking junk food or wanting to watch telly programmes I didn't enjoy.

'You don't need to do that,' I said. 'I wouldn't want you to.'

'You don't have to worry that I'll think you're rude. I understand. This is your home, your space. I've invaded it and haven't even given you time to prepare. But you won't offend me, whatever you do.'

Did he really think I was concerned only that he shouldn't think me rude or ungracious? That was, after all, the most logical conclusion to be drawn from my apparent reservations. The truth was something I must never reveal. Simon was simply the most beautiful man I'd ever seen. I couldn't bear the thought of letting him go. I'd memorised every part of him – the shape of his mouth when he smiled; the way his hair fell over his right eyebrow; his particular smell that defied description. I couldn't look at his hands without imagining how they would feel against my face. I couldn't look at his neck without wanting to kiss it.

'Gabrielle? What's up?'

'Sorry. Thinking.'

'You think too much. The snow'll be gone in a day or two.'

'Your room is very small. The cottage is quite dark. I have a cat.'

He laughed. 'But I like cats.'

I was being ridiculous. Of course it would be all right. We'd sit up late, drinking wine, talking about books, art, love, maybe some music in the background. We'd become good friends – the best!

But how could we? How *could* we?

In a moment of largesse, I'd agreed to help out with the church Christmas fete. Mr Latham's most stalwart helpers (virtuous tenders of flowers, pourers of tea, providers of biscuits) had both succumbed to flu.

'I know you're not a great joiner-in,' he'd said, 'and I'm not a person who generally takes advantage of ladies,' (I smiled, biting back a crude rejoinder to this singular admission), 'yet I know you to be a most reliable person and I should take it as a great favour if you could force yourself, just this once.' He said no more, but his eyes pleaded his case and pleaded well, for I needed no further persuasion to pitch in, as he put it, like the trouper I was.

The day after Simon arrived I found myself standing

behind the cake stall in a musty church hall decorated with the bright rainbow and fanciful Noah's Ark beloved of Sunday school painters everywhere. A dove hovering over my head, I accepted the greetings of the stallholders either side of me (white elephant to the left, knitted goods to the right). During slack moments, one or other of these excellent women offered to fetch "refreshments" (lukewarm beige tea in a thick china mug and a couple of stale digestives) and, somehow or other, I found myself telling them I had a friend staying with me until the trains were running normally again.

'A friend? You should have brought her along.'

'A young man, actually.' Rashly, 'And I barely know him from Adam.'

'Is that wise?' Not crass enough to suggest Simon was a potential axe murderer, the knitted-goods lady was moved to remark that one couldn't be too careful these days.

'Well, on your own head be it,' was her response to my feeble protestation that the majority of people were basically good and the odds were against Simon being either psychopathic or a kleptomaniac.

Word got round, as it always does, and Mr Latham requested a quiet word in my ear on the subject when we took the unsold goods back to the vicarage at the conclusion of the fete.

'You of all people ought to approve of looking for the best in people instead of assuming the worst,' I said. 'The Good Samaritan and all that.'

A tight frown, a hint of annoyance. The clergy, too, are only human.

'Or is it my morals you're worried about?'

31

'I'm sure you're too modern a person to care about such things, my dear.' A mild reproach? But why, indeed, should I have cared? 'My only concern is that this young man will take advantage of your kindness. I shouldn't like to see you being upset.'

He seemed to appreciate the risk Simon posed. I had no fear that Simon would murder me or rob me or ruin my reputation. The danger was that I'd fall in love with him, and I was more than halfway there already.

Mr Latham gave me a sad smile. 'I preach the power of love all the time. Often I think I should remind people that love can be as destructive as hate.'

'We all know that, deep down,' I murmured.

'You're a writer, of course, which doubtless makes you unusually perceptive about such matters.'

'I'm no longer a writer. I haven't been a writer for over twenty years.'

'You don't dabble at all?'

A curious word. One dabbles in the water because one is afraid to submerge one's whole self, or because one can't swim. My debut novel had been acclaimed as wholly assured, perfectly realised; not the work of a tentative writer, but of one who held out her arms to embrace the riptide.

'All or nothing,' I said, echoing Simon's avowed attitude to his writing career.

'A pity. When one has a vocation, it seems a great shame to renounce it.'

'I didn't. It renounced me. But anyway, to get back to the point, I'm not a silly schoolgirl and I'm quite alive to the dangers posed by handsome young men to vulnerable women of a certain age.'

Mr Latham blinked rapidly several times like one of Trollope's timid clergymen when confronted with foreign ladies of charm and dubious taste.

'Any passion could never be requited,' I added. 'I'm too old to be one of those interesting mature women who capture the imagination of young men in French novels. Unrequited love won't kill me, I do assure you.'

No, it wouldn't kill me, but I suspected I was trying to convince myself as much as Mr Latham. I told him I recognised the risks I was running, but it wasn't true that I was indifferent to those perils. Hadn't I found consolation in the fact that the President of France was married to a woman twenty-four years his senior? The twenty years between Simon and I were nothing!

I wondered if Mr Latham had ever been in love and how much he knew from personal experience of the lusts of the flesh. He must have been in his late thirties, but he was one of those men who give the impression of having always been an old soul, never entirely at ease in the modern world, the whiff of the vestry clinging to him like cigarette smoke. He took his job seriously, but more, I suspected, from reverence for the office than because he felt any great fatherly love for his congregation.

It was on the tip of my tongue to ask if he knew the pangs and pains of romantic love; I was restrained only by a glimpse at his bony fingers worrying a corner of pink blotting paper on the desk. They were not, surely, hands that had ever caressed the skin of another person. Hard, cold fingers more accustomed to cradling a Bible as he intoned the funeral rites than to offering succour to the still vertical.

Fearful of saying something neither of us would be able to forget, I forced a cheery smile and closed the conversation with a few brusque words to convey thanks for his concern, assurance that no great harm would befall me, and certainty that his anxiety was misplaced.

'I trust you're right,' he said eventually. 'I hope… That is to say, I realise you're not a person inclined to confide in others, but my door, you know, is always open.'

What kind of advice did he imagine he could dispense that would be of any use? His shoulders were hardly there to be cried upon and any outpouring of emotion would have ruined our sterile but satisfactory working relationship. A formula; the kind of thing he believed he was expected to say, and I accepted it in the same spirit. Or was I doing him an injustice? I'd always believed him to be as little inclined to make a friend of me as I was of him, but I might have been wrong.

'I'll bear that in mind. Thank you.'

CHAPTER FOUR

I returned home bearing two cakes: a seed cake and a Victoria sponge oozing buttercream and jam.

'Sorry I had to whizz off like that,' I told Simon after asking if he wanted a slice of cake.

'It's okay. I checked the weather forecast. Doesn't look likely to get above freezing for another day or two. I hate imposing on you like this,' he said, pushing back his silky blond hair. 'Stupid of me to travel in the first place, but the forecast is usually wrong.'

'I tried to phone to stop you coming. You never answered.'

'Yeah, sorry about that. I gave you the number for my old mobile by mistake. I've got a new one now.'

'You could have rung me. My number hasn't changed.'

'Yeah, well, it's done now.'

He said he'd never tried seed cake but would like to, so I cut us each a hefty wedge. I thought about bringing out the best tea cups from a set (blue and white, decorated with dragons) inherited from my grandmother, but decided on mugs in the end. Men often find fiddly handles a trial. I was fussing, I knew I was, and that would make me seem strange, but I couldn't relax.

'My grandmother always had seed cake whenever we visited,' I said. 'I suppose she made it herself, although

I'm not sure. You can't buy it now – not in supermarkets anyway – but it's very easy. Just a Madeira with caraway seeds thrown in. The recipe calls for two teaspoons, but I use more than twice that amount to give the proper flavour.' All this was nonsense. He'd likely never made a cake in his life and there was no reason to suppose he'd care how a caraway seed cake was made.

There were so many things we needed to talk about. He could be living under my roof for a week or more. Should we mention money? I'd never intended to rent out a room, I wasn't that hard up, but he'd eat a lot, wouldn't he? A young man of his age? What had I done?

'More cake?'

'Not right now, thanks. It is lovely. I've been thinking, we haven't really discussed terms. I mean, is it okay for me to use the kitchen?'

'You're welcome to eat with me if you want to.'

I couldn't, after all, bear the thought of him eating alone in his room. I'd lay the table properly – the good tablecloth, the silver cutlery...

Candles? Roses?

He gave a timid laugh, his eyes nervous. 'It's kind of weird, this, isn't it? I never really thought what it would be like. We barely know each other, do we?'

Yes, it was odd. We were nothing to each other, but here we were, living together; not quite friends, not quite anything.

'Do you need to let anyone know where you are?' I asked. 'You should let them know you're safe.'

'I made the necessary phone calls while you were out. It's fine.' A soft, kind smile. 'You've been so good. I hope you don't feel I'm taking advantage of you. I mean, foisting myself on you like this. I'm sure you were just being polite.'

At this point Pushkin made an appearance, slinking out from underneath a flowery armchair. She'd made herself scarce since Simon's arrival. Not even her favourite pouch of food had coaxed her from her hiding place. She stared at the intruder, her body hunched up, nose sniffing the air.

'She's sizing me up,' he said. He made no move to pet her, which pleased me. Cats must make up their minds about people in their own time. And for my part I refused to make any "I think she likes you" type comments. Maybe she would, maybe she wouldn't.

Maybe I would, maybe I wouldn't.

Two days later I began to realise the extent to which Simon had made himself at home. He went out, ostensibly to the station to check on the trains, and came back with a portable typewriter he'd bought on impulse from a junk shop.

Morevale was a large, sprawling village with a population of four thousand or so, many of whom lived on the housing estates that had been built in the sixties, although many more lived in the remoter areas on the other side of Minster Hill, which dominated the landscape for miles around. These days, most people travelled by car to do their shopping in Shrewsbury, but we did have a relatively busy main street that lacked only a shop selling Barbour jackets to make it more or less identical to any other rural high street.

The junk shop where Simon found the typewriter had been there since I was a child, though it had expanded over the years and was something of a honeypot for anyone searching for quirky objects of the type so beloved of *Bargain Hunt* participants. Madeleine had loved it; she'd enjoyed buying things that horrified her parents: a moth-eaten stuffed crow, a death mask, a creepy doll in the form of a grinning clown with demonic eyes. They were missing from her room after she died, so I assumed her parents had binned them.

'I hope you didn't pay much for that,' I said to Simon, examining the typewriter he'd bought. I'd owned a similar one when I was in my early teens. It wasn't antique or even a particularly good model.

'I've always wanted one of these,' he said. 'When I saw it, I couldn't resist. I've got a laptop, but you can't pretend to be Ernest Hemingway when you're tapping on a computer keyboard – you need good, solid keys that make a noise when they hit the paper.'

The macho writer literally forcing words on to the page, making his mark. I amused myself with an image of Simon crouching over his typewriter, pretending to be a genius. Maybe he'd pour himself a glass of whiskey and leave it sitting on his desk for inspiration.

'I like the sound of people typing,' I said.

He sat on the edge of the sofa, hands loosely touching. 'This is just your standard portable job. I've always fancied one of those huge black iron things – you know the sort?'

I nodded. 'They weigh a ton. Hardly portable.'

'Maybe I should try writing longhand.'

'Why? The words won't be more authentic for having been written with a fountain pen.'

He gazed at me, appraisingly. 'There are so many

things I want to ask you. Things you probably won't want to talk about.'

'We'll have to see how it goes, won't we? I might end up revealing all kinds of secrets.' I spoke lightly, teasingly, but I think we both appreciated the weight of my words. 'Did you get as far as the station?' I asked. 'Did you find out about the trains?'

'Yeah,' he said, pushing his fingers through that silky hair I loved so much. 'Would it be a terrible imposition if I stayed for just a couple more days? The thing is, I haven't been entirely straight with you.'

My scalp prickled. 'Go on.'

'I don't have my own place; I still live with my parents. Only we had a massive bust-up. I told them I was going to spend a few weeks with a mate of mine who lives in Carlisle, but I don't really want to go there. Can I stay here, just till the heat dies down at home? I promise I won't be a nuisance. And I've got everything I need in my rucksack if you don't mind me sticking a few clothes in your washing machine.'

He must have thought I was a pushover and he wouldn't have been wrong. The way he looked at me; his blue, blue eyes. How could he not realise how I felt about him? Was it loneliness, the absence of a man in my life that made me so susceptible? Was I that pathetic, that soft a target? I told myself to keep my guard up, to be wary. I couldn't let him see what he was doing to me. I avoided standing close to him in case I should find myself reaching out to touch him.

What *had* he done to me?

'If it hadn't snowed, you'd have gone to Carlisle, I suppose?'

'I guess.' He grinned disarmingly. 'But it's nicer here than in Carlisle.'

On Sunday morning he insisted on going out to pick up a newspaper before I'd started to prepare breakfast. While he was out, I couldn't resist sneaking into his room to see what he'd made of it. His typewriter sat on the dressing table. I had an old typing chair he could have, and a small table if he wanted it. Beside his typewriter was a Moleskine notebook. I was tempted to imagine it filled with lines of deathless adolescent prose, but what did I know? For all I knew, he might have been a genius.

I felt rotten for snooping, even though it was my house and I'd not so much as tampered with a drawer. When he returned with fresh croissants from the little artisan bakery, I felt even more guilty.

'I didn't expect you to get up so early,' I said. Perhaps it was only teenagers who slept in until lunchtime.

'I don't like the deadness of Sundays, but it's worse if you don't make an effort. Have you got any jam?'

I pointed to a cupboard, pleased we were in agreement on the subject of Sunday. It was a day I'd always disliked – that back-to-school-tomorrow feeling that never goes – but if I dragged around all day in a dressing gown I felt more like an invalid than someone taking it easy.

My kitchen was just big enough to accommodate a table that barely seated two people. We had to sit with our legs to one side to avoid bumping knees.

'I like your crockery,' he said.

Nothing matched. All the plates and bowls were inherited from my grandmother. We're not talking Clarice Cliff, just ordinary china that people ate from in the forties and fifties. Occasionally I toyed with the idea of treating myself to a proper antique service, but I'd probably have been too nervous to use it.

'I like everything about your house. It's got style. Real style, I mean, not something copied from a magazine.'

He was flattering me and I was vain enough to fall for it.

After breakfast we tidied up and settled ourselves in the sitting room with the papers. Normally I wouldn't have bothered with a Sunday paper, a bloated mass of themed sections and supplements, but it passed the time.

It was only after dinner (shop-bought pizzas), when it was getting dark and we sat down with a bottle of wine and chatted, that I began to feel more relaxed with him.

'I almost left and got on the next train after lunch,' he admitted. 'You were totally pleasant and polite, but it's like you were a cat flexing its claws, waiting for the right moment to lash out.'

'Goodness, was I really that bad?'

He shrugged, gently swirling the wine in his glass. 'I can understand it. I think I'm quite easy to live with, but you don't really want me here, I know that.'

'I'm used to my own company.'

'And prefer it?'

'On the whole, yes. I'm sorry if I made you feel unwelcome. I was trying very hard to do the opposite, but clearly I failed.'

He stretched out a leg, touched Pushkin with his foot and wriggled his toes in her fur.

'It doesn't matter. Honest. But I really do like it here – the house, the village, everything.'

Me? Did he like me?

41

'If you can bear to have me around,' he continued, 'I'll do my best to respect your personal space.'

'I'd hate you to think I resent you being here. I don't.'

He grinned. 'You worry too much. You surely don't care what I think about you? I'm a nobody, nothing I say really matters.'

I wondered how well we would learn to read each other and which of us would learn the most, and gain the most, from the exercise.

I topped up our glasses and asked him, for no particular reason, if he liked Baudelaire.

'Get drunk and stay that way. On what? On wine, poetry, virtue, whatever. But get drunk.'

He smiled and clinked his glass against mine and I thought, yes, it will be all right, if only we can stay drunk – on wine, on poetry, whatever.

But it wouldn't be all right, would it? I told myself we could never be more than friends, at best, but as soon as I got into bed and closed my eyes, the fantasies emerged out of the darkness. I pictured him walking into my room, our eyes locking, reading the same desires there. Idiotic enough to sleep naked in the ridiculous hope this would happen. Giving myself to him, tasting him, feeling his heart beat against mine. My hand sliding between my legs, the moment when reality and fantasy merged. And then tears of self-pity, emptiness, a grinding sense of loss for what could never be.

He must never know, never guess. I would be ordinary with him, give him no reason to believe I thought him extraordinary. And he wasn't; he was a young man like millions of others. Brash, gauche, unaware of all the nuances of human behaviour. It would likely never cross his mind that a woman twenty years his senior would think of him in sexual terms. I staked everything on this thought. Somehow I must teach myself to write this off as a crush. It would pass, it was nothing, I was old enough to know better.

But I wasn't.

CHAPTER FIVE

I paused for a moment before inserting my key into the lock. Simon and I had breakfasted together and he'd told me he intended to use my absence to explore the village and then perhaps "bash out" something on the typewriter.

'I want to talk to you about my writing,' he'd said, 'but I don't want to be pushy. I mean, I don't expect you to read what I write or anything, but any tips you might have—'

'Maybe. I don't know. I'll think about it.'

Madeleine was the only person I'd ever talked to about writing, unless one counts the journalists who'd interviewed me during my brief glory days. Too young properly to appreciate what I'd achieved, I'd resented the repetitive questions, the prying into my "backstory", and most of all the inevitable "What are you working on now?"

But of course Simon wasn't interested in any of that. I didn't think the young were necessarily more selfish than the rest of us, but it would have been strange if he hadn't been interested in me for what I could do for him as an adviser, mentor, networker. He was sadly mistaken if he believed I had any privileged contacts in publishing. I had none. I'd never had an agent and my editor had probably retired by now. Even if she hadn't, I would bet she had only the haziest recollection of me. Any friendship that might have developed between us had been knocked dead when she tried to persuade me to write a memoir about my friendship with Madeleine.

'It would plug the gap between this novel and the next, if you're struggling,' she'd said.

'How can I? I've never come to terms with losing her.'

'Writing about it might help.'

'No. Absolutely not.'

'You won't even consider it? I could help you – we could brainstorm ideas.'

A lump in my throat, I had shaken my head, very much wanting to chuck at her the plate of biscuits she always provided at our meetings. Somehow I'd found my way back to Paddington station, grateful my carriage wasn't packed, so I could hunch into a corner seat and gaze tearfully at the passing scenery, the fields of cattle and sheep, the bleak beauty of the British countryside at the fag-end of autumn.

Madeleine, Madeleine… How can I put you into words?

She and I sat next to each other on our first day at infants' school. People said we looked alike and it wasn't long before we pretended we were sisters. Both of us only children, we instinctively understood each other's need for quiet time away from the big groups of children who shrieked and argued and pushed one another over on the playing field.

I can't, of course, remember what it felt like to be a child, but I do know that Madeleine was always there, always willing to stick up for me, always ready with a comforting arm whenever I was upset. She was the first to congratulate me when our teacher chose the poem I'd written to read out in assembly. The teacher made a point of talking to my mum at home time, telling her how impressed she was with the poem. In later years I used to tell journalists that was the moment I knew I wanted to be a writer, but I doubt it was as clear-cut as that. Here, I might have thought as a young child, is something I can do for which I can earn praise from other people.

Madeleine and I spent hours in her bedroom writing stories. The first ones, I seem to recall, were brief character sketches of our parents, our teachers – vignettes based on the small dramas of our lives. We then moved on to writing stories about things we wanted to happen. Cue tales along the rags-to-riches meeting-a-handsome-prince lines. Often I would write the stories and Madeleine would illustrate them. We talked about working together when we were adults, collaborating on children's books. Naturally they would be brilliant and we would become rich and famous.

Our friendship survived secondary school and puberty, though Madeleine lost interest in our stories, dismissing them as kids' stuff. For a while she wanted to be a vet, then a barrister. She was the clever one and her parents, unlike mine, were ambitious for their daughter. They paid for flute lessons, dancing classes, Girl Guides. Everything she did she excelled at, but nothing held her interest for long.

I, meanwhile, continued to write in secret, frustrated at my inability to come up with anything original. My poems were either sentimental or hopelessly pedestrian. My stories fizzled out after the first couple of paragraphs.

'Show me some, then.' Madeleine lying on my bed on her stomach, legs crossed in the air. After school, both of us still in our school uniforms, only the ties discarded. The air sweet with the smell of her Juicy Fruit chewing gum. She held out a hand, a charm bracelet hanging loosely from her wrist, her long nails painted pearly pink.

'You'll only laugh.'

'When have I ever laughed at you?' Her deep-set dark eyes ringed with kohl, a bit smudged. Her Theda Bara look, she called it.

I handed her the ring-binder, decorated with pictures of famous writers, in which I kept my poems.

We were fourteen and I hadn't shown her anything I'd written since we'd started secondary school. As she read, she twisted her hair around a forefinger. I wanted to lock myself in the bathroom until she'd finished. She liked reading, but she never appeared to be overly bookish, her preference being for the glitzy Danielle Steel type of novel, embossed covers with the titles in foil lettering. That's what she claimed and those were the only books I ever saw her reading. It wasn't until I was allowed access to her room after her death that I found a cupboard stacked with books I'd never guessed she'd owned: Flaubert, Jorge Luis Borges, Christina Stead, Dorothy Richardson and dozens more, some of them so obscure I'd never heard of them, let alone read them. I didn't understand why she'd kept them a secret from me. She'd have told me if she had a drug habit, but wouldn't tell me that she read serious literature.

'These are pretty good,' she said as she leafed through the ring-binder. 'Very clever.'

The right words, but the lack of enthusiasm in her tone was damning. I think I'd have preferred her to laugh at me.

47

'They need work, I know that.' I had to say that, even though I thought them perfect.

'They're a bit Plathish.'

Of course they were. Who else would a moody school-girl try to emulate? Madeleine had teased me often enough for my Plath fixation, calling me a Plathologist when I lingered too long over the facts of the poet's suicide. One of our few arguments was over the issue of whether or not she had intended to take her own life. Madeleine insisted Plath had intended to be found.

'It was a classic cry for help,' she maintained. She thought suicide was a wicked, selfish act that accomplished nothing except the grief of innocent people. I accused her of being unfeeling, lacking in understanding, the disagreement escalating until it reached the tipping point and we didn't speak for several days.

It was she who offered the olive branch, making light of the argument.

'I don't want us to fall out ever again. If we start arguing, one of us must say "*Pax*" and we'll talk about something else, okay?'

We both stayed on at school for A-levels, though I'd scraped through with the minimum number of GCSEs required. Madeleine had achieved nine, all As except maths. That one B dented her pride, and we came near to arguing again when she went into hysterics over it.

'What about me, then?' I said, furious at her lack of sensitivity. 'One A, one B, three Cs. How do you think I feel when you go all drama queen over one lousy subject?'

She apologised, but after that things changed for a while. I'd always known she was clever, but now I resented it. Most of all, I found it hard to accept the

48

marks she got for English, since she claimed she never did more than skim our set texts. She even talked about reading English at uni. I fell in love with the books we studied, but my marks rarely hovered above average. It simply wasn't fair! She was my best friend, I loved her, and I couldn't bear the fact that I wished, more than anything, for her to be ordinary.

And then there were the boys. In that respect our relationship was the classic combination of beautiful girl with plain girl in tow to take up the slack. Madeleine had her pick; I was lumbered with the best friends who, if they were kind, liked me for my personality or, if they were cruel, gazed at her while they caressed me.

Her boyfriends were a heady mix of high achievers and bad boys. She got through them at quite a rate and only a few stick in my memory. The bad boys left a deeper impression than the clever ones, because they were generally nicer to me.

She was the reckless girl who'd happily go the whole way, I the timid girl who would go so far but no further. Sometimes we compared notes. Sometimes we got down to business with our respective partners side by side. She always got the bed, I'd be on the floor. Bra pushed down, tits out, zip undone, my hand clasping a stiff dick like it was an ice lolly. Watching Madeleine out of the corner of my eye, her head thrown back, lips parted, one leg dangling on the floor. Yet I don't think sex meant much to her beyond the relieving of a simple need, and love was a word that never crossed her lips. When a relationship ended she was rarely upset for more than a few days, her misery prolonged only if the boy concerned decided to blab about how "easy" she was, and many did.

'Am I a whore?' she once asked me. The question took me aback, left me speechless. 'I don't want to be known as the village bike,' she added.

'Why do you let them, then?'

She frowned, gazing at the green foil strip of Microgynon pills she held in her hands. She'd just shown me where she hid them in her bedroom, her parents having no idea what their daughter got up to. Years later, when I watched the BBC production of *I, Claudius*, I was struck by a line spoken to the amoral Messalina by her lover. He accused her of wanting to crack the world apart just to see what would happen. That's what Madeleine was like.

Despite her "wild child" tendencies, she was essentially a nice, polite girl. Teachers liked her. She didn't show off or arse-lick and, her maths GCSE meltdown notwithstanding, she was modest about her abilities and achievements. She also did her best to encourage me to go to uni, which I'd decided against. My grades were unlikely to be good enough to get me into the university of my choice and I wasn't prepared to settle for second, let alone third, best. I had no idea what I was going to do once I left school and I could hardly bear the prospect of being parted from Madeleine, but she was destined for great things and places to which she would travel without me.

'You should be a writer,' she told me. 'You love books so much. More than I do.'

'I've no talent.' Never again had I shown her any of my hard-won, disastrous poems and stories, and she'd never asked.

'What *do* you want to do, then?' Not that she had any idea what her eventual career might be. In those days, if you had a degree in any subject, lots of doors automatically swung open for you. Anything I might have enjoyed doing required a degree, and Madeleine was probably right to scorn my stubborn refusal to consider studying at one of the minor universities.

'A degree's a degree,' she'd say. 'Who's going to care what class it is or where you got it?'

'But I'd know.'

'I still don't understand why you think it's better to have no degree at all than a poor one.'

'No, you wouldn't.'

'Tell me, then. Explain it to me.'

How could I? The world *was* split open for her; she took from it whatever she chose, whereas I could feel my choices narrowing. I wasn't clever enough; I wasn't talented enough.

'I wish I were more like you. I wish I *were* you!'

A strange look came into her eyes when I said this. Sadness; a kind of fear; a soft wince of pain. Envy is often misplaced, but when I looked at her I saw a glowing golden girl who would win all the prizes.

'Are you happy?' I asked. 'With your life – with what you think your life will be like, after?' I meant after university, but I could easily imagine her staying on, gaining a PhD, becoming the sort of brilliant academic whose appeal is so great she finds herself the darling of the press, of television, of popular culture.

'I think I'd like to ask the cards.'

She kept her Tarot cards, a Rider-Waite deck, wrapped in a pale green square of silk that had belonged to her grandmother and still smelled faintly of the old lady's Coty L'Aimant. I sat on her bed and watched her shuffle the cards, her eyes closed, chin tilted upwards. Cut and cut again. Ten cards arranged in the Celtic Cross spread. I doubt she really believed in this hokum any more than I did, but often it gave her consolation: a sense that fate could be manipulated if one knew the hazards to avoid.

The card representing "final outcome" was the one that interested us the most. Sometimes she used the whole deck, sometimes only the major arcana, and today – with the whole deck to choose from – she'd picked the sun card as her final outcome.

'That's good, isn't it?' I said.

'Yes; it's a very positive card.'

'Then why do you look so glum?'

She glanced up. 'Do I? Maybe I wanted more. The High Priestess. The Lovers. Something... Oh, well.' Roughly she pushed the cards together, returned them to the deck. 'It doesn't really *mean* anything, does it? You can't cheat fate.'

I had no idea what was bothering her. I was the one with the uncertain future, the probability that my life would be swallowed up in some awful, menial job that I'd resent. I snatched the cards from her, decided to ask them to guide me, to tell me simply whether or not I should follow Madeleine to university.

'The Tower.' Madeleine picked up the card to examine the picture. A stone tower struck by lightning, a golden crown falling from its apex. 'It means you have to destroy the fortress you've built around yourself, not lock yourself away like an anchorite.'

'Anchoress,' I softly corrected her. Two people fell headlong from the tower, suspended for ever in mid-air.

'It's all nonsense, isn't it? You can interpret the pictures any way you want.'

True enough, and I don't for one moment ascribe anything that happened later to warnings we should have heeded from the cards, but I did have a sense when I looked at the tower that I had accepted my fate without quite knowing what that fate was.

In the weeks leading up to our final exams, Madeleine decided to stop seeing the boy she'd been going out with for several months.

'I can't afford to be distracted,' she told me. 'I can't stomach the idea of hanging around waiting for re-sits.'

Less bothered about the outcome of my exams, I became a sort of surrogate lover, meeting Ben for coffee, going to the pictures with him, allowing him to slip his hand up my t-shirt while we watched the film. He often talked about Madeleine, missing her, berating her, telling on her. I reminded him she was my best friend, I didn't want to hear him badmouthing her, but I wondered at some of the things he claimed she'd done. How could she? Did she have no sense of self-preservation, no self-respect? Was there a core of self-destructiveness in her nature? Why else would she have agreed to play strip poker with three young men?

'We cheated, of course,' Ben said, his smile half apologetic, half callous. 'We got her naked, but then she took fright, darted off and hid behind the sofa, crying until we gave her clothes back.'

It could have been so much worse had they not been essentially decent young men, but the question remained – what possessed her to do such things? When I tried to ask her, she got angry – with Ben for sharing the information and with me for listening.

'How could I not listen? I didn't know what he was

going to say!' I'd been doing her a favour, hadn't I, in taking him off her hands?

Her eyes brimmed with tears. 'Soon I'll be away from this stinking place, away from little people and their small minds.'

Was I included? 'You did it, then? He wasn't lying?'

She shook out her long hair, dark and dull, in need of a thorough wash. 'It was just one of those stupid things you do. Someone had a bottle of wine. I don't even know how to play poker. I'd forgotten all about it.'

Ben hadn't. I doubted the other lads had, either. And neither could I. The image of Madeleine crouching behind a sofa, the young men teasing her, refusing to hand back her clothes immediately, hurt me. For all her brilliance, all her beauty, she was terribly vulnerable. Compared with her, I was slow-witted, dull, a dud rocket to her spinning Catherine wheel, but I had my tower, my fortress of thick bricks, and I'd wall myself up sooner than allow myself to plunge into the starry vastness.

CHAPTER SIX

Simon hadn't heard of Barbara Pym, so before I went to work I plucked my copy of *Excellent Women* from the bookshelf and handed it to him.

'You'll probably find it quaint. No vampires or murders.'

'Sounds refreshing. I prefer books that feel as if they needed to be written, not those with one eye on the best-seller lists.'

'You're not interested in writing a book that makes a lot of money, then?' He was young enough to be in love with the romantic idea of suffering for one's art, but also young enough to feel that riches were his due. At that age, you rarely write unless you're fairly sure you're going to produce a masterpiece. Or perhaps that was simply me being romantic about youth.

He grinned. 'You know what they say. Money might not buy you happiness, but it's more comfortable to cry in a Mercedes than on a bike.'

'I'd best get off to work. I thought we might go out for a drive somewhere this afternoon.'

'Oh yes – your little car.'

'Not exactly a Mercedes, but still.' A beige Fiesta, in fact, the sort of car garage mechanics like to call a "good little runner". I hadn't forgotten that Simon claimed to be researching Mary Webb and I'd compiled a list of places associated with her. For all I knew that had been another lie and he had no interest in Mary Webb at all.

My car was a luxury. I didn't need it to get to work and its one regular weekly outing was to the supermarket. Even that I could probably have managed on the bus. Madeleine and I both learned to drive as soon as we turned seventeen, for the vague reason of "independence". My parents bought me a second-hand Mini to learn in, but Madeleine – despite the fact her parents were wealthier than mine – had never wanted her own car.

'Can you drive?' I asked Simon.

'I have a licence, but no car. I don't like owning stuff, makes me feel too responsible. A car's just something else to worry about and spend money on.'

'Speaking of money, presumably you're aware it doesn't grow on trees. If you're going to stay here for a while, would you be willing to make a contribution to your food?'

'God, yes, why didn't you say?' He pulled out his wallet from a back pocket and presented me with five tenners.

'Exactly how long are you intending to stay?'

'Just a few days, then I promise I'll leave you in peace. If that's okay with you?'

I left him sprawled on the sofa with the Barbara Pym novel that, I suspected, he would hate. Timid people leading more or less timid lives. Would he get the irony or would he find the characters and their concerns utterly perplexing in their ordinariness?

Today I viewed Mr Latham with a jaundiced eye when I took his lunch in to him. Doubtless he saw me as an excellent woman, although I didn't quite come up to scratch where church activities and volunteering were concerned.

'How is your young man settling in?' he asked.

'He's not my young man.'

'Oh, I didn't mean – Good heavens, I never meant to imply any kind of improper liaison.' He unwrapped his cutlery and spread the napkin across his lap. How comfortably he would have fitted into one of Pym's novels.

'He's bought a typewriter. He wants to write a novel.' As I spoke the words, I knew that Simon intended to stay for longer than a week. But why? All right, he'd had a ruck with his parents, but he must have had other relatives or friends he could have stayed with. It made no sense that he should prefer my company to that of friends his own age, and there were few arguments so insurmountable that parents wouldn't be glad to see their child, however difficult or annoying he was, once they'd had a few days to calm down.

'I don't suppose I'll see him in church – will I?'

'I never questioned him about his religious beliefs.'

'In any case, I should like to meet him. Bring him round one afternoon if you wish. Not that I mean to pry, but it's always nice to see a new face.'

Bored with the old ones, are you? I thought. And probably he was simply curious to see the person who was staying with me. I would have been, in his place.

'Thanks, I'll ask him. I thought I might take him for a drive this afternoon. He's studying the books of Mary Webb.'

'Oh, good. Plenty of places of interest, then.'

'Sorry. You want to get on with your lunch in peace.'

He chuckled and sliced into his poached egg. 'I must say, I am rather peckish. And do, please, bring young, er—'

'Simon.'

'Simon, yes. Any time.'

I couldn't begin to imagine what Simon would make of Mr Latham. We were relics from another age, the vicar and I, and not even an age we had personally known.

As soon as I got home I felt I must explain Mr Latham to Simon, but he'd drifted to sleep on the sofa, the Barbara Pym novel open, face down, on his chest. He couldn't have read much beyond chapter three. And oh, how beautiful he looked lying there, the sun kissing him, the sun allowed...

'Simon!'

He took his time regaining consciousness, rubbing his eyes with the heels of his hands. 'Sorry.' His voice thick, sticky with sleep. 'The sun always makes me drowsy.' He removed the book from his chest, marking his page with a Post-it note. 'And how was your vicar today?'

'He's not my vicar. I don't even go to church.'

'Don't you?' A frown. 'Is it quite right for a vicar to have a heretic cooking his meals?'

'I'm an atheist, not a heretic. I don't hold beliefs strong enough to qualify as heresy.'

'Has he never tried to convert you?'

'Don't be frivolous.' I went to the kitchen to make a pot of tea.

'Sorry.' He stood in the doorway, his hair dishevelled, t-shirt shapeless from having been washed too many times.

'What for?'

'For taking the piss. No one in my family ever bothered with religion. It's like a different world. Well, it *is* a different world, isn't it? God, the Devil.'

'I never speak to Mr Latham about religion. It would hardly be wise.' I put down the tea infuser and gazed at him. 'We know nothing about each other, do we? The essentials, I mean. The things that are important to us.'

'Finish making the tea, then come and sit down. We'll talk. I want to *know* you, properly.'

'What about our drive? I was going to show you some of the places connected with Mary Webb.'

'It can wait. I think we should talk first.'

He wandered back into the living room. I wasn't sure what to think. Pleased, for a start, that he hadn't frowned at the mention of Mary Webb, so I assumed that part of his story wasn't a lie. Confused by this wish to "know" me – what did that mean, exactly? We get to know people gradually. We make a special, concerted effort to do so only when the person concerned is a potential partner. That couldn't be the case here.

Only occasionally did I miss Russell, but to lose a golden person like Simon would be a far heavier blow. In slow motion I finished preparing the tea, wondering – most pointless of exercises – how to avoid falling in love with him. It wasn't something I wanted to happen, but how did one elude such things?

'Is this Earl Grey?' he asked.

I nodded, not trusting myself to speak on even so banal a topic.

He leaned forward, his eyes – his beautiful blue, blue eyes – gazing straight into mine. 'Well?'

'Well?'

'All right, let's start with your job. How did you come to be doing something like that?'

A safe topic, and something I didn't mind talking about. 'I needed a bit more money, simple as that, and as I have few qualifications and little practical experience—' I shrugged. 'It was either that or work in an office. I was a typist after I left school. It bored me stupid.'

'Go on.'

'What else is there? I wanted something part-time in more or less pleasant surroundings. I like it.'

'It's suitable. Writers shouldn't have careers.'

'I'm not a writer.'

'You have the soul of a writer.'

'Even proper writers have to pay the bills.'

'Yes, but they should take jobs they don't have to think about. Writers need to dream, to breathe, if they're to create anything worthwhile.'

His idealism was understandable. I was perhaps not much better, since I'd never had a family, never had to handle the day-to-day responsibility of running a home in any meaningful way. Who cared about the dust? Not me and certainly not Pushkin.

I'd brought out cups – it seemed wrong to drink Earl Grey from a mug. He handled the dainty cup well, not fumbling it or drinking in the slightly camp manner some men affected. Perhaps if I could think of him simply as a potential friend, all would yet be well.

But then he said, 'And what about your lovers?'

'My what?'

'Tell me about them. Who were they, and what happened to them?'

'I—'

'I'll share mine if you'll share yours.' His smile was almost cheeky, but that didn't stop me feeling the situation had tilted in the wrong direction.

'Why do you want to know?' I set down my cup and scooped up Pushkin, hoping the rhythmic action of stroking her fur would restore some sense of order.

He shrugged. 'I'm interested in human nature. I can't begin to understand you until I know what kind of men have shared your life.'

I doubted that was true. Wasn't it even rather a sexist thing to say? Or was I in danger of misreading and over-analysing everything he said?

'No one has truly shared my life. I've never lived with anyone.'

'All right, then. What was your last lover called?'

'Russell. He was married. He took me to Paris, but it rained.'

He laughed, as I'd hoped he would. 'I like the idea of Paris in the rain,' he said. 'I've never been, but I would like to, and I hope it rains when I go.' A pause, and then, 'He went back to his wife?'

'He never left her.' I hoped I didn't sound bitter. If I'd examined my feelings carefully, I would have realised quite soon after meeting Russell that we were a bad match. I'd known his wife – impossible not to in a village, albeit our sprawling village was as large as some towns – although I'd never done more than pass the time of day with her. If she knew about me and her husband, she never let on.

'And before him?'

I gazed at my hands, my ringless fingers, my carefully-trimmed nails. 'Why go there? The past is—'

'I know. I've read *The Go-Between*.'

'You're young enough not to have a past in any real sense.'

He raised his eyebrows. 'Says you.'

'Sorry. That was patronising.'

A rueful smile. 'I probably deserved it. But I'm no nearer to knowing who you really are.'

'You can fire questions at me and I might even answer most of them, but that's not how you get to know someone.'

'No.' His voice soft, filled with meaning. He touched his cup, but didn't pick it up. 'I think we should go for that drive. Or visit your vicar. Both, if you like. And then, tonight, we should buy some booze and get seriously pissed, and then I might learn who you are.'

'"*Get drunk and stay that way*"? All right. But you might regret it.'

He pushed back his golden, silken hair and shook his head.

We decided to save the drive for another day, since it was now nearly three o'clock. I wasn't entirely happy about the prospect of taking Simon to meet Mr Latham; it felt too much like a parody of taking a boyfriend home to meet one's parents. What I feared was not the vicar's disapproval – or his approval, for that matter – but, rather, that I would find myself imitating too closely and grotesquely the nervous teenage girl whose role I was mimicking.

'How should I address him?' Simon asked on the walk to the vicarage. 'Do I call him sir?'

'Just Mr Latham will do.'

'Nice place,' he said once we'd reached the rectory.

'It's only his for as long as he's vicar here. Apparently there's a Church of England scheme to help retired vicars find somewhere to live. They're encouraged to retire to somewhere outside of the parish where they worked.' This, I felt, was one reason why Mr Latham would be vicar here for as long as he was able. I'd done a bit of Googling, curious to know what kind of salary he earned, and discovered he was probably on around £25,000 a year. No family or expensive hobbies, so I imagined he saved a good deal from his earnings.

'So soon?' Mr Latham said when I knocked at his door and introduced Simon.

'Is this a bad time?'

'Not at all! Do, please, come in – both of you. Shall I make coffee? Or would you prefer tea?'

'We're fine, thank you,' I said. The kitchen was my domain. Mr Latham and I had never sat down together as equals and I shrank from doing so now.

He ushered us into the living room.

'It's a nice place, this,' Simon said, sitting down.

'Far too big, of course. And it can never feel entirely like your own home. It isn't, after all. Still, I can't complain. Miss Price tells me you're a student – English literature, is that correct?'

'Sort of. Did you always know you wanted to be a vicar?'

'Not at all. I wanted to be an engineer. Have you settled in all right?'

'Yes, thanks. It's a pretty village. Not that I want to outstay my welcome. I ought to be moving on soon. I'm running out of clothes for one thing.'

63

'It is indeed a very pretty village; I'm glad someone of your tender years appreciates it. I've been very happy here. Tell me, would you be interested in seeing my collection of Mary Webb books? I have a couple of rather fine first editions.'

I watched them discuss Mary Webb with some relief, pleased they'd found a topic of mutual interest, wondering why I cared. Did it matter so much that Mr Latham should like Simon?

We left after forty-five minutes or so.

'Well, what did you think of my vicar?'

Simon grinned. 'He's exactly as he ought to be. Sweet and sincere. If it's an act, it's a bloody good one.'

'Why should it be an act?'

'No reason. Just me being cynical.'

We made a detour to buy wine and food from the local Spar.

'I love places like this,' Simon said, grabbing two bottles of Pinot Noir. 'They sell all kinds of unexpected things.'

'I preferred the old days when you had proper corner shops that weren't run by multinationals.'

'You're a romantic.'

'No, just old.'

'Daft,' he said, nudging me with his elbow. 'Fancy a spag bol for dinner? I can do a vegetarian one.'

He insisted on cooking the entire meal himself. My job was to lay the table, which we'd dragged into the living room.

'You do like red wine, don't you?' he asked.

'Yes, it's fine.'

'It always seems more grown up, somehow, than white.'

Over dinner we talked about books: our favourite authors, our guilty pleasures, the books we most wished we'd written.

'So why didn't you go to university?' he asked.

'The simple answer is I don't know. Maybe I should have done.'

He cleared away the plates and refilled our glasses. We put the table back into the kitchen and sat side by side on the sofa: a dangerous thing to do, though Pushkin sat between us, a curled-up chaperone.

'You don't give much away, do you?' Simon said, wine glass in one hand, the other stroking the cat's head. 'Have you ever had a best friend in whom you confided everything?'

Madeleine. 'Yes, I did. But she died.'

'Long ago?'

'More than twenty years ago.'

'It must have been rough.'

'It was. I'd rather not talk about it.'

'Sure; sure.'

For a while we sat in silence, sipping our wine, Madeleine as well as the cat between us. I couldn't bring myself to share Madeleine with him. Nor did I wish him to take on the role of confidant. If I started spilling secrets, I feared I might drown in them.

'Drink up,' he said, picking up the bottle and holding it out, ready to top up my glass.

'I shouldn't... I oughtn't.'

'Speak to me, Gabrielle.'

I took a big gulp of wine. 'Ask me something, then.'

'What were you like when you were seventeen?'

'Why seventeen?'

'Why not?'

'All right. I was ordinary. I read a lot of books, I listened to depressing music, I dyed my hair black, I lost my virginity.' Deliberately provoking him. Blame it on the wine.

He took a long, slow sip, then looked me straight in the eye.

'And what was that like, Gabrielle?'

I shrugged. 'He was no one special, just some guy I got off with at a party. It was at someone's house – big house, the dad was a solicitor. I've no idea whose bedroom we were in. We'd smoked a few joints downstairs, then we went upstairs and into the first room we came across. He found a box filled with records, proper vinyl ones, and he put on an old Sisters of Mercy single.'

'Go on.' His gaze was intense. 'What was his name?'

'James. I think he was Scottish. Nice looking. But when I saw him again the next evening, he didn't want to know. Blanked me.' Odd how much that still hurt, after all these years. 'What about you? Your first time?'

'It was at a party. It's always a party, isn't it? She was the host's sister. She was the only one who wasn't drinking. I was in the kitchen, bored out of my skull, in the middle of phoning for a taxi. She took the phone off me, killed the call. Grabbed my arm, took me outside. Said she wanted to show me the flowers her mother grew in this greenhouse thing at the bottom of the garden.'

'You were interested in plants, were you?' I said. Keep it light; don't think about Simon, that girl touching him, holding him, so easy, just kill the phone call...

He grinned. 'Couldn't have cared less about the plants. Great monstrous things they were, like triffids;

66

they didn't look real. You know what hothouses are like, all that heat and humidity, and this terrific smell coming from the plants: kind of fleshy, if you know what I mean.'

I did. I could see the plants, feel the hot, clammy air on my skin, the smell of rainforest flowers.

'She pulled up her dress. No knickers. She was surrounded by all these plants, I felt leaves and tendrils and things brushing against me; it was like the plants were trying to devour us. And afterwards, she just pulled her dress down and took me back into the house. She never said a word, neither of us did. She handed my phone to me, smiled, and walked away.'

'I'm guessing she was older than you.'

'Twenty-eight, something like that. I was eighteen, she seemed really sophisticated; it was like something in a movie. She lived in London; I never saw her again.'

It sounded so much like a scene from a film that I wondered if he'd made it up. Too much like a stereotypical zipless fuck, too perfect in its details. I told myself it wasn't true, that he'd invented the scenario to turn me on. Why else would he want to talk about sex? But hadn't I started it?

'You haven't told me what yours was like,' he said.

'Uncomfortable. Embarrassing.' It should have been comical, but wasn't, the fact that I'd lost my virginity while Andrew Eldritch sang the death-in-sex "Bury Me Deep" in that sombre bass-baritone voice of his that would have made a nursery rhyme sound ominous and funereal.

'You'll have to do better than that,' Simon said. 'Did you take all your clothes off? Did he kiss you? Did it hurt?'

67

I couldn't do this. This was not a conversation we should have been having. Was he as aroused as I was? Why was he doing this?

Simon's voice now quiet, almost a whisper: 'Did he make you come?'

My eyes locked on his. I spoke in a whisper too: 'What do you want from me, Simon? What do you want me to say?' How could we move past this, and how could we put down our glasses and return to chatting about books?

'Only the truth. Honesty. Did he?'

One word. Yes or no. Honesty didn't enter in to it. He'd asked one question, but in his eyes there was another much more dangerous one. *Yes*! I wanted to scream, but I couldn't take that risk.

'No.'

'No,' he repeated. Softly, oh so softly, he reached out to touch my hair, his thumb brushing against my cheek. 'The wine has stained your teeth. I'll wash up, shall I?'

'You can leave it, if you want.'

He shook his head, his fringe falling gently over one eye. 'Best not. It always looks worse in the morning, doesn't it?'

CHAPTER SEVEN

The last person I ever expected to hear from again was Russell. Six months earlier we'd parted in acrimonious circumstances with much shouting and name-calling on both sides. I was dead to him, he'd said, and the feeling was mutual.

He phoned in the morning around ten. I'd sat down with a cup of coffee having first taken one upstairs to Simon, who had decided to work on his novel.

'I'm at work,' Russell said. 'I can't talk for long.'

'Why do you want to talk at all? Surely we've nothing to say to each other.'

'It's my wife. She's found out about us.'

'There is no "us". And how can she have found out?'

He gave me some rigmarole about credit card bills and letters relating to his – our – trip to Paris.

'I told her it was over, that it never amounted to much—'

'Well, thanks!'

'The point is, for as long as I've known her she's wanted me to take her to Paris and we never got there. We should have gone there for our honeymoon, but by then she was pregnant. Terrible morning sickness. She didn't feel up to it.'

'I don't need to know all this, Russell. Why are you

phoning me? This is your problem, not mine.' *Your affair, your rules.*

'I just needed someone to talk to. You've no idea what it's like.'

Of course I hadn't. I'd never been married, never had to deal with the compromises and petty resentments that most marriages, I imagine, entailed. I'd always known Russell was married and that I had no prospect of any kind of a future with him, even if I'd wanted it. If he'd been found out while he and I were still seeing each other, the affair would not have survived, and I certainly didn't want to become embroiled in his tawdry marital problems now that we were apart.

'I'm sorry, it must be hellish, but I should have thought I'd be the last person you'd want to speak to.'

'There isn't anyone else. She says she wants a divorce. I'm sure she doesn't mean it, she'll change her mind once she calms down. But in the meantime, it's bleak.'

Well, yes, it would be. Perhaps the wagon would stutter to a halt, or else pick up and drive off at top speed. Either way, I'd already hopped off and wasn't about to scramble back on.

'I don't want to get involved. I don't want to know,' I said. My coffee was cooling and I wasn't sure I could be bothered to make a fresh one. I could hear the muffled sound of Simon hitting the typewriter keys. What story was he telling? Whose?

And then, 'Are you seeing anyone?' Russell asked.

'No business of yours.'

'No. Quite right. Do you ever think about me?'

I was in no mood for maudlin reminiscences. 'Rarely.' Enough time had passed for any wounds to have healed, so that I could feel little more than a kind of disinterested contempt. I hadn't the patience to prolong this phone call, which could benefit neither of us. 'I'm sorry things have turned out badly,' I said, 'but I can't offer you anything.'

'I'd very much like to see you again. Just someone to talk to.'

'That wouldn't be a good idea.' I didn't want to be unkind; I've never seen the point of cruelty for the sake of it, but his suggestion was ridiculous and he must be made to see that. 'Honestly, there would be no point.'

For all I knew, Simon might have been typing the same word over and over, but I was glad for the sound that reminded me I wasn't alone, that I needn't accede to Russell's suggestion simply for the sake of having someone to talk to.

'For God's sake, Gab, I only want to talk to you!'

It seemed little enough to ask. Would he have understood the reasons for my disinclination? I was no longer in his game, no longer bound by his rules. He had no right to expect anything from me, no right even to ask. He'd untied me as easily as a slip knot, would have resented me if I'd made any attempts to contact him once he'd ended our relationship. We were neither lovers nor friends.

'I don't want to argue with you. You ended it between us and I accepted that. Why can't you accept that I don't want to see you now?'

It even crossed my mind that he wanted me as a reserve in case his wife followed through with her threat to divorce him.

'At least say you'll think about it. I wouldn't expect anything from you.'

'You're already expecting too much.'

71

'Is it so terrible for me to admit that I've missed you?'

'That's not why you phoned, though, is it? If your wife hadn't found out, we wouldn't be speaking now.'

'There *is* someone else, isn't there? Why else would you not want to see me?'

Lost for words, I reached out and touched my coffee cup. Stone cold. Nothing I said to Russell was likely to get through to him, to pierce that bullet-proof vest of insensitivity. Old habits, though: one doesn't hang up until both parties have said goodbye.

'I thought you said you couldn't talk for long?' I said. I pictured him sitting in the staff room of whichever school he now worked at, teachers gazing at him quizzically as they wandered in to make hot drinks during their breaks.

'I know. I've got a pile of marking to do and another lesson in ten minutes.'

'You'd better go, then.'

'But nothing's settled.'

'It is as far as I'm concerned. Do I have to be blunt? I don't want to see you. Not because it would upset me – don't think I've been pining for you or anything like that. Your problems bore me, Russell.'

I thought I heard a sharp intake of breath, but I might have been mistaken. Was he going to tell me I'd changed, that I'd become a cold, hard bitch? No doubt that's what he thought.

The wasted coffee was a nuisance, but I was rather enjoying being the cool one, the one in charge for a change. His life was, so he thought, falling to pieces. He expected me to provide the dustpan and brush, the bandages, the sweet tea and biscuits. I would do no such thing.

In the early days of our affair, we'd lent each other

72

books that meant something to us. He gave me Primo Levi, Milan Kundera, George Orwell. In a misguided attempt to explain something about myself, I lent him books by Colette and Jean Rhys. The effort was wasted. The books annoyed him, confused him. He dismissed Jean Rhys's female characters – those lonely, vulnerable women who don't quite fit in anywhere – as flaky drunks.

'We're not responsible for each other,' I said. 'I don't owe you a thing.'

'It's because of you that my marriage is in trouble.'

'Don't you dare hang that on me! You were the married one – you chose to get involved with me. And I wasn't the first, was I?' If I weren't careful, the conversation would degrade into a futile exchange of accusations and recriminations. I'd allowed him to rile me in spite of my good intentions. 'This is absurd,' I said before he could cut in. 'Can't you see what a mistake it was for you to contact me? Can't you see how impossible it is for us to talk without being hurtful?'

'I didn't want it that way. I'm trying to offer the olive branch here.'

'No, you're not. You're pissed off with your wife and you want someone to moan to about her.'

'Is that what you think? I don't want to lose my marriage. I thought we could be friends, you and I.'

'Then you were mistaken. I'm sorry, and I hope you and your wife manage to patch things up, but I'm not involved in this any more. Don't call me again.'

I hung up. I remained annoyed that he'd called me at all, wished I'd done more to make him see how inappropriate it was, but more than anything I felt bone tired.

Simon was still typing, the sound oddly soothing

despite its disjointed rhythm. If he asked me who'd phoned, I would tell him. I hoped he would. I'd be able to say all the things I wanted to say to Russell but couldn't, for there's no point in speaking to someone who isn't listening.

When I returned home from work, I called up to Simon and asked if he wanted a drink. He was still hammering away on the typewriter. Could he really have been typing all that time? I envied his dedication, if that's what it was.

I prepared the coffee and took a mug upstairs. His door was open. He sat in front of the typewriter, at an angle from the window, peering at the paper in the machine. Dressed in jeans, feet bare, naked to the waist.

I wanted him, oh how I wanted him! I wanted to kneel at his feet, beg him to touch me, to let me touch him. *Let me love you!* His fingers in my hair, my teeth grazing his skin, my mouth—

'Simon?' Too shrill. 'I've brought your coffee.'

He squinted at me, then grinned. 'Guess I should put some clothes on, shouldn't I?'

'I'm surprised you're warm enough.' Something a mother would say. And of course he was warm enough; the central heating was on and the low winter sun hit the south-facing window in an explosion of light.

'I must be cold-blooded. My typing isn't annoying you, is it?'

'Not at all. I like it.' I walked across and placed the mug on the table next to him. His golden, sun-kissed shoulder. What did his skin smell like? How did it taste? To accept that I might never know almost made me cry out. *It's not fair!*

'How's the writing going?'

He pushed his fingers through his hair. I caught a glimpse of the coarse, darker hair in his armpits. Every bit of him beautiful, desirable, fixed in my mind.

'I tell myself just to keep writing, that it doesn't matter if it's drivel as long as I've got something down on paper. But I don't know. I think it's good to write off-the-cuff sometimes, blocking out the inner editor, but I know I'll read it back tomorrow and it'll be so bad it'll depress me.'

'We should talk.'

He rested his arm over the back of the chair. He hadn't done much to personalise the room, but he'd marked it with his presence, his smell. It could never be the same ever again.

'Did I hear the phone ring earlier? Not that it was likely to be for me.'

'It was Russell, my former lover. Too boring to talk about.'

'I doubt I'd find it boring. You must tell me all about him.'

'Later. After dinner, maybe.'

I tried to settle down with a book, but the sound of typing now proved a distraction. Simon. Simon typing. A glisten of sweat down the middle of his back. His hair, warmed from the sun. I didn't give much thought to what he was typing; I couldn't think past that picture of him: his frown of concentration, his toes digging in to the carpet as he filled the paper with words, words, words...

Simon uncorked another bottle of Pinot Noir. I'd never drunk so much wine as I had since he moved in.

'I want to hear all about Russell. That's his name, isn't it?'

'Always Russell, never Russ. Yes, that's his name.'

I kicked off my house shoes and tucked my legs under me on the chair. Simon slouched on the sofa, his feet still bare, but now he wore a t-shirt with a faded picture of Kurt Cobain on the front.

'He's the married one who moved away?'

I nodded. 'He phoned because his wife got suspicious about some of the items on a credit card statement from when he took me to Paris. He'd told her it was a school trip. Someone must have said something to her. I'm sure he could have bluffed it out, but I don't think he has the imagination for that.'

'Stupid of him, then, if all she found was that – no love letters or anything.'

'God, no. I've never written a love letter in my life.' Did the two letters count that I'd written to a boy after he admitted – without much shame or embarrassment, it must be said – that he'd cheated on me while on holiday? I could still muster a cringe of mortification as I recalled begging him not to split up with me; that it was okay, just a holiday fling, I could live with that. More bizarre than that, perhaps, was the fact that I'd copied out the letters, folded them and slipped them inside my diary. In those days I believed everything I did, everything I wrote, was material for stories.

'Sounds to me like he wanted an excuse to get out of a boring marriage.'

'I've no idea what his marriage is like, but he seems to think I should be willing to listen to him moan about it.'

'Does he want you back?'

'I shouldn't think so. Anyway, he doesn't care what I want. I don't think he ever did.'

'So what did you tell him?'

'That I wasn't interested. That I didn't want to hear from him again. He doesn't think I mean it.'

'But you do?'

'Enough time has passed for me to see him clearly for what he is.'

'Sure?'

'Quite sure. Simon, I need to talk to you. I don't want to make you feel unwelcome, but surely your parents will want you to go home to them for Christmas?'

'I told you, we argued.'

'Was it such a dreadful argument? Families should be together at Christmas.'

He gazed at me with an incredulous smile on his face. 'Seriously? You still believe all that Tiny Tim, festive cheer bollocks?'

'Not entirely. I'm not a sentimentalist as a rule. But wouldn't it hurt your parents terribly if you weren't there?'

'They don't care about me, they never did. I wasn't wanted. Don't ask me how I know, I just do. I've got two younger brothers, they're the ones who matter.'

'But it's only one day – two at most.'

'Just shut up about it, will you? I don't want to discuss it.'

'I can see that. But you are staying in my house as my guest. I do have some say over who stays and who goes.'

'So you're going to kick me out too, are you?' he sneered.

'If that's how you're going to talk to me, then yes, I bloody well will!'

He held up his hands. 'All right, I'm sorry, okay? It's a sore subject, that's all. You wouldn't know what it's like to watch your brothers being showered with love and attention and just getting the scrag-end for yourself.'

There was real pain in his voice and his eyes, but could it really have been that bad? Wasn't it more likely he was exaggerating for my benefit, to make me pity him, to make me feel guilty for suggesting he leave? As if I wanted him to. As if I could bear the prospect of watching him walk out of my life.

'They think I never realised,' he continued. 'They're both educated, they've read all the childcare books, all the heavy theory about how to bring up well-adjusted children. But it's only the theory they're good at. When it came to me – to *me*,' he repeated, thumping his chest with his fist, 'they hadn't the first clue. All the music lessons and educational toys in the world can't make up for knowing you're the cuckoo.'

I wondered if he meant he was adopted, but it seemed too direct to come out and ask. Not that an adopted child would necessarily be less loved than any other, of course.

'Why did you argue?'

'This time, or the thousands of times before that?'

'This one.'

He shrugged. 'They found some weed in my bedroom. It was the smallest amount, barely enough for a couple of joints, but they carried on as if they'd found needles and tourniquets. It's all right for them to booze till they're cross-eyed, but not for me to smoke the odd joint.'

'It's the sort of thing that would worry many parents, I imagine.'

He shook his head vigorously. 'You don't understand.

It wasn't my welfare that concerned them. They blasted me for keeping the stuff in the house, where my brothers might have got hold of it. I told them no one had any business going into my bedroom and it's not as if they're little kids. They're fifteen and seventeen for Christ's sake!'

'I'm sure they'll forgive you. Parents do.'

'I don't want them to forgive me. I want them to accept me. It's not the same thing.'

No, it wasn't, but I felt some sympathy with the parents. I was glad I'd never had a child. Whatever parents do, they're always wrong in someone's eyes. Not enough love, or too much, or not the right sort.

'So what will you do? You can't stay away for ever, and isn't Christmas a good time to bury the hatchet?'

'Goodwill to all men, even useless sons? Maybe. I'm just not ready to face them yet. If you want me to go, that's fine, I can doss at a friend's house. I'd just rather stay here, that's all.'

'But you need to make plans for the future.'

'I'll get by.'

He was young enough to believe that, and young enough not to care about things like long-term financial security. His world was still small and revolved around himself. What he wanted, rather than what he needed, came first.

'At least send them a card,' I said.

He grinned. 'I knew you'd say that. Well, maybe I will. Can I talk to you about my writing?'

'Not now. I'm not in the mood.'

'I want to know if you think Roland Barthes was right about the death of the author.'

'That's a bit random.'

79

'Just something I was thinking about while I was working. Was he right?'

'I think it's probably asking too much. People are free to interpret any book as they please, and any work should always stand first and foremost on its artistic merits, but that doesn't mean there wasn't someone behind it with a personal agenda, a set of ideas, a backstory.'

'A backstory – exactly – because we all have one.' His gaze too sharp, as if he was testing me, trying to catch me out.

'And what's yours, Simon?'

He finished the wine in his glass and poured out another generous measure. His eyes on the bottle as he spoke: 'Just an everyday tale of a would-be writer with too much education and not enough ideas.'

'Bullshit. If you really thought that, you wouldn't be writing a novel.'

'*Trying* to write a novel. I'm not going to have a breakdown if no one wants to publish it.'

'Then why bother? Why not do something more likely to give you what you want, whatever that is?'

He shrugged, flexing his toes. 'Because I like the idea of being a writer. The image appeals.'

'I don't understand you. You seem so cynical, but is that just a pretence?'

'No one actually needs novels, do they? So I hate it when I start getting too precious about it. Especially as I might not have enough talent to do it anyway. Whereas if you have a true vocation and it doesn't work out, how painful must that be?'

I hoped my expression didn't give me away. 'Few writers would say they had a true vocation. They just write.'

'If I make it, I'll dedicate the book to you,' he said with a sudden, surprising grin.

'No, don't,' I said quickly. My own book was dedicated to someone dead: to Madeleine. The most important person in my life, reduced to a few words in italics. I didn't want his thanks.

'Oh, well, I needn't, then.' His face sulky, his gaze fixing again on the wine bottle. Sometimes he looked so young and I felt light years away from him; such a vastness between us, of things unspoken and undone, and probably better for being unspoken and undone.

CHAPTER EIGHT

The speed at which Simon typed surprised me, although I suppose in these computer-dominated days kids learn keyboard skills from toddlerhood. I wondered if traditional secretarial courses like the one I'd taken even existed any more. They'd likely been subsumed into generic "business studies" courses.

I sent Madeleine a letter to tell her when I'd landed my first job as a copy typist with a law firm. I was a quick learner and I got the job barely three months into the secretarial course, having sailed through the typing test during the interview.

She scribbled back a postcard: *Fantastic news! Hope it goes well! Come and stay with me sometime!*

Just that; no more. She was at Warwick University studying English. A train would have got me there in a little over two hours, but I never did go to see her.

We kept in touch by letter (no mobile phones in those days), but I rarely had much to say and her letters were always filled with anecdotes about people I didn't know. For the first year she seemed happy. She enjoyed studying and the social life. Occasionally she'd mention someone she was seeing, but she never seemed to get serious about anyone.

We saw a lot of each other when she came home for the

summer holidays, although I didn't have the luxury of two months with nothing to do except laze around and enjoy the warm weather. Of course I was jealous; madly jealous. She complained about the number of books she was expected to read over the summer and I'm afraid I snapped at her, telling her she didn't know how lucky she was.

We were seated outside a country pub on a sweet summer's evening, all gently dying sun and chirping birds. She adjusted the cardigan draped across her shoulders and grinned.

'Up the workers, eh?'

I gazed into the distance: rolling fields, that quintessential Englishness, an "Is there still honey for tea?" moment. I'd made a mistake. I could have been like Madeleine, immersing myself in books, obscure music and student politics for three years.

'I hate my job. I know it's my own fault for choosing to do something I don't want to do. I thought I'd feel happy when I got my first payslip. But it just reminded me how many more years of this I have to get through.'

'Pack it in, then. Do something different. It's not too late.'

'I could never be as good as you, that's the trouble.'

'I'm not that good. If I were, I'd be at Oxford or Cambridge.'

Even so, she let slip that her tutor was confidently predicting she'd get a first. Not a boast; a simple statement of fact.

She reached across the table and touched my hand. 'You can't put up with being bored for the rest of your life!'

I snatched my hand away. 'I don't know what I want instead, that's the trouble.'

'Are you still writing?'

I shrugged. 'A bit. When it's quiet at work, sometimes I start writing something.' I didn't tell her that I liked the feeling of emulating Stevie Smith, who typed out her stories on the famous yellow notepaper while at work.

'What about when you're not at work? What do you do with yourself?'

An odd question. Had we really drifted so far apart that she must ask about my life? Too caught up in her own social and academic whirl to pay me much heed when we were apart. In the letters we'd exchanged I always asked what she was up to; she never asked what I'd been doing.

She tucked a stray wisp of hair behind her ear. Everything she did, even the most casual gesture, had a careless elegance I couldn't hope to emulate.

'Do you care?' I asked. An argument was not what I wanted, but everything about her was golden. I felt there was nothing she couldn't do, couldn't have, if she wanted it enough. It might have been better if I'd told her straight, 'I'm jealous of you and I'm sorry for that.' But I couldn't.

'Of course I care. You're my oldest friend. It's just that I never know what to say to you. I hate feeling that you resent me. Shall we have another drink?'

I sat alone while she went inside the pub, my hands tucked between my knees, my gaze on the birds lined up on telegraph wires in the distance, my vision blurred with tears.

'Here we go.'

'Thanks.'

'You're crying!'

'It's nothing.' I fumbled in my bag for a tissue.

She leaned forward, frowning at me, the sun glinting off the gold heart-shaped locket around her neck, a present from her parents for passing her A-levels.

'Look, I don't want to pry, but if you're depressed—'

'I'm not; I'm unhappy. It's not the same thing.'

'Is it only the job? Or something else?'

How idiotic I was back then. At nineteen I thought I was old, that it was too late to change direction. I could have applied to a university – what did it matter if I didn't begin studying for my degree until I was twenty, or twenty-one? For some reason – for no good reason – I'd decided that avenue was closed to me; that I must make the best of, quite literally, a bad job.

'Don't envy me,' she said when I failed to respond to her question. 'Chances are I'll still end up in some badly-paid godawful job when I get my degree.'

'You'll only start at the bottom, though. I'm stuck there.'

She sighed, and I knew my pig-headed refusal to consider other options irritated her.

'It's not just the job,' I said. 'No one really kept in touch with me after school. They've all moved on. Either they're at uni or they've got steady boyfriends and aren't interested in hanging out with me.'

The other women in the office where I worked were married, settled, both of them "trying for a baby", not interested in pubs or clubs. Not that I was, particularly, but where else did one go to meet people?

'Well, I'm here now. We'll see lots of each other when you're not at work.'

So I became her holiday challenge. She introduced me to people she knew, picked up leaflets from the library

85

about local groups of potential interest, even accompanied me to a meeting of the nearest writers' group. I promised her I'd keep attending, but I dropped out as soon as she went back to uni. They were a decent enough bunch, but there was something musty and fossilised about even the youngest members. I would have felt less desperate trying to pick someone up in a bar.

I did, however, sign up for evening classes to study for a GCSE in maths, and there I met Tim. I often think I went out with him mainly so I'd have something to talk about in my letters to Madeleine. Even so, I struggled to dredge up any enthusiasm when trying to describe him to her.

She read easily between my unenthusiastic lines.

Don't settle for second best, she wrote. *Better to spend the rest of your life alone than with someone who doesn't make you happy.* It was the sort of cod philosophy my mother might have uttered. Did Madeleine think I was too stupid to understand why I pursued my relationship with Tim? If he didn't make me happy, neither did he make me miserable. At thirty he was significantly older than I. Steady, reliable, unadventurous. I told myself he was what I needed, that he'd help me to adjust to the humdrum nature of my life.

I told him about Madeleine, showed him photos, boasted about her academic prowess.

'Almost sounds like you're in love with her,' he joked.

We usually met at his place, since he had his own flat – tidy, neutral, a bit bleak. He was the sort of person who framed and hung up his certificates, and in the living room, not the bathroom.

'I suppose men don't have best friends in the same way women do.'

86

'We don't talk about our feelings all the time, if that's what you mean.'

'I'm not sure it is. Anyway, sometimes I hate her.'

He raised his eyebrows. He liked to introduce me to people as his bookish girlfriend, but when I said things like this he seemed almost disapproving. In his world, things were clear-cut. A simple man, he called himself, with a measure of pride.

'It's not a straightforward relationship,' I told him.

'What does she want to do after she gets her degree?'

'I don't know. She could do anything she wanted.'

'Not likely she'll come back to live round here, is it?'

Stupidly, this had never crossed my mind. I realised I'd been assuming she'd come home and our friendship would return to the way it had been in the old days. I now saw how improbable that was. Wasn't it likely she'd want to find work somewhere more vibrant than Shropshire? London, even. She'd never talked about her plans for the future and I wondered now if this was a deliberate policy to spare my feelings rather than an indication that her plans really were vague.

I must have turned pale, because Tim asked if I were all right.

'I never thought, that's all – about Madeleine moving away.'

He shrugged. He was shuffling through his CDs and the noise was grating on my nerves.

'People move away and drift apart all the time.'

'But we can't!'

He turned to me and grinned, a CD hanging loosely from his hand. 'We don't need to, do we? Nothing to keep us apart.'

Did he really think I was referring to him and me? And I wonder what he'd have thought if he'd found out that right there, at that moment, I was visited with the realisation that my relationship with him was all wrong; dead in the water, unfixable.

Somehow I got through the rest of the evening without giving any sign that something was amiss. I'd never had to end a relationship before. How did one do it without seeming like the bad guy? I could give him no reason for not wanting to see him any more. None, at any rate, that would have made sense. "Because you're not Madeleine" came closest to explaining my feelings, but he would misinterpret, believe my feelings towards Madeleine were sexual. Not that I cared if he thought that, but it wasn't true. Perhaps it might have been kinder, though: he could have hated me cleanly instead of not understanding. So I took the coward's way out, telling him I wasn't sure where our relationship was going and I needed a break to think things through.

He responded coldly, albeit politely, and I sensed he knew my rejection had something to do with Madeleine.

'Call me when you're ready,' he said.

I nodded, promised I would, but we both knew it was over. I told him he was welcome to see other girls in the meantime. That, too, was cowardly.

On paper I poured out my feelings to Madeleine. She responded with a few scribbled lines on the back of a postcard: *So glad – never thought he was right for you! Will write more when I've got time. Mad xx*

But I didn't hear from her again until Christmas when she came home for the holidays. She phoned from her parents' house, said she had a bitch of a cold and hadn't been to lectures for a fortnight.

'Honestly,' she said, 'I don't even know if I want to do this any more.'

A crisis of this nature was the last thing I'd expected.

'I need to see you, Gabs. I've got to get out of here, my parents are driving me insane. Can you meet me down the pub in half an hour or so?'

Don't be late, she'd said, but I still had to wait fifteen minutes for her to turn up.

'God, I hate this place,' she said when she finally arrived. It was an ordinary country pub, a bit gloomy, heavy on the horse brasses and sepia photos of rural activities, but no worse than that.

'Not trendy enough for you, is that it?'

'That's not what I meant,' she snapped.

I'd have to tread carefully. She was clearly in a foul mood, worse than having a head cold warranted. Her hair was tangled and dull, her make-up badly applied, or she'd been wearing it too long.

A couple of drinks later, she softened enough to smile and apologise for being such a grouch.

'I know this isn't a great pub.'

'It's not that.' She pressed the palm of a hand against her forehead. Was she in pain, and was that pain literal or metaphorical?

There was no point pestering her with questions. She'd tell me in her own time or not at all. Instead, I told her about my break-up with Tim and the Christmas card he'd sent me, with the message *Love (????) from Tim*.

She smiled wanly. 'That's a bit childish. Aren't you glad you got rid of him?'

'Mostly.'

'I've been a cow to you, haven't I?' she said. 'I keep meaning to write to you – to explain everything properly – but I can never find the words, so I end up sending those stupid postcards.'

I gave her a weak smile. I had quite a collection of her cards, most of them National Gallery ones, lots of Cézannes and Picassos.

She placed her hands palms down on the table, her nails bitten and without their usual glaze of pale pink varnish.

'I'm sick of studying,' she said, gazing at the table. 'Sick of books! Sick of the books I'm meant to be studying, anyway. It's not true that you get to think for yourself at university. They tell you that, but in the next breath they tell you what you're supposed to think, and you'd better not veer too far from that.'

'Can't you put up with it for just a while longer? You're halfway through, practically.'

She looked up, her eyes swimmy with tears. When she shook her head, two teardrops fell neatly down her cheeks on to the table.

'Maybe I could, if it was only that. But there's something else.'

For one horrible moment I thought she was going to tell me she was pregnant, which would surely have been the end of university for her. I waited.

'I've been seeing someone,' she said. 'It's been going on since the beginning of term – since October. It's not long, is it, but it feels like for ever.'

A doomed love affair? Clearly it wasn't making her happy.

'He's a lecturer,' she said. 'I know it's not the same as a secondary school teacher and a pupil, but it's frowned upon. And he's married.' She gulped, or sobbed, I wasn't sure which. 'I love him. And I can't help thinking about the Christmas he must be having with his wife. They don't even have kids. Why can't he leave her if he really loves me?'

Odd, how disappointed I felt. Of course men would fall in love with her, that was inevitable, but thus far she'd never allowed one to overwhelm her. "Love" was a word she'd never used about any man. But now, seated before me, was every love-struck teenager; every damp-eyed, doe-eyed cliché. She had wept over boys before, but in an indulgent, almost luxurious way, accepting the brief pain as an inescapable, even necessary, rite of passage.

'You disapprove, don't you?' she said. 'I knew you would. And I don't blame you.'

'I can't bear to see you so unhappy, that's all.' There was nothing I could say to make her feel better, so I didn't try.

When we'd finished our drinks, we wandered aimlessly around the village, speaking only to comment on the coldness of the weather.

'I hope it snows,' she said. 'But it won't, will it?'

That year we didn't even exchange presents. I'd bought her a charm bracelet to replace the one she'd broken a year or so earlier, but she made it clear Christmas was something to be endured, not celebrated. She wanted only to get back to uni to speak to her tutor about switching courses and to see her lover. I kept the bracelet for myself, but I never enjoyed wearing it. It was hers, chosen for her, and whenever I put it around my

91

wrist I remembered the desolation I'd felt at tearing off the wrapping paper.

Between New Year and Easter I received occasional postcards (Bronzino, Titian, Rembrandt's self-portrait with his Saskia), but she gave no hint of unhappiness until May, shortly before she was due to sit her second-year exams. The letter she sent ran to three pages, the writing tiny rather than her usual scrawl. It was mostly incoherent and I was worried enough to speak to her parents. They were aware she was, as her mother expressed it, "having a bit of a crisis", but they put it down to the pressure of studying for exams, Madeleine's highly-strung nature (their words, not mine), and her own ridiculously high expectations.

I couldn't think of anything more I could do and should perhaps have been less relieved than I was when I received a postcard from Madeleine saying she'd been in a bad place when she'd written the letter and that I should ignore it, ending with a quotation she attributed to Byron: *Adversity is the first path to truth*. I had no idea what to make of this, deciding it was prudent to wait until her exams were over before pressing the point.

Could I have done more to help her? Should I have persisted, pestered? I chose to follow her parents' line of reasoning. What could I have done, anyway? Her doomed love affair had to be allowed to play itself out in its own time. Didn't I always provide the shoulder for her to cry on, the tissues to mop up her tears? She knew I was there, waiting. I always was.

CHAPTER NINE

Another phone call from Russell.

'You've got to stop pestering me like this,' I said. Only now did it occur to me that, in choosing him for a lover in the first place, I had been subconsciously emulating Madeleine. But surely that couldn't have been possible? Our relationship began with him offering me lifts home on days when it rained, since I only bothered taking my car in the winter when I didn't fancy the otherwise pleasant half-hour walk home.

I thought it kind of him to offer, and eventually, on one damp day when my car was in for servicing, I accepted.

'I was starting to wonder if I had a BO problem,' he said. 'I've lost count of the number of times I've asked if you wanted a lift.'

'It was nothing personal. I like to walk when the weather's fine. My car's off the road today.'

'Seems daft us both taking cars in when we live so close to each other.'

'How do you know where I live?'

'I've seen you. At least, I assume that sweet little cottage is yours?'

'Yes, it's mine.' I'd lived with my parents until they divorced, and then with my mother until she'd died, when I was thirty-four. I told neighbours and acquain-tances that I sold the family home because it was too large for me, but the fact was I couldn't bear the prospect of living there alone. Not that my mother and I had been particularly close, but her death raised ghosts and memories I needed to shake off.

We car-shared regularly that winter, Russell and I, although usually in his car. He said he was a nervous passenger, which I took to be a euphemism for disliking women drivers. On the short journey to and from work we chatted about the school where we worked, the weather, but rarely about ourselves. There must, I suppose, have been some gradual exchange of personal information that led to our affair, but it's difficult to pinpoint when a casual friendship between two colleagues became something warmer, and finally sexual.

I do remember that the first time he kissed me, he'd stopped the car outside my cottage, lingering for a while to finish some anecdote he'd been telling me. Curious and flattered rather than overwhelmed with passion, even then I seem to recall reflecting on Madeleine's affair with her lecturer, wondering if it had begun in the same casual fashion. Knowing Madeleine, it had probably been intense from the start.

'You know I'm married.'

'I could hardly fail to know.'

Madeleine had loved her lecturer. I never loved Russell. But he started it...

'I'll never leave her.'

Oh, yes; he made that clear from the start.

'I'd never ask you to.' *Easy to say...*

I soon wearied of being his bit on the side; of knowing

94

that whenever he was with me he'd had to invent some small lie to placate his wife; of knowing that I could never phone him at home, no matter what; of knowing, most of all, that – whatever her faults – his wife would always come first. One accepts these things in theory without realising how sordid and cheap they make one feel in practice.

Sometimes, when he was away with his wife for the weekend, he'd nip out to a phone box and call me. 'Just because I needed to hear your voice,' he'd say, but I pictured him glancing round, worried in case he was spotted, a clever lie neatly lined up to be unwrapped if the need arose. We could do nothing spontaneous together, could never be seen in public as a couple. What a life!

Glad I'd left all that behind, I slammed the phone down. Immediately I felt relieved, even euphoric. Then I started to tremble. I didn't imagine he was a mad stalker or anything like that. I shook with anger, not fear, my head swimming with images of the presents he'd given me during our affair; my lukewarm reception of them; his disappointment, his inability ever to understand what it was like for me.

'But I have more to lose,' he'd said.

'But I have already lost,' I'd replied.

If he was now paying the price for his indiscretion, his lapse in concentration, he was going to make damn sure I paid with him. That hardly seemed fair.

Simon stood in the doorway. 'What was all *that* about?'

I rolled my shoulders. 'You heard?'

'I heard you shout at someone. I heard you slam the phone down. You didn't break it, did you?'

'No, I didn't break it. Oh, God,' I groaned, 'I'm going to have to change my number if this carries on.'

'Russell again? Got a nerve, hasn't he?'

'You could say that. In any case, I don't see what good it would do him if we met. I can't repair his marriage; I can't even sympathise with him particularly. I wasn't his first extra-marital fling.'

'Really?' Simon sat on the sofa, one leg tucked under him. 'Can I see a photo of him?'

I had only one picture, taken at my work leaving do, a non-event lunchtime thing notable only for some very pretty cupcakes baked by the school secretary. I found the correct album and passed it to Simon.

'He's the one on the far left with the cheesy grin.'

'You don't look happy.'

'I wasn't. Whenever a teacher left, they'd have a big after-school piss-up. I got a lousy ten minutes in the staff room at lunchtime, everyone checking their watches, and a lot of people didn't bother turning up at all. Stupid to care about such things, I know.'

'It's the same in any big organisation. Maybe that's partly why I want to be a writer. I know you have to please your agent and your publisher, but it's not the same as having a boss and having to go to an office every day.'

'No, it's not. Maybe that's why I like working for the vicar so much.'

Simon wandered off to the kitchen to make coffee. When he came back, he asked why I'd quit my job at the school.

'I was only a temp. I stayed longer than I intended. I'm not rich, but I've got a bit of money my mother left me and I can manage with part-time work. I used to tell myself I'd use the rest of the time for writing, but that never happened.'

He gazed at me quizzically. 'Never? You never wrote anything again?'

I shrugged and stared into my coffee. 'I won a couple of minor competitions with short stories, but I couldn't seem to come up with a single idea that could be dragged out to the length of a novel.'

'Didn't mean to open up old wounds.'

I shook my head. 'It doesn't matter. Are you going to tell me what you're writing? Don't if you don't want to.'

He dragged his fingers through his hair. 'It's hard to describe. I kind of want to go a bit experimental, but it's hard to pull off without sounding pretentious. Maybe when I've written a bit more I'll discuss it with you – if you don't mind, that is. You might be able to help. One of my characters is a guy who's cheating on his wife. He's based loosely on my dad.'

'Is that wise?'

'He'll never recognise himself, too much of a narcissist. The thing is, I want it to sound credible. I don't want to make the character totally unsympathetic.'

'Your dad—'

'I've seen him with other women. He's not particularly discreet. I can't stand men like that, but I guess no one is totally bad. That's what they tell you in books about creative writing. Always give your worst characters a redeeming feature, even if it's only that they love their pet Jack Russell or never kill spiders.'

'I'm not sure you can write effectively about someone you don't like,' I said. Did he despise his father's mistresses? Did he despise me for having taken up with a married man? He was young enough to conflate me with those women his father knocked around with; to see us all as home wreckers, the enemy.

'It's weakness I can't stand,' he said. 'If he'd had enough of being married and walked out, or filed for divorce, that would have been honest. Instead he sneaks around, doing all the lame stuff your Russell probably did. Telling his wife he's working late at the office, listing his girlfriend under a bloke's name in his contacts list, spraying the car with air freshener to disguise the smell of her Miss Dior.'

God, he was brutal. And accurate. Of course it was a sordid business, and in Simon's eyes there was no room for tenderness, for human frailty.

'Sorry,' he said, but he didn't sound it.

That same day, Mr Latham also wanted to know what Simon was working on.

'I shouldn't pry,' he told me. 'He's a very personable young man, isn't he?' He adjusted the napkin and knife on his tray. 'Always a treat to speak to someone who knows the work of Mary Webb.'

'I don't really know what he's working on. A novel of some sort, but I don't know what it's about.' I didn't even know if he could write. The letters he'd written to me had been chatty, bookish, but far from literary. 'Is there anything else I can get you?'

'No, that's fine. I'll let you know how I get on with the sandwich.' He'd expressed a fancy for a half-baguette filled with sliced Brie and white grapes. For Mr Latham this was cutting-edge stuff. I think he worried that I would get bored serving him endless poached eggs and ham salads.

'If you like it,' I couldn't resist saying, 'perhaps we

might branch out into paninis and ciabatta.'

He chuckled, for he was not without a sense of humour, albeit rather a simple one. 'Quite so, quite so. I'm afraid I've never been terribly adventurous in the food line. Taste buds killed by all those dreadful meals at boarding school.'

'I never knew you went to boarding school.'

'Not a very good one. Rather a brutal sort of place. If I had a child, I most certainly wouldn't send it away to school. Character-forming, they call it. Not a phrase *I* should use.'

He interested me when he spoke about himself and his life, and I rather wished he'd do so more often.

'Tell me, Miss Price—'

'Gabrielle. Please call me Gabrielle.'

He smiled. 'A beautiful name. Thank you.'

'I interrupted you.'

'I was simply going to ask if you felt able to provide the catering and waitressing for a small festive gathering I'm having on the twenty-second. Please feel free to say no if you have other plans.'

'What sort of food would you want?'

'It will be mostly rather elderly clerical men – not famous for pushing the culinary boat out, I'm afraid. Sandwiches, salad, perhaps a quiche or two and some sort of dessert.'

'I should be delighted.'

'God, that's too precious!' Simon said when I told him of the vicar's request. 'Please say I can come – I've worked as a waiter. I'd love to hear what a bunch of priests talk about.'

I flicked his wrist with a magazine. 'You're certainly not coming if you're going to gloat. And I don't want you gossiping about them, either.'

'I wouldn't, I promise, but you must let me come!'

'Maybe. I'll think about it. But only if you swear to behave.'

That evening, Simon insisted on cooking dinner.

'Why?' I asked.

'No reason. Does there have to be one? I like cooking. Call it a general thank-you for letting me stay and being so considerate and everything.'

'I'm not aware I have been, particularly.'

'You've made me feel welcome. You don't mind the racket of my typing. You don't want to know every detail about my life.'

'Maybe I do, I just haven't asked.'

'Comes to the same thing. I think you would ask if there was something you especially wanted to know.'

That wasn't true. I'd brushed aside as irrelevant, as none of my business, the things I most wanted to know: what sort of girls did he fancy? Did his friends and family wonder where he was? What did he really want from me?

He nipped out to buy the extra ingredients he needed to make his meal, refusing to let me see the contents of the carrier bag when he returned.

'No fun unless it's a surprise,' he said with a grin. So I let him get on with it, torn between expecting burnt offerings or something worthy of *MasterChef*.

'Go and change into something spectacular,' he called out.

Spectacular? I had a couple of good dresses I'd bought in the days when I was described as a "breakthrough fresh voice" with "gifts that will ensure her books are read for many years to come". Classic dresses that fashion couldn't harm, they had the stale, bored look of clothes that had been left undisturbed on their hangers for too long.

I even slapped on a bit of make-up, something I rarely bothered with these days. I put on the bracelet I still thought of as Madeleine's, the one I'd bought her for Christmas but never given to her. It was no good, I felt like a thief, or worse; stealing from the dead. I removed it and put it away in my jewellery box. Perhaps I should have thrown it into her grave, but such grand gestures have always struck me as affected, even rather tasteless.

'You can come down now!'

He'd laid the table and set it with a candle and a small vase filled with sprigs of holly.

'I might have to move the vase,' he said. 'The table's not really big enough.'

'This is very nice.' Nice? Romantic, surely?

Of course not!

I'm not enough of a foodie to go into ecstasies over the details of the meal. Steamed artichoke with melted butter for the starter – a dish that wouldn't tax even the most kitchen-phobic cook. The main course a rather more complex ricotta and walnut ravioli with sage butter. For a student he clearly knew his way around a kitchen; or my cookery books, at least. Dessert, passion fruit fool with hazelnut biscuits. His constant need for reassurance ('Is it okay? Really okay? You're not just saying that?') rather spoilt things.

'Do relax,' I told him. 'You're making me nervous.'

'All right, let's talk about something else.'

'How is your book coming along? Mr Latham was asking me about it earlier, wanted to know what it was about. I had to say I had no idea.'

'Do you ever talk to him about your book? Has he read it, do you know?'

'He's never said. And no, we don't talk about it. It's the elephant in the room sometimes, but it all happened so long ago it seems largely irrelevant.'

'To you? Or to other people?'

'To everyone. It's old news.'

After we'd eaten, Simon cleared the table, washed up and opened another bottle of wine.

'I really do like your house,' he said, wandering around the room, touching things. 'Lots of books. Lots of mad ornaments.'

They weren't mad and I hadn't chosen them. My grandmother had spent the last few years of her life trawling auctions for pottery and glass. She wasn't interested in collecting valuable pieces, only things she found pretty: Japanese eggshell china, Mason ware jugs, Willow pattern plates.

'You've got style,' he said.

'I'm old enough not to care what anyone thinks of me, that's all.'

'No, it's more than that.' He sat next to me on the sofa, his knee gently bumping against mine as he spoke. 'It's a quality some people just have. You can't fake it.'

'If I didn't know better, I'd say you were flattering me for some nefarious purpose I can't guess at.'

He chuckled, swirling the wine in his glass. 'I hope I'm not that predictable.' He pulled a small hexagonal table towards him, placed his wine glass on it, then took mine and put it next to his. Then he turned to me, laid a hand gently against my cheek and softly pressed his lips to mine. It wasn't a passionate kiss; neither was it a platonic one. I'd imagined what it would be like to feel his mouth on mine, and now that it had happened it had been too unexpected, too fleeting for me to capture it.

'What was that for?' I asked.

'Does there have to be a reason?'

'There usually is.'

He handed me my glass of wine. If he noticed that my hands trembled, he didn't mention it. His were perfectly steady.

'I thought it would be nice, that's all,' he said. 'Wasn't it?'

I nodded, too overcome, too bereft to speak. I wanted more. I wanted too much. I wanted all of him.

Don't spoil the moment, I told myself. Accept it for what it is: a pleasant moment, a lovely gift. That's all it was, all it could be.

But gifts are never entirely free, are they? One rarely gives without expecting something in return.

CHAPTER TEN

Things didn't improve for Madeleine during the remainder of her second year at uni, and when she came home for the summer break she announced her intention to take a year out.

'And do what?' I asked.

She sighed and leaned back in the armchair while I took the typing chair. My parents had moved my bed into the box room to give me more space in what was now my personal sitting room.

'I think I'll travel,' she said. 'Work my way around Europe – isn't that what students do?' She pulled strands of hair from her ponytail, twisting them between thumb and forefinger. She'd never had so much as a paper round, so I wasn't sure how she thought she'd find work, but maybe the kind of places she had in mind weren't that fussy.

'Come with me,' she said. 'You hate your job and you must have saved a bit of money by now.'

I was half-heartedly saving towards the deposit on a flat, my grandmother having offered to give me half the sum I needed for my twenty-first birthday. Madeleine snorted when I told her this.

'Is that what life's about? Saving up for a poky flat that'll keep you trapped in a dull job you need to pay the mortgage?'

'It's what life is about for most people,' I said. 'What else is there?'

'Yes – what?' She gazed out of the open window, thumb and forefinger stroking the gold heart-shaped locket she always now wore, at a not very picturesque view of the backs of other semis and their pocket-handkerchief gardens.

I still wrote in my spare time, but once I'd started work my dreams had shrivelled. A couple of my poems had been published in small magazines, but the money I earned from these was never going to buy me a mansion: a fiver in one case, nothing except three complimentary copies of the magazine in another.

'Isn't that the point of going to university?' I asked her. 'Getting a degree so you can go after the interesting jobs?'

'Plenty of graduates end up in dead-end jobs. It's not as if I'm studying anything useful like medicine. English grads are ten a penny. I'd like to get into publishing, but I don't think it's that well paid and it's jammed with people called Tristan and Cressida. My face wouldn't fit.'

'It can't all be like that, surely.'

'I bet most of it is.'

'You'll be all right, then. You've got a posh name.'

She chuckled softly. 'So have you, come to that. Wanna start up a publishing firm with me?'

I managed a weak smile. 'I could be your secretary.'

She narrowed her eyes. 'You never did know how to aim high, did you?'

She was more than likely right, but until you've walked in someone else's shoes...

'So that's your great plan, is it? Work in a few Spanish

bars, soak up the sun, smoke a few joints, then go back to uni?'

'Why not? If I go back in October I'll resent it. I'm burnt out, Gabs.'

'Maybe shagging a lecturer didn't help.' Below the belt, certainly, but wasn't it true? Hadn't she made everything a whole lot harder for herself by getting involved with him, whoever he was?

'Ouch, the pain,' she muttered. 'All right, but who's to say I would have had a better time going out with another student? I didn't plan any of this.'

'So are you still together?'

She glanced away. 'I suppose not. I told him to choose. I guess he chose.'

She brushed away tears. I reached out to her, but she shrank away.

'I've never been much use to you, have I?' I said.

'No, but that's my fault, not yours. I didn't want you involved in this stupid mess with Hugo – yes, that's his name, don't laugh.'

'I wasn't going to. How old is he, anyway?'

She shrugged, examining her chewed fingernails. 'Not that old; thirty-six maybe. Doesn't matter, does it? He's married and that's that. I wanted to keep you out of it; I didn't want to... well, it sounds daft, but I feel like you're clean, innocent. I didn't want you knowing about all the shit I went through with him.'

I crouched at her feet, my arm resting on her knee. 'I'd rather have known, if I could have been any help – just someone to talk to, I mean.'

'I suppose so.'

I moved away from her. I could feel how tense her

muscles were. She didn't want me to touch her. Sometimes I wondered if she liked me at all.

'Is it because of him that you don't want to go back to uni?'

'I shall go back eventually, but I need to be away from him for a long time. I want a break from it all.' She pushed her fingers through her hair, dislodging her ponytail completely. 'I don't see the point of any of it.'

I sympathised. Over the following weeks I let her talk, I let her sulk, I bought her drinks; but there's a limit to how far you can push anyone. About me she never asked, beyond sniping at the little I'd settled for. She had the luxury of being able to do what she wanted for a year, knowing she could walk straight back into university and, more likely than not, sail through her final year.

Her dramas felt real and tragic to her, of course they did, but by the end of August I wasn't sorry to see her go. How far she would actually have to slum it on her travels I wasn't sure, but I hoped it would do her some good to learn how to budget, and walk instead of relying on people to give her lifts. I suppose I hoped it would help her to grow up a bit, to realise that not everyone had options, and there's no point in whining and bitching and wringing your hands if life doesn't turn out the way you want it to.

I heard from her very little during her year out. Postcards bearing foreign stamps fell through the letterbox during the first couple of months. From these I gathered that Barcelona was awesome, Paris was littered with bearded men who wanted to read Rimbaud to her, and Amsterdam had the best nightlife. And then nothing. Complete silence. She didn't even come home for Christmas.

'Not worth it, she said,' her father told me when I went to the Andersons' on Christmas Eve. They'd invited me and my parents round for drinks and mince pies, but it proved a gloomy occasion.

'Not worth it, my foot,' her mother muttered, ripping her Christmas cracker hat from her head. 'We would have paid her airfare.'

'Not that we know which country she's in,' her father added.

'They've reached that age, I suppose, when they want to do their own thing,' my mum said.

'I don't see your Gabrielle gallivanting off around the world when she ought to be at home with her family.' Mrs Anderson scrunched the orange paper hat in her hand. 'It's too bad of her, it really is.'

'Doesn't she tell *you* what she's doing?' Mr Anderson asked me.

'All I've had from her is a few postcards.'

'She didn't even send us a Christmas card.' This from Mrs Anderson, squeezing the paper hat like a stress ball. 'We've never interfered in her life. We gave her everything she wanted, within reason. I don't understand why she's chosen to ignore us.'

Mr Anderson held a plate of mince pies under my nose. I shook my head. If Madeleine had been there, we would have played charades and Trivial Pursuit. There would have been music and laughter. Even the tree seemed to have lost heart, a mound of dropped needles scattered around the pot in which it sat.

My parents made their excuses, saying they still had

a lot to prepare for "the big day", although it would just be the three of us, and they didn't even bother with a turkey since I'd turned vegetarian. I followed along a few paces behind them on the short walk home.

'You'd think she'd died the way they're carrying on,' my mum said.

'They spoilt her to hell and back, that's the problem,' my dad added, 'and now they want something in return.'

'Her presence is all they want,' I said, treading carefully to avoid slipping on the frosty ground. 'It was a bit rotten of her not even to send a card.'

'Still, not much of a party, was it?' Dad said. 'They should have put us off if they weren't in the mood for guests.'

I heard nothing from Madeleine until February when she finally bothered to send me a proper letter, although it said very little and mostly comprised a sad string of excuses for why she hadn't been in touch sooner. Mrs Anderson came round to our house brandishing her own letter from Madeleine.

'What am I supposed to think?' she said, flapping the envelope in the air. 'I can't even write back, there's no return address.'

I sat on the sofa with her while Mum made tea.

'My only child,' Mrs Anderson kept saying.

I felt for her, I really did, but at least we knew Madeleine was safe, and she had to come back sooner or later since she was due to begin her third year at uni after the summer. We could all tell her then how selfish she'd been.

'Did she say much in her letter to you?' Mrs Anderson asked.

'Not much.'

'She doesn't even say when she's coming back.'

Mum brought in the tea. I felt, as Madeleine's oldest friend, it was my duty to sit and talk to her mother, but when Mrs Anderson started to sob, Mum said I'd best leave it to her.

It wasn't until late July that Madeleine phoned me from Heathrow to say she was back in England and coming home.

'Have you phoned your parents?' I asked.

'What? Sorry – tons of people here, I can hardly hear you.'

'Your parents,' I shouted. 'Have you phoned them?'

'Not yet. Listen, I don't have much change left, can you go and let them know I'm back? I'll get the train, so I'll probably be home around seven or eight this evening. Gotta go – someone else wants to use the phone.'

I duly went round to tell Mrs Anderson I'd heard from Madeleine. At first she was silent, her lips pressed together.

'I think she didn't have much spare change,' I said.

Mrs Anderson shook her head. She'd gone very pale. 'Thank you,' she said, her voice clipped, and shut the front door in my face.

Don't shoot the messenger, I wanted to say, but I understood how she felt.

'I know I should have made more of an effort to keep in touch with them,' Madeleine said later, seated once again in my armchair. 'There were reasons why I couldn't – reasons I can't even share with you.' She took a bottle of duty free Finnish vodka from her bag. 'No, I didn't get as far as Finland, but a Swedish guy told me this stuff is the best.' She poured some into two shot glasses.

For someone who'd spent the best part of a year travelling around Europe, she had precious little to say about her experiences. I'd been abroad only once, on a school trip to France. I wanted to know about the places she'd visited.

'Let me know when you've had your photos developed,' I told her. 'I really want to see them.'

'I hardly took any,' she said. 'Besides, it wasn't really a holiday. I was working a lot.' She was vague about this, too, saying she'd mostly done bar work, plus a bit of tour-guiding (she spoke good French and passable German). Nothing about her year out added up. I knew better than to press for details, but it irritated me that she refused to confide in me. Did I mean so little to her?

'Did your parents blow up at you?' I asked. 'You should have phoned them. It was bad tactics to phone me instead.'

'I know. And I do feel bad about that, but I couldn't bear to speak to them.'

'But now you have.'

She shrugged and sighed. 'If I wasn't their only child, I'm sure they'd have washed their hands of me. They keep saying they don't understand me, but I don't even understand myself. They want everything nice and straight, but it isn't. There were things I had to do that I didn't want anyone else to know about.'

That was as near as she ever got to explaining her lost year.

She claimed that the break had done her good, that she was looking forward to her final year at uni, but in the event she graduated with only a third-class honours degree. For a girl who'd been expected to ace a first this was a bitter disappointment, although Madeleine seemed oddly unaffected.

111

'What does it matter?' she said. 'It was all wrong from the start. I'm glad it's over.'

It was hard to believe a messy love affair was at the bottom of everything, but what else could it have been? She started to apply for jobs and her good A-levels, plus a glowing personal reference from our former head teacher, got her a post as a teaching assistant in a primary school. She was no happier than I in her work, and I disliked myself for feeling that I'd got what I wanted – Madeleine here, not in London pursuing some glamorous publishing career.

'Don't tell my parents, but I'm writing a book,' she told me one evening while we were sitting in the pub.

'A novel, you mean?'

'It'll probably be rubbish, which is why I'm only telling you. I wrote some notes for it while I was away; couldn't get the idea out of my head. Have you placed anything recently?'

'A couple of poems.'

Her novel was the only subject about which she showed any animation. The rest of the time she seemed strangely disconnected from the world around her. She did her job competently by all accounts, but evinced no ambition to move on to something better. Men asked her out, but to my knowledge she turned them all down. I even wondered if perhaps her crisis had concerned her sexuality; that the male lecturer had been a smokescreen. Her parents were hardly the most liberal-minded of people.

We met every weekend, and often she spent Saturday afternoons in my room, reading through my recent poems. She never offered to share her writing with me and I began to wonder if it was a figment of her imagination. She'd pour vodka into the shot glasses, a little ritual by now, although the Finnish vodka had long since gone and she was forced to make do with a regular supermarket brand.

Despite seeing so much of her, I felt I knew her less and less. Her interest in clothes had diminished to the point that she only ever wore the same pair of jeans and baggy grey sweatshirt, the heart-shaped locket her only jewellery. She'd been so ambitious, so full of life; now I felt she was hardly there half the time. She'd sit on the floor in my room, sipping her vodka, reading my poems avidly, but she rarely made any comment on them and I didn't like to ask. I would read or type – she said she liked the sound of me typing. We spoke very little, for we had little to talk about. The shared confidences of our teenage years were gone.

She must have made some friends at uni, but she never spoke about them, never invited them to stay, never went to see them. Her life seemed to have shrunk, and whenever I tried to say this to her, all she offered was a bland smile.

'I just can't get through to her,' Mrs Anderson told me. We'd bumped into each other in the newsagent's. 'Is she drinking too much, do you think? I'm sure she drinks vodka because it doesn't smell.'

We walked back from the shop together, she carrying a blue nylon shopping bag, I with magazines and a bag of crisps.

'She never seems drunk,' I said. 'She doesn't drink much when we go out.'

'She keeps saying, "I've got a job, haven't I? What more do you want?" I only want to see her happy, and I don't think she is.'

I thought this oddly perceptive of Mrs Anderson.

Madeleine never wept, never moaned, never showed any signs of distress, but her mother was right: she wasn't happy. Not sad, simply neutral. As if she didn't care about anything or anyone.

'Can't you get through to her?' Mrs Anderson said. 'Girls tell each other things they'd never tell their parents, don't they?'

Her desperation moved me, pained me, but I had to tell her that Madeleine was no more forthcoming with me. Naturally I didn't tell her about Madeleine's novel, the existence of which I strongly doubted.

'Poor woman,' my mother commented when I told her about my conversation with Mrs Anderson. 'That's the trouble with high achievers: people expect too much from them. Madeleine's got herself a nice little job; most parents would be pleased.'

But Mrs Anderson was right: it was Madeleine's lack of interest in anything that was so troubling. All the vibrancy seemed to have leaked out of her like sawdust from an antique doll.

'Did you ever get those photos developed?' I asked one Saturday. Surely she must have had them processed by now?

'I never bothered,' she said. 'You should only keep photos of things you want to remember.'

'Your mum's worried about you.'

'I know, and she needn't be. I'm perfectly all right.'

'Are you? Really?'

She laughed. 'Of course I am. Everyone worries too much.'

'About you?'

'About everything. Stuff generally. Why does no one

understand that contentment isn't the same thing as happiness and that you don't have to go around smiling like a maniac to prove your contentment to other people?'

'*Are* you contented?'

'It's a work in progress.'

'You used to have a go at me for letting go of my dreams. What happened to yours?'

'They've changed. Sometimes you need to review them and see if they're really what you want.'

This sounded to me like something she'd heard from the lips of a charming Frenchman as he passed a joint to her. Maybe she was right. Maybe what we were all interpreting as disinterest, lack of engagement, was simply Madeleine taking stock of her life and, as she put it, reviewing her dreams.

'I would have liked to see your photos.'

'Photos of someone who no longer exists,' she said, and would say no more on the subject. She did, however, show me a picture of the man she'd been involved with at uni, the married lecturer.

'The Lecherous Lecturer,' she said.

'*Love in a Cold Climate*. I know. I've read it.' An ordinary face, but what can one tell from a photograph? 'Do you still love him?'

She shrugged. 'I don't think I feel anything for him. It's the best way.' Then she took the picture back and tore it neatly into four pieces. 'Don't look so shocked, it's only a bit of paper.'

But I shivered and looked away, a little in awe of her, a little scared of her, and I think I understood then that, of the pair of us, she was the true writer, for she had the necessary splinter of ice in her heart.

CHAPTER ELEVEN

Perhaps I should have acted sooner to change my landline number, but the complications involved seemed insurmountable: so many people would have to be notified, and what if I missed an important call during the changeover? Was it even possible to change one's number? It wasn't as if I were being stalked, simply mildly inconvenienced.

At any rate I didn't change my number and was unprepared for the next unwanted call I received. At first I assumed myself to be the victim of a crank call, for the person on the line didn't speak. No heavy breathing, just noises indicative of someone trying to catch his or her breath.

'Hello? Who's there?' I said, feeling foolish. An Indian call centre, perhaps. 'Oh, for goodness' sake,' I muttered when no one spoke.

I was about to slam the phone down when a voice finally said, 'Gabrielle Price?' A voice I didn't recognise.

'Yes? Who is this?' Silence. 'What do you want?'

And then, sobs. Hardly the usual sort of nuisance call, and presumably not a wrong number, for the person had clearly spoken my name. I waited for the sobbing to subside.

'Look, who is this?'

116

'I'm Michelle,' she said at last. 'Michelle Poole. Russell's wife.'

I gripped the receiver. What fresh hell was this? 'What do you want?'

Sniffs, snuffles, the sound of a nose being blown. 'I want to talk to you.' Her voice nasal from weeping.

'About what?' A foolish question, but I had no idea what else to say.

'What do you think? I know all about you. He's told me.'

I raised my eyes and tried not to make my sigh too obvious. In her shoes I'd probably have wanted to confront my rival, too. Although I wasn't her rival, not now, and really never had been.

'It's ages since I've seen him.'

'He says he broke it off with you. Is that true?'

'Yes, that's right,' I said. I didn't care about Russell, didn't want him, didn't even have to deal with his presence now that he'd moved away. In the circumstances I was more than willing to paint the situation in the manner most likely to please his wife, the woman who did have to deal with him.

Her voice rose to a pitch that was almost a squeal. 'He took you to Paris, didn't he?'

'I did go to Paris with him, but it wasn't the romantic tryst you're probably imagining.'

'A dirty weekend,' she spat. Well, let her. Her venom was pretty useless on me. 'Women like you are a disgrace. You're evil!'

She needed to vent. I understood that. I still winced, though. 'It never amounted to much,' I told her.

'That's your sort all over. You have your bit of fun, never caring who you're hurting, and when he dumps

117

you, you're all "Oh, it was nothing!" But it's not nothing to me!'

'I'm really not the heartless bitch you think I am. I know what I did was wrong. There are no excuses. I never meant anything to him.'

'You must have meant something. He's never taken me further than Dublin. I'm sick of being a doormat, sick of it.'

Her words dissolved into sobs. I wanted to feel sorry for her, but an overwhelming wave of tiredness swept over me. I *did* feel sorry for her, but she didn't really want to speak to me, she wanted a punch bag.

'Are you still there?' she demanded.

'Yes, I'm still here.'

'I'm too upset to think straight at the moment. I want to meet you, to speak to you face to face.'

'There wouldn't be much point.' Almost amusing, perhaps, that both husband and wife were so desperate for my company. Except it wasn't funny at all. It wasn't even tragic; it was too mundane for that.

'Are you scared to face me, is that it?'

'No, I'm not scared, I'm just not sure what purpose it would serve.'

'If I'm going to forgive him, I need to understand.'

What on earth was there to understand? A tawdry, unsatisfactory affair had petered out into resentment and bad feeling. Could she be made to believe that?

'Please,' she said. 'We can meet in a café if you're frightened I might attack you, although that kind of thing isn't in my nature.'

I believed her. After the "dirty weekend" shot, I'd expected a tidal wave of four-letter abuse, but she seemed not to have enough spite to carry through with what she'd started.

'All right, then, I'll meet you, for all the good it will do.'

She told me when she would be in the area to visit her parents. 'Russell won't be with me,' she said. 'My parents never liked him.' She said she could leave the kids with them for an hour or so to come and see me. Our venue was to be the café where I'd first met Simon.

'Thanks, then,' she said with another sniff when I agreed. Why did I not hesitate when I'd gone out of my way to avoid a confrontation with Russell? If I owed Russell nothing, neither did I owe anything to his wife. But I disliked Russell, despised his weakness. His wife was a different matter. A casualty, the innocent bystander who catches the shrapnel. I owed her nothing, therefore I felt no obligation to meet her, therefore it was in my gift to do so, and I chose to do it. Better the clean cut that drew blood than the wearying, bruising sense of obligation towards someone who no longer meant a thing to me.

'You really will be there?' she added, sounding like a teenager worried that her first date might stand her up.

'I really will.' Russell might let her down, I would not. A stupid thought. He was her husband, I simply the woman who had done the dirty on her. I knew only that I cared more about Michelle's feelings than those of her husband. I would meet her, offer my wrists to her; the rest was up to her.

In the meantime, I had food to organise for the vicar's little festive gathering.

'Should we wear outfits?' Simon asked.

'Outfits?'

'Waiters' uniforms.'

'You as crusty butler, me as frilly French maid? I don't think so, somehow.'

'Vicars and tarts,' he said with a grin.

'The only tarts they're getting are the sort with vegetables in.'

I confirmed all the details with Mr Latham, and on the Wednesday morning before the event Simon and I set to making the quiches, piles of sandwiches, two salads and a lemon drizzle cake. Mr Latham said there was no need for traditional Christmas food apart from a few mince pies.

'And you'll probably end up taking those home with you,' he'd said. 'It's one of the minor burdens of priesthood that one gets offered festive fare on a daily basis from the first of December.'

'You're getting paid for this, aren't you?' Simon asked.

'He told me to keep a receipt for all the food and he's paying us each £8 an hour for serving and waiting.'

'He doesn't need to pay me, I'm only going along for the fun of it.'

'Fun?'

He shrugged and leaned forward to shut the kitchen window. 'Research, then. If I'm going to be a writer, I need to experience as many different things as I can.'

How painfully he reminded me of my early ambitions, when I thought I could learn something about writing from listening to mundane conversations and scribbling them down verbatim.

We covered the plates and dishes with cling film, and for once I used the car to drive to the vicarage, since there was too much for the pair of us to carry. Simon sat on the back seat to stop the plastic crates filled with food from toppling over and I drove particularly slowly.

I'd arranged to be at the vicarage for six, a good ninety minutes before the guests were due. Mr Latham had kept his Christmas decorations to a minimum. A small, tastefully decorated tree with a star at its apex had been placed in a corner of the sitting room, and on the sideboard in the dining room he had on display a wooden Nativity scene. Even that, he felt, was a little too much, but it had been a gift from the Sunday school children.

He helped us carry the food from the car into the kitchen. '*So* good of you,' he said. 'And how kind of young Simon to come along to lend a hand.'

I glanced back at Simon, who winked. He got a frown from me in response. In my own house, Simon was welcome to make fun of the vicar all he liked, but not here.

My fears turned out to be groundless. Simon behaved impeccably. The conversation between the guests proved a small revelation, since very little of it seemed to have much to do with religion. There was a lot of moaning about keeping parish accounts and chairing meetings, but perhaps admin is the curse of every job.

Over the washing up, Simon whispered, 'Did I do all right? I didn't disgrace you, did I?'

'You were fine.'

He pouted. 'Only fine? Is that the best you can say?'

I flicked soap suds at him, with a quick glance round to make sure Mr Latham wasn't there. Not that he would have cared – why should he? – and I wasn't sure why I would have minded being caught out in some frivolous action in his house.

121

'The all-seeing eye of God,' Simon murmured against my ear.

'He's not God.' I snapped off my rubber gloves and started to stack the crockery in the plastic crates.

'God's representative, isn't he? You're different with him; you sort of tighten up.'

'I hadn't noticed. Why would I do that?'

'Because most people are superstitious even if they're not religious. Think about it. Would you ever swear at a vicar?'

'I don't go around swearing at anyone as a rule.'

'All right, bad example. But the point is you talk to him differently from how you talk to other people, and only because he wears that dog collar.'

'I'm the same with policemen,' I said.

'A policeman is someone in authority, like the man from the water board. A vicar isn't; he's got no earthly powers to arrest you or cut off your water.'

'I don't quite see—'

'It's just interesting, that's all. Maybe we're all secretly hedging our bets even if we call ourselves out-and-out atheists.'

Mr Latham poked his head around the kitchen door. 'All right in there, you two? I must say, I think that went swimmingly. I'd rather hoped there would be some of the lemon drizzle left for me to have tomorrow, but not so much as a crumb remains.'

Did I really speak to him in a different way? But don't we all adjust our persona depending on whom we're addressing?

'I'm glad it went well. We'll be finished soon.'

'Take your time – no hurry – though I'm sure you

want to get off home.' He beamed – yes, he beamed, and I saw that Simon was right. When I looked at Mr Latham I didn't see a man; I saw someone who was on a higher moral as well as spiritual plane. I couldn't imagine him ever having a dirty thought.

It was of Mr Latham I thought when I hesitated on the threshold of the café where I'd arranged to meet Michelle. How would he handle such a situation? But he would never have found himself in a dilemma similar to mine in the first place. If he'd ever hurt anyone it would have been accidental. And yet I'd never intended to hurt Michelle – had never, in truth, given her more than a passing thought.

She gave me a wan smile. I was pleased that she'd chosen a table in a secluded corner. Would she weep? Perhaps she was past that.

She already had a cappuccino, which she cupped with both hands. We didn't speak until the waitress arrived with my coffee.

'Thank you for coming,' Michelle said. 'I wasn't sure if you would. I'm not sure I would have done in your position.'

It was an ordinary weekday morning, therefore no great surprise that the few other customers were elderly ladies treating themselves to tea and a cake. I hadn't told Simon where I was going, since he might have insisted on tagging along.

'I read your book,' Michelle said. 'It's Russell's copy.'

I was relieved I hadn't written a message in it. I hadn't even signed it. 'He never read it.'

'No. It's very good. You should write another.'

'You don't really want to talk about my book, do you?'

'I hoped it would tell me something about you – about what you're like. But I think it's too clever for me. You'd probably despise the kind of books I generally read.'

She wore a little discreet make-up and her medium-length dark hair was shiny and well-cut. The pale grey pearl studs in her ears and her delicate silver necklace suggested a woman who cared about her appearance. She hadn't yet abandoned her wedding ring, a thin gold band.

'When did you last see my husband?' she said. We both smiled, for the phrasing sounded so music-hall.

'Not since you moved away. He – well, he did phone me a couple of times, you may as well know that.'

She nodded. 'I suspected. What did he want?'

'To meet me, to talk about – about what he'd done; what had happened.'

'Me finding out, you mean? I gave him hell.'

She lifted her cup to her lips with both hands, then carefully dabbed her mouth before replacing both hands around the cup. Her calmness surprised me, but I got the feeling she was struggling to keep her emotions in check. Every movement she made was careful, deliberate.

'He's a shit,' she said, her mouth turning down at the corners. I couldn't disagree, but he was still her husband. Running him down wouldn't help her to come to terms with what he'd done. I assumed the fact that she still wore her wedding ring indicated her intention to remain married, but what did I know about marriage or the complicated business of negotiating one's way through the marital minefield?

'What will you do?'

A small sigh expressing great weariness escaped from

her lips. 'He wants us to try again, to make another go of it, all the usual clichés. But really I think it's just the hassle and expense of divorce that stops either of us doing anything about it.'

'You do know I meant very little to him, don't you?'

'It doesn't help. He says the kids and I have always come first in his mind, but that doesn't help either. He says it's not my fault, but that sounds like a cop-out. If he was happy with me he wouldn't go after other women, would he?'

The *cri de cœur* of every neglected wife.

'Do you work?' I asked.

She laughed softly. 'You think I need to develop more interests outside the home? That's exactly what Russell said.'

'I'm sorry; I didn't mean to sound patronising.'

'I work part-time in a charity book shop. It's only voluntary. He didn't want me to work when the kids were little, so he's only got himself to blame that I can't find anything much now.' She leaned back, hands still not letting go of her cup. 'It's odd, don't you think, that I can sit here talking to you as one sensible woman to another? I was a bit hysterical when I phoned you. I didn't want to leave you thinking of me as an unhinged harpy.'

'I don't have that impression at all. And if I'm honest, one of the reasons I agreed to meet you was that I didn't want you to run away with the idea of me as a home-wrecking scarlet woman.'

'Scarlet woman – there's an old-fashioned phrase. But if I really loved Russell, wouldn't I want to scream at you and tear your hair out? I don't understand why I don't.'

'Maybe you do. It would be reasonable, I think. Not

125

that I'm any threat to your marriage, but still, these things aren't logical, are they?'

'I think I just feel that if I start screaming at you, the bastard will have won.'

This didn't seem like a great basis for the rest of her marriage, but neither was it my place to tell her what she ought to think about Russell. I'd told him that his marriage was not my concern. The same applied to Michelle. I felt she had a right to confront me, but not to solicit my opinions. Not that she had. But she might.

'It might be easier to hate you,' she said, 'but I'm fairly sure I don't. He might have already started cosying up to someone new for all I know. I don't have the energy to hate every woman he's screwed.'

It might have been easier for me, too, if she'd hated me; then I might not have felt such pointless sympathy towards her.

'We shan't meet again,' she said. 'I got what I came for.'

'Which was?'

'To find out what kind of person you are. We might have been friends, in another life.'

I should have been happy with the way our meeting had gone, but it left me oddly dissatisfied. Her attitude had been exemplary and maybe that was the problem. I would have been upset, embarrassed, if she'd shouted and made a scene, if she'd cried, but that might have been more cathartic for both of us. I felt the problem of Russell had merely been shelved, not solved – for her as much as for me. Certainly if he rang me again I could tell him he had a wife who was too good for him and mean it, but wasn't that too glib? Too easy to align myself with the injured wife when I must shoulder my own share of the blame for her injury.

Russell's marriage, his problem, but I'd known he was married and had given very little thought to Michelle. Clever of her, really, to present herself to me in the guise of a reasonable and likeable human being. If she had struggled to keep her composure, doing so effectively had ensured I was troubled by a searing sense of guilt not even Mr Latham could have assisted me in shaking off.

CHAPTER TWELVE

As Christmas Day was fast approaching, I again asked Simon if he had any intention of going home to spend Christmas with his family.

'I can't face them,' he said. 'I can't face the hell of a family Christmas. I know I'll have to go home sometime, but later rather than sooner. I've got used to being your lodger. Unless, of course, you've got other plans.'

I had no plans. Christmas meant nothing to me. Generally I popped in to the vicarage over the break, simply to give some structure to my days. I envied Mr Latham who had services to plan, parishioners to visit, bonhomie to dispense.

'No, I've nothing planned,' I told Simon. It was just another day, wasn't it? If he hadn't been there, I might have cracked open a box of mince pies and sipped a Baileys while half-watching whichever blockbuster movie the BBC decided to show, but otherwise I would have carried on as normal.

Neither Simon nor I could muster the necessary festive cheer to make a special day of it. We had no tree, no presents, no tinsel or crackers. On New Year's Eve, we drank a bottle of prosecco and watched one of those depressing review of the year shows on the telly and, as Big Ben chimed, Simon rooted around in his rucksack and pulled out two Eurostar tickets. At first I thought he was letting me know he'd decided to leave after all; I didn't realise one of the tickets was for me.

'But why?' I said.

'Spur of the moment thing,' he said. 'It's cheaper this time of year. I remembered you telling me about Russell taking you to Paris and the lousy time you had there.'

'Yes, we did.'

'I've never been to Paris. Wouldn't it be nice to go and not have a lousy time?'

Nice! Could he possibly be as naïve as he appeared? He was offering himself as a substitute for Russell, wasn't he? Or was I over-analysing? Had he simply fancied a trip to Paris and felt there was no time like the present? Didn't everyone make an impulsive decision from time to time?

We checked into a hotel conveniently near the Gare du Nord in a shabby back street, all takeaway espressos and shisha bars, too down-at-heel to be hip. While we were on the train, I'd half hoped he'd booked one room; a double bed. But of course he would never have done such a thing.

Two small rooms, each with a single bed. Simon lying on his, testing the springs, I suppose; me slowly unscrewing the cap from a bottle of warm Evian, gazing out of the window on to a deserted patio scattered with wooden tables and chairs where hotel guests were required to go if they wanted to smoke.

Après moi, le déluge. But no flood, however cataclysmic, could have been worse than this sense of being dragged along by something I couldn't control; some

129

force that would leave me battered, bruised, half-dead. Because it was only after I said goodbye to Michelle that I understood the reason for my dissatisfaction. I was free of Russell, of whatever ties had bound me to him, only because my heart belonged to someone else. The poignancy of watching Michelle walk away was far surpassed by the pangs I felt when I imagined a future scene in which I was the watcher and the person walking out of my life for ever was Simon.

I'd tried so hard to muffle my feelings; told myself it was ridiculous, that if I ever expressed those feelings I would make a fool of myself. Too bad. The damage had been done, the shadow firmly fixed on the x-ray. He could never be mine, but I was his. Disgusting, obscene, oh yes! Instinctively I knew his lip would curl if I told him how I felt. That kiss he'd given me had been nothing; a little experiment, a dare. Well, he'd done it: he'd kissed the hag, and there, as far as he was concerned, the matter ended.

Being besotted with someone makes you see them in a strange light. Every small thing they do seems miraculous, every quirk is endearing, every smile, every movement, every sweep of their eyelashes. There he sat on his bed, toes pointing up, the soles of his feet grubby, the prominent bones of his wrists and fingers giving him the look of a gangly teenager. He was not a teenager, it wasn't criminal for me to want him, but if my love wasn't immoral, it was certainly unwise.

Where else should we find love except in Paris? What else should we find in Paris except love? And pain. And the lonely cries of the soul Jean Rhys described so well in her novels – stories that made sense to me only when

I reached an age when I understood what it meant when a woman grows older and wearier but still wants to be loved, desired.

Oh, God...

'Hm?'

'What? I didn't say anything.'

'Sorry. Thought you did. So where do you want to go tomorrow? Eiffel Tower? Sacré-Cœur? Notre-Dame?'

Simon was young enough to find delight in the smallest of things, even something as mundane as an all-you-can-eat buffet breakfast: a feast of croissants, brioche and *petit pains* spread thickly with Nutella. We stuffed our pockets with what we couldn't eat (even sachets of jam) so that we wouldn't have to bother finding somewhere to buy lunch.

The Eiffel Tower, Sacré-Cœur, Notre-Dame...

My fingers surreptitiously pressed against a marble statuette of the Virgin Mary, a furtive prayer.

If you grant me this, I will believe.

Wet flagstones and bare branches in the Place du Tertre under the cold winter sun. A black cat, its tail forming a question mark shadow on the wall behind it. A window opening above us, a lace curtain whisked by the breeze; a girl calling down to her lover, a young man astride a shiny red motorbike. Simon's hand loosely catching hold of mine, fingertips against fingertips. And later, in the evening, drinks in a fashionable bar. A French guy with all the ooze of a practised Lothario, asking me if Simon and I were married. Engaged?

Just good friends.

He laughed, disbelieving, Simon and I dropping our gazes, blushing; but did we blush for the same reason?

Lothario quoted a passage about lost love, which he then helpfully translated from the French.

'Colette.' My voice without colour. I recognised the quotation, taken from *The Last of Cheri*. Poor Cheri, discovering that the sexy, fascinating older woman he'd loved had become fat and jolly, sexless. If Simon understood, he didn't say. And Lothario, how did *he* know? Was it – was I – so obvious? Surely it couldn't be that the French have a special radar that picks up the subtleties of love – of desire – in strangers?

'Ah, you know Colette,' Lothario said. 'That is good.'

'Why good?'

A suave Gallic shrug. 'I am French. We're proud of our writers. The English use their best writers to teach schoolchildren to hate literature for ever. We celebrate ours. We *live* them.'

I'd spotted a young woman reading Rimbaud on the Métro and I'd enjoyed the moment, but there was nothing to say you couldn't hop on the London Underground and find someone reading William Blake. Maybe it wasn't the same thing. There is no British equivalent of poets like Rimbaud and Baudelaire. Edith Sitwell, perhaps, but who reads her?

'The French think they have a monopoly on literature and romance,' Simon said. He looked very much at home sprawled in a velvet-upholstered chair, forefinger brushing against his lower lip, a glass of Pernod and water on the zinc table in front of him.

Lothario had an entourage of several young women, brunettes dressed in black, all mascara and red lipstick like the three terrible women who attempt to seduce Jonathan Harker at Castle Dracula. Their ravenous gazes shifted between Simon and Lothario (I wish I'd known his name so that I could refer to him in a more sensible fashion). Occasionally they bent their heads and whispered to one another. Simon paid them no heed, but neither did he take my hand as he'd done when we strolled around Montmartre.

He might not be mine, I wanted to shout at them, but he'll never be yours, either. And I'm the one who's going home with him tonight. You don't need to know about the separate rooms. Imagine us (as I will) squeezed into one of the small beds, blankets on the floor, his body curved around mine, our fingers laced together.

But in reality there was only awkwardness, Simon and I standing in front of our respective doors, a thin wall and so much else separating us.

'Sleep well,' he whispered before inserting the key card into his door, and all I could do was smile and hope he couldn't read the yearning in my eyes.

He wanted to go shopping at Les Halles. I wanted churches, cemeteries. We argued.

'It won't be any different from any other mall,' I said. 'Why waste time trailing around shops?'

'I want to buy some clothes.' Determined, like a child.

I shrugged, sulked, didn't respond when he suggested I take a look around the church of Saint-Eustache while he shopped.

'Oh, be like that, then,' he snapped. 'I'll see you back at the hotel.' And he stalked off, abandoning me. A petty squabble that left me with a stone in the pit of my stomach. I wanted to take home only pleasant memories. I wanted to remember the carousel at the foot of Sacré-

Cœur, murky lamplight, cobbles slick with rain; his hand holding mine.

I could have taken myself off to a cemetery, but the idea lost its flavour without Simon. I took the Métro straight back to the hotel and sat in the patio area with an espresso and a book, a tartan travel rug around my shoulders, woollen gloves doing little to warm my hands. Too cold a place to sit for long, yet I preferred to be alone outside than in my small hotel room. In any case, I couldn't settle to read; couldn't get past the feeling that the whole holiday was now spoiled.

Simon turned up a couple of hours later carrying two shiny carrier bags with designer names on them. He was smiling, pleased with himself, eager to show off his purchases. I had little interest in women's clothes, still less in menswear.

He dumped the carrier bags on the table and sat down opposite me.

'How can you afford designer clothes if you're a student?'

'My dad might not be my greatest fan, but he's generous. Guilt money, I suppose.'

'You're happy to let him bankroll you, are you?'

'It's the least he can do,' he said, refusing to meet my eye. 'What have you been doing with yourself?'

I brandished my book.

'Did you look round the church?'

I shook my head.

'You should have done. In the guide book it says Madame de Pompadour and Molière were baptised there. Shall we do the Louvre tomorrow?'

'If you like.'

'Rihanna had a private tour of the place and took loads of selfies in front of the paintings.'

'Very postmodern. But maybe no worse than all the tourists who snap away at the *Mona Lisa*. It's not even much of a painting.'

'Still in a bad mood, then?' he said, more than a hint of sarcasm in his voice.

'Just fed up.'

'How about I get rid of these bags and then we find somewhere nice for coffee and cake? My treat.'

I was the petulant child and he the grown-up trying to humour me, to get me back on side with sugary snacks. I had to snap out of this black mood, didn't want him to think me one of those annoying women who must have everything their own way and can do nothing without a man in tow. Only the very young and the very beautiful can get away with such behaviour.

Over coffee and a slice of Tarte Tatin, Simon told me about a novel he'd recently read, *The Hopkins Manuscript* by R C Sherriff, about a catastrophic natural event resulting in most of the earth's population being wiped out.

'Because there were so few people left,' he explained, 'all the old rules broke down. One survivor decided to live in the National Gallery. There was no one to stop her, no one cared about art any more, so she basically took ownership of all the paintings. Imagine if you were the only person left on Earth and you could live anywhere you wanted – any grand or public building – all yours for the taking. I'd go and live in a library.'

'Presumably there wouldn't be any electricity. You could only read on days when you could see to do so by natural light. Or with candles, until all the candles ran out.'

He gave me an odd, uncertain smile. 'Forget the practicalities.'

'But I can't. It would be cold in winter, too. You'd have to burn the picture frames, if you could find any matches to light a fire with.'

'Do you have to be so literal? Can't you just see the romance in it?'

'I would like to.' Impossible even to contemplate the idea of having a relationship with a man so much younger than myself. He would live for the moment. I would always be conscious of the fact that at some point, while he was still in his prime, he would look at me and see an old woman. The horror of imagining that moment would haunt me, ruining all the good times.

Paris is not really for lovers. Paris serves only to remind one of the transience of love, of life. The Pont de l'Alma, covered in graffiti: outpourings of grief and remembrance for Princess Diana. The Catacombs, thick with skulls and bones, the air sour, thin, signs near the payment kiosk warning those with heart or respiratory problems not to attempt it. And, of course, the cemeteries and their printed maps, checklists of death. How many can you find, photograph, cross off? Opposite the great wall enclosing Père Lachaise, a long row of funeral directors, florists, shops with sober black signs and tasteful gilded lettering, hearses parked in front of them. On every notable grave, scraps of paper bearing messages, weighted down with stones; small plaster angels; flowers, candles, even a tangerine on the double grave of Sartre and de Beauvoir.

Simon indulgent, less enthusiastic than I'd hoped, bending down to stroke each cat that wandered over the graves. When he came across a black cat, he said, 'We've got one like you at home.' We? Home? For surely he was referring to Pushkin; and yes, he was, for he added, 'I hope Pushkin's all right.'

'Of course she is. She's in an excellent cattery. She'll come to no harm. Cats don't miss their owners the way dogs do.'

Simon perched on the white grave of Paul Éluard, lifting the black cat on to his knees. The blond boy, the black cat, fugitive sunlight falling through the branches of bare winter trees. I took a photograph before Simon realised what I was doing. I wanted him to look exactly as he was, not even a suggestion of the tightness that results from knowing you're having your picture taken.

He held out his hand. 'Let me take one of you.'

I shook my head. 'Not here. You made a nice composition, that's all, you and the cat.'

The cat soon sprang away from him and sat in the middle of the path to wash itself.

Simon looked up at me, squinting against the bright sun. 'Do you think either of us will ever write a story about Paris? About *this* Paris?'

'This Paris?'

'Our Paris, then, if you like.'

'It doesn't belong to us,' I said.

'You know what I mean. You're being too literal again.'

I took a drink from one of our bottles of Evian and handed another to him. 'And yet I'm the one who finds cemeteries appealing. They seem to bore you.'

He shrugged, the bottle dangling between thumb and forefinger. 'I prefer the living to the dead, that's all.'

'How odd. That you should see it in those terms, I

mean. Aren't memories a kind of death, in that case?'

He grinned. 'Too philosophical for me.'

I stretched out my arms. 'This is France. Philosophy runs in the water.'

'I hope not,' he said, shaking the last few drops from his Evian bottle. 'Philosophy's worse than death. It makes you worry too much about the purpose of living instead of getting on with living. Come on – let's leave the ghosts alone.'

We took the Métro to Montmartre and spent the rest of the afternoon strolling along the back streets. He held my hand – to stop us losing each other, he said – and I wished I could accept the gesture lightly. I recalled my mum telling me to hold the hand of whichever neighbour was bringing me home from school. Each hand felt different, with its own smell and texture. Some clammy, some floury. One was rough, one smelled of Gingham perfume.

But Simon's wasn't just another hand. I couldn't catalogue it, couldn't even begin to describe it; it was just *his* and therefore perfect. I longed to take it to my lips, brush my mouth against his skin, inhale the smell of him.

We paused to watch a thimblerigger taking money from unwary tourists, his routine polished, presented in English; his expression entirely shifty. I felt Simon's thumb caress my palm.

'Should we warn them they're being conned?' I said.

'Why bother? They're not putting their life savings down, are they? A euro or two at most.'

And they laughed when they lost, a rueful shake of the head, plenty more euros where that came from, and a quick photo op with the cheeky conman, all good fun.

I felt suddenly depressed, my spirits lowering with the sun. My lips dry, unkissed. I wanted more than this chaste holding of hands; I could hardly bear the prospect of another night sleeping in my mean little bed, feeling like a child again. I envied the thimblerigger his glib sleight of hand, his easy patter.

Simon put down a euro, winked at me, guessed right, right again, then wrong, as we all three knew he would.

'What did you do that for?' I asked.

'It's only money, isn't it?' He took another euro from his pocket, pressed it into the hand of an Algerian girl with outstretched arms. She ran after us. 'No – no more,' Simon said, shaking his head, then shrugged and gave her another euro.

'Simon.' I felt oddly irritated, as if the beggar was a rival for his love. She gave a graceful bow, didn't try for three in a row. She was one of those wise people who understand when it's time to back down, and that to expect too much is foolish.

CHAPTER THIRTEEN

A period of mild depression invariably follows any holiday, even an unsuccessful one. Mine had started on the journey home, the tears falling as our train drew out of the Gare du Nord.

Simon squeezed my hand. 'You'll come back,' he said. Not "We", I noticed. Who would be with me the next time I visited Paris, or would I be alone? I didn't see myself as a solo traveller. I liked the vision of renting a room for a month, spending my days in Paris as a *flâneuse*, wandering wherever the mood took me, getting by with a mixture of bad French and simple English. But I wasn't that brave or resourceful.

I sniffed, nodded, told myself not to be so childish.

'When we get home,' Simon said, 'we'll draw the curtains, pour ourselves some good red wine and read *Les Fleurs du Mal* to each other.' He turned his face away to gaze out of the window, though for most of the journey there was precious little to see, and even the French countryside we passed through was flat and bleak, rather like Suffolk.

It was a long journey with three changes of train. Before I unpacked I collected Pushkin, arriving home to find that Simon had already dealt with the suitcases and had even hung up my clothes.

140

'Wasn't sure if I should,' he said, 'just wanted to help.'

'Thank you.' I coaxed Pushkin from her carrier. She bolted upstairs. 'I can't face cooking. And we don't have any milk or bread.' The final straw. Simon sat beside me and let me sob, passing me the tissue box.

'The Spar will be open,' he said once my crying had subsided. 'I'll get bread and milk, though they might not have much left, and I'll get wine, and while I'm out you can order pizzas.'

He would have made a good nurse. He did some magic with wires and gadgets so that we could watch a slideshow of our Paris photos on the TV screen. We ate pizza straight from the box and drank overpriced plonk, both of which served to soften the jagged edges of my misery.

'We'll always have Paris,' he said. 'I know that's just a thing people say, but it's true.' But memories would fade even if the photographs didn't. In five, ten years' time, I would remember only a few details in sharp focus, and they would likely be the ones I would prefer to forget. And Simon, what interest would he have in preserving the holiday in any but the vaguest of outlines?

"Paris, yes, I first went there a few years back with a friend – acquaintance, really – just someone I knew for a short time…"

There was no "our" Paris. There was his Paris and there was my Paris. There was some overlap, but the roads forked in crucial places. The memory of our separate rooms wouldn't haunt him as it would me.

After I'd finished work at the vicarage, Simon insisted we go for a walk. 'We both need some fresh air. Everyone finds January depressing.'

I lent him a scarf, though he insisted he never felt the cold.

'Where shall we go, then?'

'Just a walk around the village. You could show me the house where you grew up.'

'It's just an ordinary semi, same as millions of others.'

'I'd like to see it anyway.'

I always averted my eyes on the rare occasions when it was necessary to pass the house. Simon had to shake my arm to make me look at it properly.

'Who lives there now?' he asked.

'No idea.' A Christmas wreath was still fixed to the front door and there was a red Ford Kuga on the driveway; otherwise it looked much as I remembered it.

'Did your friend live near here?'

'Madeleine? Just down there.' I pointed further down the road, but had no desire to be more specific.

'The river's over there, isn't it?' Simon asked.

'Yes. Just beyond the cul-de-sac where Madeleine lived.'

We were standing barely five hundred yards from the spot where Madeleine had drowned. I'd never been near the river since her death and had no intention of doing so now.

'Why did you never move away from here?' Simon asked. 'Why stay in the same place if it holds such bad memories?'

'I suppose I always hoped the memories would fade or become overlaid with better, stronger ones.'

'You should go back to where she died. The actual spot. Then you'd see it's a place like any other. You'll feel nothing, I promise.'

I shook my head. 'It's getting dark. I don't have a torch.'

'We won't need one. Don't you want to start writing again? Don't you want to start living? You never will until you've laid her ghost. This is part of it.'

Eventually I agreed, but it had nothing to do with writing, everything to do with proving she was really dead. Whenever I dreamed about Madeleine, which was often, her face was caught in a rictus of horrified surprise, her clothes sopping, her skin pale, almost translucent. One hand splayed out, but no one there to grip it, to save her.

'How old did you say she was when she died?'

'Twenty-two.'

'That's younger than I am now. It must have been rough for you.'

'And for her parents.' Could one ever get over the loss of a child? In the early days, shortly after Madeleine died, I spent a lot of time at her parents' house. Together we mourned. We swapped memories, pored over photo albums, passed tissues to one another. My parents tried to dissuade me, told me it was morbid, and over time the Andersons' attitude changed. They shut the door on the past, changed the subject whenever I brought up Madeleine's name. I wanted them to look upon me as a surrogate daughter. They picked up on that, but they knew it wouldn't do. I didn't compensate, I merely reminded them of what they'd lost.

Their response was muted when my book was published. I was careful not to brag about it, but it hurt me deeply when I overheard Mrs Anderson speaking to a woman in the post office.

'All the while she was pretending to grieve for Maddie

143

she must have been writing that book, feathering her own nest.' Of course it hadn't been like that at all, and I didn't understand her sour attitude. After that, I avoided her.

'It's a pretty spot,' Simon said. 'No fishermen, either, to spoil the view.'

'Hardly, at this time of day.' My gaze travelled to the river. Water that sparkled under the sun's rays now took on a leaden, sinister appearance. 'I've always been frightened of water. With the trees and everything, I'm always reminded of that painting of Ophelia lying on her back, palms up, flowers trailing after her.'

Ophelia's lips slightly parted, her dress reminiscent of a bridal gown. A pretty corpse, not twisted and bloated, hair and limbs tangled in river muck.

'Don't think about it,' he said.

But I did. And I thought about Virginia Woolf searching for stones to put in her mackintosh pockets, placing her hat and cane on the river bank and then wading purposefully into the Ouse. Did she weep?

'Don't think about it,' Simon repeated. 'Come on.' He dragged me to the river's edge. 'Look into it,' he said. 'No dead bodies, no ghosts.'

But the branches of the trees overhanging the river whispered like the murmurings of a ghost. I didn't believe in spirits, in any kind of life after death, and I knew that any ghost I thought I heard was my own conscience. I was alive and she was dead – where was the sense in that? I'd done so little with my life; the mark I'd made on the world was no more than a dirty thumbprint. But self-pity was even more loathsome than blaming myself for a death that wasn't my fault.

'I just wanted her to live, and I'd rather be haunted by her ghost than think of her spirit being snuffed out completely. I tried—' To live through her? To make her live through me? Not quite that. Not really. 'I tried to keep her memory alive, but everything fades eventually.'

'Even love,' Simon said. He took my face in his hands and kissed my forehead. The kind of kiss a priest might bestow on a penitent. Simon's lips were cool against my skin.

'D'you remember that first letter I wrote to you?' he asked.

'Of course I do.' I'd kept it, slipped inside a plastic wallet and stored in the box I risibly called my cuttings file.

'I had this fantasy of you teaching me everything you know about writing. Of turning me into a great writer, no less.'

'You'd do better to sign up at one of the universities that offer creative writing MAs.'

'I'd rather become a writer – *if* I become a writer – through trial and error. Blood and tears. Writing – serious writing – is kind of like a love affair, or should be. You get to know your story, it intrigues you, if you're lucky it enthrals you, and ultimately it ends, leaving you wretched and abandoned.'

'I think writers overplay the creative aspect of their work. It's a trade like any other. Unless you write purely for your own pleasure, you write a book of a length and style you think publishers will want. Writers have to sell themselves. Puffing a book isn't much different from a tart decking herself out in satin and sequins. It all comes down to money in the end.'

145

Simon bit his lip. 'I think art's more important.' He looked me straight in the eye. 'I'm young enough to think that, you see.' But he didn't grin. He looked suddenly, briefly defeated. By his own youth? By his ideals, knowing they would inevitably be knocked about, assaulted, defiled?

'I'm glad,' I said. 'You're too young to be cynical.'

'Was Madeleine? Was that why she killed herself?'

'It was an accident. I'm sure it was an accident.'

'What was she doing here? Why would she be here in the first place? How could she have got close enough to the water to fall in? Could she swim?'

Questions fired at me without mercy. 'I don't know,' I said. 'I don't know!'

'Then you don't know she didn't do it deliberately. You can't know that for certain.'

'What does it matter how it happened? She's still dead!'

'It matters,' he said. 'It always matters.'

I'd believed the purpose of this excursion was to bring me some sense of closure, not to rehash events long buried. 'Don't you realise I've spent the last twenty-odd years wondering, grieving, going over it again and again?'

'You'll never stop thinking about it. Closure is about coming to terms with a tragedy, not forgetting about it altogether.'

'But how she died— What actually happened—'

His gaze was impassive, but he wasn't fooled.

I shivered. He was right; it mattered.

146

CHAPTER FOURTEEN

Gently but surely Simon prodded at the soft tissue, the thin skin, the old bruises.

We'd been discussing his work in progress and I'd been trying to help him negotiate a blockage: one of those points in a novel when you feel it's all a hideous mess; your characters made of cardboard, your plot full of holes. My PC was littered with half-completed manuscripts like so many car wrecks. All of them write-offs, their scrap value negligible, some of them so old the rust on them was lacy and friable.

Pitilessly I gazed at Simon hunched forward on the sofa, dragging his fingers through his hair. He was young, he hadn't known tragedy. His angst was temporary; it was nothing.

'I just wish I knew what to *do*!' A self-indulgent moan.

'No one said it was easy. You just have to plough on.'

He glowered at me. I daresay I deserved it. Still pitiless, I continued, 'Creative people shouldn't get a special dispensation. Surgeons don't get surgeon's block. They just—'

'Plough on? Like *you* did?'

That hit home. What had I been saying so breezily, so thoughtlessly?

'I wasn't blocked,' I said. 'I just... I ran out of steam,

that's all. I kept trying, but nothing was ever as good. It reached the point where it seemed useless to continue.'

'I don't believe you,' he said. 'That novel was so good – I mean so, so brilliant – it's not credible you couldn't have written another one as good, or better.'

'You know as well as I do the number of writers who produced only one novel.'

'So you're content to number yourself among them? Gloating at everyone else who perseveres?'

'I'm not gloating and I did persevere. I've just told you, I kept trying more times than I can count.'

'How do you explain the first book, then?'

'I can't. The first one is different; you've nothing to live up to. No one has any expectations. You can write what you like, knowing no one will care whether it's any good or not.'

'You're full of excuses, aren't you? You've never really *done* anything, have you?'

Did he believe I needed some kind of shock therapy, something to shake me out of my apathy? Perhaps I did, but Simon barely knew me and had no right to sit in judgement.

'If I were you, I'd remember that you're a guest in my house. I can boot you out any time I please. The middle of the night, if I choose.'

'You'd do that, wouldn't you? You don't really care about anyone, that's your problem.'

'Do *you*? You've no time for your family and I've never heard you mention a single friend by name since you've been here.'

'And where are *your* friends, Gabrielle? Madeleine's the only one you ever talk about and she's been dead how long?'

'Why do you care? What is any of this to you? Why did you have to come and poke your nose where it's not wanted?'

'That's rich,' he said, leaning back against the sofa and crossing his arms. 'You wouldn't have let me stay if you didn't want me to be here. I think you're lonely. Lonely and frightened.'

'Frightened?'

He nodded. 'You're as timid as the respectable ladies in those Barbara Pym novels you like so much.'

I told myself he was a silly kid who knew nothing of my life, but his arrows pierced where they hurt the most. I couldn't deny his accusations, though I didn't see why my failings warranted so much vitriol. Didn't most people simply bumble through their lives, ticking over, aiming not for greatness or even happiness, but simply trying to get by?

I took a deep breath. 'We're all flawed, Simon. I've made mistakes and often I've taken the easiest route, but that doesn't make me a terrible person.'

'*That* doesn't, no. But some mistakes are more forgivable than others, aren't they? Can you honestly say you forgive yourself for every bad thing you've done? It's the ones you can't forgive yourself for that matter.'

'That's between me and my conscience,' I said, wishing I smoked or had a strong drink to hand. 'I'm going to make some coffee,' I said, moving towards the door.

'That old cop out! Go on, then, go and make your coffee.'

My eyes smarting, I stood with my hand on the door handle. If I walked through the door, I was a coward. If I didn't, I was weak, doing what Simon wanted me to do.

'I can't win with you, can I?'

'That's life,' he said with a self-satisfied smile. 'There are winners and there are losers. It's not my fault you blew it.'

'Blew it? Blew what? You have no idea—'

'Of what, Gabrielle?' He edged forward on the sofa, stared at me as if daring me. 'You didn't get the breaks, is that it? Write one brilliant novel and that's it, game over?'

'It wasn't my fault,' I said through gritted teeth.

'Course it wasn't. Always someone else's, isn't it?'

'It wasn't my fault,' I repeated more loudly. 'It wasn't! I never meant—'

'What did you never mean? You might as well tell me now.'

'I'll tell you nothing.'

He gave a disdainful sniff. 'You never meant any harm, is that it? A sheep could say as much if it could talk.'

'You really are a shit.'

'Aren't I just? And what are you?'

I quailed beneath his appraisal of me. He was nothing to me; he was nobody! My home, my life. He didn't belong in either.

'Fuck off, Simon,' I muttered.

'What about the voices in your head, though?' he said, tapping the side of his head for emphasis. 'What about them?'

I swallowed the lump in my throat.

'If none of this matters, why do you look as if I've threatened you with a gun? You can't use your brilliant book as a shield against life. That's what you've done, isn't it?'

'No! I hate that damn book! I wish she'd never written it!'

I caught my breath. Surely he'd never notice my slip of the tongue? But of course he did. He missed nothing. His eyes glinted. He'd scented blood and went in for the kill.

'Of course you never wrote it. How could you? Someone like you?'

Now what? Should I invite him to make himself comfortable while my story poured out like a thin trickle of sour Spanish plonk?

'Look, hang on a minute—'

'She. Madeleine. Why else would you be so obsessed with her, so haunted? She died, so you helped yourself to what she'd left behind, which just happened to be a work of literary genius. My God, that takes some beating!'

Tears fell from my eyes. For many years the truth had ceased to matter because I (the 'I' who wrote *The Song of the Air*) had ceased to matter; had been buried beneath a drift of dry leaves, covered up like some perpetually hibernating creature.

He picked at his bottom lip so hard he broke the skin. Roughly he scrubbed at it with his knuckles, a smear of red against his pale skin.

'You've no idea, have you, what you've *done*?'

What had I expected? Understanding? Amusement? I'd misjudged him. I hadn't reckoned on his disgust.

'Look, I can explain—'

His eyebrows shot up. '*You* don't believe in the death of the author, do you? Which is either deeply ironic or a bit macabre. I mean, you *knew* the author was dead – literally dead – and you just... took over.'

151

'It was what she wanted.' Cling to that, the stubborn root that refuses to yield its grip on the compacted soil. 'She did!'

'You don't get it, do you?'

'It was one book no one much cares about any more. It's not like I'm claiming the novels of Virginia Woolf as my own, for God's sake. And fiction itself is just a bundle of lies. It's not *real* – only the ideas are real.'

'*Her* ideas, not yours. Anyway, this isn't about authorship, it's about me and you. You lied to me.'

'You want to be a writer because you're in love with the idea of being one, not because you've got something deeply important to say. It's a job like any other.'

'So you did what, exactly – hot desking with Madeleine? Job share? She did the work and you took the glory?'

'Glory – what glory? My fifteen minutes? Barely that! The book would have sold better if people knew she – the author – that she was already dead.' I paused, expecting him to speak, but he didn't. I had no choice except to bluster on, to fill the oppressive silence. 'Plath, for God's sake – look at her. If she'd lived to be an old woman, who'd still be reading her? It doesn't change the poems – they're not better or worse. It's all smoke and bloody mirrors!'

We stared at each other. He was the first to break eye contact, and I knew that was somehow important. I was determined to brazen it out. No cowering, no excuses, no apologies.

'What would you do if I went to someone with what I know?'

'Like who? Who would care? Who would believe you?'

'Her parents might.'

152

'So you'd be willing to cause them massive pain just to plant your flag on the moral high ground.'

'There's more to it than that. You owe it to posterity – to *her* – to have a true record somewhere of what happened.'

'My confession?' I sneered. 'Bless me, Father, for I have sinned.'

He nodded. 'Why not?'

'And what would I do with this ludicrous confession? Hand it over to the police?'

'Don't be daft.' His face softened slightly. 'You wouldn't have to do anything with it. Stick it in a safe deposit box with instructions that it's only to be opened after your death.'

The phone rang. We both stared at it.

'Don't answer it,' Simon said, glaring at me.

I picked up.

'What the fuck did you see Michelle for?' Russell demanded.

I'd given little further thought to my conversation with Russell's wife. Water under, etc.

'She asked to meet me. We had a perfectly amicable chat. Why are you cross?'

'Jesus Christ! You're as bad as each other,' he shouted. 'Bloody women, you're worse than a pack of monkeys!'

'Monkeys? What *are* you on about?' Most of my mind was on Simon, who had slipped from the room. I heard him switch the kettle on.

'You're all the same,' Russell continued, 'rubbishing men is what you like best, isn't it? God, I can just imagine it, the pair of you picking me over, telling yourselves you're "bonding" but really just using me as your Aunt Sally.'

'It wasn't like that. There was no question of anyone being picked over. You can't bear to accept that two women could have a perfectly reasonable and sensible conversation; you have to turn us into cackling witches to suit your plot.'

'That's rich! That's *really* rich! Female solidarity my arse! You didn't stop to think about Michelle while I was banging you, did you?'

'Neither did *you*, and you're the one who made all sorts of vows to her. Love, honour, cherish – ring any bells?'

'Well, you must have said something to her – she's left me. Gone to her mother's, of all the pathetic clichéd things to do.'

Back to the womb, to unconditional love. 'She probably wants you to realise she doesn't want to be taken for granted any more.'

'*Thank* you, Professor bloody Greer.'

'Oh, grow up, Russell. There's no point sniping at me. You got yourself into this mess, not me.'

He slammed down the phone.

Simon held out a cup of coffee.

'An olive branch?' I said.

'Only instant coffee. What did he want?'

'To tell me his wife's left him. Obviously it's my fault.' I sipped my coffee, but caffeine was too weak a drug to be of much use. For a woman who led an uneventful life, I seemed to have mired myself in complications. No point complaining. If I didn't deserve everything that was being chucked at me, I wasn't entirely blameless, either.

I wasn't the person Simon had believed me to be. A cheap pickpocket rather than a gifted novelist. I'd been exposed as ordinary, unexceptional. No talent, nothing to say. An empty box, a dud firework, a ripe plum with a grub curled up inside it. To know you've disappointed someone is difficult to accept. He'd admired me, been a little in awe of me. I was nothing more than the breath-taking magic trick that turns on banal mechanics.

'Don't hate me,' I said. More tears: predictable, detestable.

He took my hand and stroked it. 'I don't,' he said. 'It was a staggering thing to pull off, really. Almost impressive.' He sounded as if he were trying to convince himself, trying to pull misshapen cloth into something presentable.

'What would you have done?' I asked.

'God, I don't know! If you could have written your own book—'

'I told you – I tried. Maybe I hoped Madeleine would somehow inspire me from beyond the grave, but she didn't. I had to accept I had no talent, at least not enough. *That* was my punishment.'

A gentle, beatific smile. 'Think how much better you'll feel after you write all this down. Then, one day, people will know, they'll understand, and it might even make you famous again.'

He might have been right. If I made my confession now, it would appear tawdry. But if the seal was broken only after I was dead, wouldn't there be some grotesque interest attached to it? Maybe I could even apply a bit of spin to the tale, style myself as Madeleine's amanuensis. There was, after all, a precedent for what I'd done: Willy, first husband of Colette. So the story went, he locked her in a room until she'd written down her spicy schoolgirl recollections, then published them under his own name. The famous Claudine novels. The balance of power eventually shifted, of course, but if it hadn't been for Willy she might never have become a writer at all.

'You do see that it has to be done, don't you? It *is* necessary.'

I didn't see any such thing. The facts of a writer's life interfere with our appreciation of the work. We know too much about most writers, even the most secretive ones.

He had no hold over me. My word against his. I was a respectable, useful member of society. I worked for a vicar; I had no blots on my copybook. What was Simon? A waster. I saw him for what he was and I always had done, for what that was worth.

'I won't do it,' I said, wiping away my tears.

He walked towards me, gripped my wrists. Looked into my eyes. Kissed me. His mouth opening against mine; my body responding, leaning into him, flesh dissolving in the heat of his body.

He broke the kiss. My mouth gaping, wanting. His lips parted, wet. He shook his head.

'It's no good,' he said. 'This will always be between us and get in the way.'

Us? There was no us!

'If I write it all down, if I do as you ask—'

I saw only what I wanted to see, believed only what it suited me to believe.

'You'd be doing it for me. It would show me how much you trust me. How much I mean to you.'

But what do I mean to you, Simon?

'Does that matter so much to you?' I asked.

He nodded.

'Do you trust me to tell the truth?'

'But I don't know what the truth is, do I?'

'And if I refuse?'

'I can't force you, can I? What's the worst I can do?' *Or not do...*

'You could tell people what I've told you and hope they'll believe you.'

'Would they, d'you reckon?'

I shrugged. 'They might want to, some of them. Her parents, for a start. They resent the money and fame that came to me when I published the book. For some reason they thought it was in bad taste, as if I'd deliberately done it to rub their noses in their loss.'

Simon sat on the sofa, legs apart. 'What would they have done, do you think, if you'd given the manuscript to them instead of publishing it?'

'I think, if I'd given it to them shortly after Madeleine died, they'd have destroyed it. Books aren't important to them. They wouldn't have read it. Maybe they'd have stuck it in a drawer in her room, which – I don't know, but I bet they've kept it exactly as it was. It would have gathered dust till they died, then it would have ended up in a skip most likely.'

'So, what you did, it did at least save the book?'

'Well, yes, but I refuse to say anything that makes it seem as if I'm justifying my actions. She *gave* it to me. She even crossed out her name on the cover page, for God's sake. I didn't write it, but the book *became* mine. Look at all the celebrities who have books ghost-written for them. What's the difference?'

'I'm an English grad, that's my context. Integrity of the text and all that.'

I raised my eyebrows. 'Is it really that simple? Aren't there shades of grey? All right, I'll write out the confession, but only because it seems like the only possible conclusion, the final full stop to the book. And only because it's probable Madeleine's parents will never have to read it – assuming they die before me, of course. I'll have to risk that.'

'Maybe it'll be cathartic. Maybe it'll free you to write something of your own.'

'Too late for that.'

'Do you think it was fate that brought me to you? Like it was something that was meant to happen?'

Was he being serious? His expression suggested he was.

'No; I don't believe in the workings of fate – not in the way you mean. I don't know what brought you here. Sooner or later, or maybe never, what does it matter?'

'Maybe you're right. But maybe these things matter more than you know.'

I shut my eyes. *I'm tired*, I wanted to say; *tired of thinking about the past, which is gone, over and done with. Let it alone. Let it be. Love me.* But when I opened my eyes he'd still be there, that expectant look on his face. Merciless.

158

CHAPTER FIFTEEN

There's something I've been meaning to tell you...

I'd never felt any compulsion to confess the truth. Not to my parents, not to Mr Latham, not to Madeleine's parents. And how to explain what I'd done? Would anyone believe that Madeleine had simply handed over her novel with the intention of me publishing it under my name? It wasn't credible. I would be labelled a thief, a fraud, a fake. My actions, however one tried to spin them, couldn't look anything other than shabby. A true friend would have wanted to see Madeleine's name glowing on the front cover of her book – a lasting epitaph.

I owed Simon nothing – no more, certainly, than I owed to Madeleine's parents, those good, damaged people from whom I'd long been estranged. Occasionally I'd tormented myself imagining their reactions if I were fool enough to blurt out the truth. Horror. Disgust. Pity? An insistence that I make a public declaration, a shifting of the crown from my head to Madeleine's?

And how the literary press would have clamoured to dip their bread in such a tasty sauce had I been tempted to tell. How they would have rolled up their sleeves, flexed their fingers and tapped out their thousands of jabbing words. What a story!

What was the point? She was dead. Brutal but inescapable fact. Fame couldn't touch her.

Madeleine's death was officially recorded as an accident. A tragic accident, but an accident nonetheless. No one to blame, no one held accountable. Nothing, of course, could have consoled the Andersons for the loss of their daughter, and I don't think anyone would have blamed them for the efforts they put into trying to persuade the council to put up some kind of fence along the bank of the river.

'These things happen,' said a council official.

'But how, but how?' the Andersons asked. A shrug from the council employee. Madeleine wasn't a toddler. And what had she been doing down there anyway? Sensing, I think, the council official implying that Madeleine's death might have been suicide, the Andersons backed off.

'What do *you* think?' Mrs Anderson had asked, grasping my hand. We sat next to each other on her sofa, a photo album open on our laps. 'I know she'd been very low in spirits, all that business with her degree and everything. But we'd have noticed, surely, if she were properly clinically depressed?'

No more than the Andersons did I have any idea of the signs and symptoms of "proper" depression. Nevertheless, I had more of an inkling of her state of mind than they did. But what good would it have done to tell them just how unhappy she was, to the point where she'd told me she wished she were dead? After all, I'm sure I'd said much the same thing myself during my drama-queen, life-is-shit moments.

'She liked her job,' I said. 'I don't think there's any reason to believe she intended to kill herself.'

Mrs Anderson winced. 'But what was she doing there? By the river?'

'I don't know. I don't suppose we shall ever know.'

'I feel I can never entirely accept her death until I understand how it happened. You do see that, Gabrielle, don't you? I know it's unreasonable, but it's the unanswered questions that are so hard to bear. I keep going over and over in my mind—'

'I know. I *do* understand.'

'Most people don't. They talk about "learning to live with it", about "moving on". I don't think they mean to sound heartless; in fact I'm sure they mean to be kind, but it doesn't help. It doesn't help in the slightest. There's no proper end with something like this, just a vague hope that somehow I will get used to this emptiness.'

Her words moved me, but I was no more help to her than the well-meaning folk who told her she must get on with her life.

Did she ever realise, I wonder, that I was keeping from her a great deal of information? I'm not sure any of it would have helped her come to terms with Madeleine's death.

No closure for me, either, but that was my own fault.

'I wish I were dead.'

'No, you don't. Why would you? Is your life so terrible? Have you some deadly disease?'

She kicked off her shoes and tucked her legs under her, the Lloyd Loom chair creaking as she shifted around trying to get comfortable.

'But what's the point of it all, really? Work, money – it's a big vicious circle that doesn't lead anywhere.'

'Circles don't, generally,' I said. I wanted to lighten her mood, get her off this pointless navel-gazing. The meaning of life, for God's sake! No meaning, no point, you just get on with it.

'I wanted so much from life,' she said, fingering the gold heart-shaped locket that represented her parents' pride and all their hopes for her. 'It's been a huge disappointment.'

I wanted to laugh, but Madeleine wasn't some doom-obsessed goth who painted her nails black and read existentialist French literature.

'Don't you remember telling me I shouldn't settle for less than I wanted? Go back to uni, get a better degree.'

She shook her head. 'I was wrong about education being the key. Trouble is, I don't know what the key is.'

'There isn't one.'

'There must be. Listen, Gabs, I want you to do something for me. But you must promise absolutely never to tell another living soul.'

'All right,' I said, more annoyed than curious. Why must she make such a mystery of things?

'Come round to my house on Friday night, seven-ish. I want to give you something. I want you to look after it for me, keep it safe.'

An item of jewellery, perhaps: some heirloom she didn't trust herself not to lose? What else could it be? I didn't give the matter much thought, but duly presented myself at her house on Friday evening. I followed her upstairs to her bedroom. Her parents had had it decorated hoping this might cheer her up a bit, the smell of gloss paint still lingering in the air.

She crouched down to sort through a precarious tower of books and papers, eventually dragging out a bundle of pages held together with a treasury tag. She thrust it towards me.

'Here. I'll give you a carrier bag to put it in. If anyone asks what it is, say I've lent you some books.'

I glanced at the front cover of the manuscript. *The Song of the Air* by Madeleine Anderson. Below that, a quote from *The Snow Queen*, Hans Christian Andersen's fairy tale about the struggle between good and evil: *Up in the little garret there stands, half-dressed, a little Dancer. She stands now on one leg, now on both; she despises the whole world; yet she lives only in imagination.*

'I don't understand,' I said. I lifted the cover sheet, but she reached out and stopped me.

'Not yet,' she said. 'Not *here*. I can't stop you reading it, but I'd rather you didn't until I've explained it to you.'

The explanation, when it came (after a couple of shots of vodka), made no sense. She'd written a novel, she believed it was good, but she didn't trust her parents not to root around in her room and find it. Then she snatched the manuscript from me and crossed out her name.

I laughed purely from nerves.

'I'm serious,' she said, clutching the pencil. 'If anything happens to me, I don't want *them* to get their hands on it. It's yours. I'm giving it to you, Gabs.'

Now I was frightened. People talk about the burning intensity in the eyes of crazy artists and I saw it: her eyes on me, but focussed on God knows what. Something only she could see.

'I don't want it,' I said. 'I'd rather have your friend-

163

ship – like in the old days, when we told each other everything.'

She cocked her head, seemed to have returned to the world. 'Did we, though? *Should* we have done? Would it have done either of us any good?'

'Is that the point?'

She shrugged. 'Anyway, we are what we are, and the past is over and done with. That's not true either, of course, but let's pretend it's true.'

'Why pretend? Why can't you be frank with me?'

'Because that's not my way. I don't even know why I wrote this stupid book. Sometimes I wish I hadn't.'

'If it's so good, why don't you send it off? Find a publisher for it?'

'I can't be bothered. There – that's me being frank. I literally can't be bothered. If you don't take it, I swear I'll burn it.'

I winced, even though I was certain I held a slush pile reject, at best something competent but derivative. The idea of burning books – even terrible ones – is something no true lover of literature can stomach.

'I'll take it, then. And look after it. But I'll consider myself holding it on your behalf. You can take it back any time you want.'

It was with some trepidation that I began reading what she'd written once I got home. In some ways I would have been less worried if it had been stiff, boring, the work of a rank beginner. Even a rambling mess would have left me less shaken than the thing of beauty it turned out to be.

I stayed up all night to read it from beginning to end. By the time I'd finished, my eyes were sore, my sleep-deprived mind spinning with questions. Where, above all else, had this come from? Surely I should have had some inkling that my best friend possessed this kind of extraordinary talent? All those years she'd watched me beavering away on stories that, if not actually stillborn, should have been strangled at birth.

Jealousy is unreasonable, insidious, damaging. I knew that. I despised myself. But how could I not have been jealous? The fact that she'd apparently donated the book to me was no consolation. I could never possess it. If anything it would possess me, and so it came to pass. I became obsessed with the book. For years, long after it was published, I continued to torment myself with it, labouring over each line, trying to work out how she'd done it, what the trick was. Always it eluded me.

My eyes stinging, I shoved the manuscript back into the Tesco bag. I spent Saturday, the first whole day I had with Madeleine's book, trying to hate it, trying to find fault, pick flaws, but there was only one conclusion to be drawn. The book was brilliant. Madeleine was a born writer, but more than that, she had gifts most us don't even dream of possessing.

That evening I went round to her house, asked if she wanted to know what I thought of the book.

'You couldn't have read it,' she said. 'I only gave it to you last night.' She looked even rougher than me. Panda eyes from going to bed with make-up on; food stains (tomato ketchup and egg by the looks of it) on her baggy jumper, which she wore with the sleeves pulled down so they almost covered her hands; her lank hair gathered into a messy ponytail with a rubber band. She wasn't wearing her locket.

'I stayed up to read it,' I told her.

'Does that mean you liked it?'

Liked it! Did she really have no idea what she'd done? And if I told her it was brilliant, would she demand it back? Would she suddenly decide she wasn't depressed after all, send the book out, become a world-famous author; money, fame, respect – ? All that I could set in front of her.

'You're the writer,' she said. 'Tell me what you really thought of it. I shan't be upset if you don't like it.'

It was supposed to be *my* glittering career, wasn't it? Didn't I deserve it, after all the hours, the tears of frustration, the work I'd put in to becoming a writer? *My* dream, not hers. *O, beware, my lord, of jealousy; It is the green-ey'd monster, which doth mock the meat it feeds on.* I knew the quotes. I knew what I was supposed to feel, what I was supposed to do. The right thing, the wrong thing: these were clear-cut, without ambiguity.

'I think you've got some really interesting ideas,' I said. Words: choose them carefully. 'But I'm probably not the right person to judge. I know you too well.' I didn't know her at all, it seemed. But then, she didn't know me.

She slumped back in her chair. 'It's no good, is it?'

'I didn't say that.' *How could she not know?* 'Look, I'll be honest, it's quite good. It's just... You know how fickle publishers are, how they're always looking for stuff that's overtly commercial – mass appeal and so on.'

She nodded, rubbing her eyes with the sleeve of her jumper.

She'd given the book to me, hadn't she? So why would she even care what I thought of it?

She sighed. 'I knew I was probably aiming too high –

trying to do something I didn't have the experience to do. Do you think you could do anything with it? To improve it, I mean? Would you try?'

I almost laughed. What craziness were we talking? 'Do you want me to?'

'You could edit it for me, couldn't you? Tidy it up, get rid of all the loose stuff, re-write the bits that don't work? Is it worth it?'

'Maybe,' I said, 'but I can't promise. It's quite an odd book, isn't it? I can't make up my mind whether it's stupidly good or complete bollocks.'

'Probably bollocks. Do your best. If it's useless I'll just have to accept that. It doesn't really matter, after all.'

It goes without saying that I didn't alter a single word. It was already perfect.

For the record, it never crossed my mind at any stage that Madeleine was contemplating suicide. It's a minor point, really, for I doubt this knowledge would have changed anything. That she hadn't been behaving normally for some time was something her parents and I had come to accept. We hoped she would "get over it". That something would happen, some course of action occur to her, that would bring her back to life, back to us.

'People do change,' my mother told me. 'She was never the life and soul type, was she? I expect she's still upset about not doing as well in her degree as she'd hoped, but she's young enough to change direction, if she wants.'

There was more to it than that, of course. More than I ever understood.

But the crucial point, the point where everything

stops, where the blame rests squarely upon my shoulders, is that I was with her when she died. I'd followed her, meaning to catch up with her to tell her what I really thought about her book. I felt it was the only thing that would help, give her something to be joyful about.

It was about eight, a gloomy February evening. I lifted my hand, opened my mouth to call to her. Stood there, as if petrified, feeling as impotent as I had on the day of my grandmother's funeral when I'd tried to reach my weeping mother, only to be shooed away by other relatives. My father and an aunt comforted my mother. My other grandmother looked after me, but I felt as if I'd been denied something. I wasn't allowed into the circle of grieving. Too young; no use at all.

Madeleine wore no jacket. Jeans, boots, an old cardigan that reached almost to her knees. Hands stuffed into the pockets of the cardigan, her hair loose. I was sure that if I ran up to her and tapped her on the shoulder she would spin round and look at me as if I wasn't there, or as if I were a stranger. Somehow I sensed she'd passed beyond me.

Following slowly behind, I decided she was going to meet a man. Which man, I couldn't guess. Someone she'd met at work? So much of her life was closed off to me.

I followed her over iron-hard ground (no rain had fallen for days), watched her push aside the branches of the trees, saw her stand at the water's edge. The man she waited for – why didn't he come? Another married man, stringing her along...

Hands pressed against the rough bark of a tree, I watched her crouch down, her head bent. Was she looking for something in the water? Praying? Then she climbed down so that she was sitting on the bank (grassy in summer, now an earthy ridge). She levered herself off the bank and into the water, slowly, as though testing the depth, her body adjusting to the shock.

Then I understood. 'Maddie!' I cried out. She gave no indication she'd heard me. I scrambled after her, my eyes fixed on her, watching her wade out to where the water was deepest.

I couldn't even swim. I removed my boots, sat on the bank, eased myself into the water. 'Maddie!' I shouted, but I knew she intended to pay no attention to me. I gulped water, floundering as the river shocked me with its iciness. She was a strong swimmer. She swam to a point well beyond my reach. I attempted an untidy doggy-paddle, but I knew I'd never reach her without going under. I should have turned back, run for help, but by then I knew it would be too late. Her calmness I read as determination. She'd made up her mind.

'Maddie, listen to me,' I called. 'Listen – about the book – I lied. I was jealous, okay? It's the finest thing I've ever read. I hate you for it, for being better than me, but I don't want you to die. Maddie!' My voice shook with tears. Either she couldn't hear me or she thought I was lying, saying anything calculated to make her change her mind. 'It's the truth, Maddie! It's the truth.'

I made one last-ditch attempt to reach her, but her head disappeared beneath the water. She didn't struggle. I couldn't make out where she was, had no clue which direction to go. I was cold, tired and scared. I panicked when I put my foot down and couldn't feel the bottom of the river. My head went under. I fought to stay alive, the dank river water washing away my tears.

I headed back towards the bank. My clothes were sopping, I was freezing. I looked back. She'd gone, surely for ever. I wept, shivering from the cold, shaking from fear. Of course I should have run for help, but I was winded and exhausted, heartbroken and confused.

I huddled down beside the tree, my arms around my body, rocking backwards and forwards, backwards and forwards, backwards and forwards...

Madeleine had been dead for six months. During that time I'd lived with her book, waiting for the right moment to mail it off. I expected to receive rejections: no work of art, however brilliant, is universally loved. To my parents I hinted I'd been writing a book (all those hours I spent alone in my bedroom – it was a credible enough assertion). I said nothing to Madeleine's parents, afraid that I might, in a moment of guilt, blurt out the truth. (And then what? Perhaps they'd insist on having her grave opened up, on burying the book with her.)

The book did, of course, find a publisher, and became one of those sensations no one can quite explain. Soon I was in a position where I could afford to give up my job. While pretending to be working on a second novel, I spent my time obsessively reading, analysing books, picking them apart, trying to hit upon the trick Madeleine had fallen upon instinctively. Surely, eventually, I would learn how Madeleine had done it? But its mysteries baffled me. Frustration and pounding headaches were the only results of my labours.

If only Madeleine had left some clue, even working notes for other novels she might have written. Her parents had allowed me to choose any of her books I wanted for myself. I'd been over every inch of her room, but I found nothing, not even drafts for *The Song of the Air*. It was as if she'd simply sat down one day and it came to her, all of a piece. There was nothing about her room to suggest it had belonged to a writer apart from the covered electronic typewriter and an unopened ream of typing paper.

How *had* she done it? It seemed I would never know.

CHAPTER SIXTEEN

Dear Mr Latham. Dear ineffectual Mr Latham. A man who wanted, I am sure, to be of service, to be useful, but who was ultimately unequal to the manifold problems of modern life.

Simon thought me a coward, not understanding how passionately I yearned to confess everything and to have my sins absolved. Seated in Mr Latham's study, still wearing my stripy work tabard, I wanted comfort, to be guided into a leafy glade in which stood a group of smiling people, all of them holding out their arms to me. I despised it and I wanted it.

'Well, Gabrielle, I feel honoured that you've chosen to confide in me.'

Embarrassed, not honoured: I knew the signs. 'I feel I oughtn't to,' I said, 'especially as I'm not even a member of your congregation. I've tried to believe in God, honestly I have. But I couldn't *make* myself believe, you see, and there's no use pretending, is there? Just so that one might *belong.*'

I spoke too quickly, too urgently, and perhaps I wasn't being entirely truthful. I didn't *want* to believe, because with belief comes a certain responsibility: deference to a being greater than oneself.

He dragged his chair over to sit next to me. 'I've often

regretted that I haven't taken the time to get to know you,' he said, his voice soft, sincere. 'All of us, I'm afraid, are guilty of taking other people too much for granted.'

Oh, God, how I needed a holy man before whom I could lay all my dishevelled sins and have them folded up and given back to me in a neat, orderly pile.

He leaned forward slightly, hands palms up on his lap. 'At some time in our lives we all need someone simply to listen to us. I can't promise to give you answers – those you will have to find within yourself, I'm afraid.'

Was this what I wanted? Too much like psychotherapy, or what I imagined psychotherapy to be – an egocentric ejaculation of one's fears and desires in front of an impassive analyst watching the ten-pound notes tick by. But wasn't it worth a try? At least Mr Latham didn't charge a fee.

'This might sound an odd question, but are you bound to keep secret anything I tell you? Like in the Catholic confessional?'

'Since I assume you're not going to confess to murder, I think it's safe to say that anything you tell me will be in the strictest confidence.'

Of course he wouldn't tell anyone. As if he were a common gossip!

'I worry that I'll shock you. That I'll become somehow diminished in your eyes.'

'I don't pretend to be a very worldly person, but I am familiar with most of the highways and byways people travel along, however twisting and obscure those roads might appear to me.'

I removed the tabard that made me feel unnecessarily servile, and at that point he asked if I'd care for a drink.

'Thanks, but I should probably just get on with it, shouldn't I?'

'There's no hurry.'

'I hardly know where to start.' I took a deep breath. 'It's an affair of the heart, I suppose. I had a relationship with a man, which sort of fizzled out. I don't particularly miss him. And I suppose I should add that he was a married man.'

Mr Latham nodded, his face expressing no emotion. I felt very sordid.

'Lately he's started ringing me up – mainly to shout abuse. He blames me for the problems in his marriage, which he's convinced is over. And I keep thinking about my mother, how much she wanted me to get married, have children. Well, the children are probably out of the question, but I keep wondering if I'm the sort of person who is destined to travel through life alone.'

Mr Latham blinked rapidly a few times, his hands perfectly still in his lap. 'If you don't love this man, any permanent relationship with him is unlikely to make you happy. Guilt, fear – these are never good reasons to be with someone.'

'There's someone else – someone of whom I'm fond – and that's complicated, too.'

'Is he also—?'

'Married? No. I'm not involved with him, and even if I were, there could be no future in it, but he has this strange hold over me.'

'He threatens you?'

'No, nothing like that. I'm a bit obsessed with him, I suppose.' That didn't come close to describing how I felt about Simon. It seemed wrong to want someone you didn't even like very much. But often I did like him. I couldn't pin him down. Was that the explanation, the reason I found him so wonderful?

It was madness, plain and simple. When I looked at Simon I saw someone who charmed me, infuriated me, hurt me; who made me want to beg him to understand me, forgive me, love me.

Madness. *For where thou art, there is the world itself... And where thou art not, desolation.*

Mr Latham mustn't guess it was Simon I was talking about. I felt he would find the idea of me yearning for a man as young as Simon more reprehensible than my affair with a married man. More unnatural, perhaps.

Mr Latham smiled sadly. 'I sense there is some deeper cause for unhappiness at the root of this. I do know a little about your background, of course, and it does seem a pity you weren't able to write more books. Perhaps you feel you lack a purpose in life?'

'I've made a mess of my life, that's the truth of it. I've always felt it was too late to put things right – I could never see clearly what I ought to do. I envy people who know exactly what they want and pull out all the stops to achieve it.'

'Are there many people like that, do you think? It's possible you're assuming people's lives are better organised than they really are. Don't you think?'

'It's just – this awful feeling that I've wasted my life. And that I'm the only person to blame for that.'

'A desire for companionship is perfectly natural, but sometimes it's a desire that masks a deeper need for a different kind of fulfilment.'

Here it comes, I thought, the sales pitch on behalf

175

of the Anglican church.

'I don't doubt for a moment that many people do find what they're looking for in religion,' I said, 'but I won't pretend to be something I'm not.'

'And what do you believe in – generally? I don't necessarily mean in a spiritual sense. Some people find consolation in nature, others in vocational work.'

Hug a few trees, listen to the birds, contemplate becoming a nun... Such consolations were precisely that: things people did to make up for the disappointment of their lives. I couldn't even believe in something vague but magnificent like the redemptive power of love.

'Would you consider coming to a service?'

God's pimp. His fee for listening to me prattling about my problems?

'I'll think about it.' Didn't I already do enough? Helping at jumble sales, handing out lemonade and ice-cream to children at the summer fete, delivering leaflets at Easter and Christmas. I had no quarrel with the Anglican church and would have described it as a broadly good thing in the same way that a regular bus service is a good thing.

'Please don't despair,' he said. 'Some people are lucky enough to know what they want and have the talent and determination to get it. If you feel your life hasn't turned out quite as you'd have liked, it's not too late to make changes. They don't have to be large changes and you don't have to make them all at once. But it would be a tragedy if you did nothing and allowed life to slip through your fingers.'

A nice speech. Sensible, practical encouragement, but not quite what I wanted. Well, he hadn't claimed to have the answers, had he? And without my admission of the deep rooted sin – the curse of the book, if you will – he could never understand why it felt so impossible for me to move on. No confession, no atonement, no closure.

'If there's anything I can do – anything of a practical nature, I mean. I can't imagine what, but I've often wondered why a woman as intelligent and capable as you is content to work in a job that doesn't come close to testing your capabilities.'

Tempted to tell him I might make a useful vicar's wife, I managed to resist the urge. It would have been a frivolous suggestion, but not an entirely stupid one.

'You've been very kind, very understanding,' I said.

'It's entirely my fault that we haven't got to know each other better, and the loss is mine. Your competence has perhaps blinded me to the fact that you are very much alone in the world.'

'Yes. Completely alone. But I should have got used to that by now, shouldn't I?'

After my parents divorced, my father emigrated. I was given to understand the marriage had been failing for some time, but they'd hung on until they considered I would not be adversely affected by the break-up of the family unit. At any rate, it was all very civilised. The divvying up of items they owned jointly was accomplished without fuss, my father in any case reluctant to haul great crates filled with the past to his new home in France.

'You must come out for a visit once I've got settled,' he told me. In his hand, a mug I'd bought for him on a school trip to some stately home or other. 'Don't be too upset, will you? I'll tell everyone I meet they must buy your book.' A gentle, playful punch on my arm. He and my mother were behaving beautifully so I was obliged to do likewise. Mustn't let the side down, mustn't be childish. Marriages failed all the time, didn't they? And there was no bitterness, no rancour, nothing to be sad about. I didn't even tell him I would miss him, and we idled away our last moments together talking about all the places in France we'd visit together some day.

We never did. No one's fault, not really. If I'd been younger when they split up I daresay formal arrangements would have been made, but I was an adult. I could see him whenever I wanted, if I wanted. Our relationship became one of postcards and brief meet-ups on his occasional trips to England. To have made more of an effort than that would, I think, have felt contrived.

'Look after your mum,' he told me whenever we parted after an awkward hug, both of us laden with bags and takeaway coffees. 'Tell her I'll phone her in the week, see how she's keeping.'

Not a tragedy, then. Not a disaster, my parents' divorce; merely a sense of the world having gone slightly awry, a gap that would never quite close.

We put on a brave face, my mother and I. She got involved in a few community activities; talked for a while about studying with the Open University, but never did; bumped up the "My daughter is a clever novelist!" thread; spun her divorce as something that had given her the opportunity to do all the things she'd never got round to before. And I think she was reasonably contented with the way things turned out. My father had a well-paid job and he was scrupulous in making sure we had what he called our "fair share".

178

Money was something my mother rarely worried about. I did, conscious of the fact that I couldn't live for ever on the proceeds of one book. Mother said there was no hurry; that I should concentrate on writing more books, make a career of it. And every day I would sit in what had once been "your father's study" and was now "Gabrielle's office" and force the words to come. In desperate moments I wondered if I might persuade the Andersons to allow me another rummage around in Madeleine's bedroom on the pretext of looking for something I'd once lent her, in case there was something I'd missed. Even a sketchy synopsis would have done, for I had nothing. Not a single idea.

My mother expressed disappointment when I told her I wanted to look for a job, but I promised I would take only part-time work, so that I would have plenty of time for writing.

'You know best, I suppose,' she said. 'But it seems such a shame – such a comedown.'

'Lots of writers have part-time jobs,' I told her.

'Journalism and book reviews, not office temping.'

'What does it matter? It drives me mad, being stuck in that little room all day.' I'd toyed with the idea of getting my own place, a modest one-bedroom flat, but it seemed extravagant when our house was more than adequate for two people. And we got on, more or less, neither of us inclined to encroach upon the other's personal space.

And so the years drifted by. Jobs came and went, boyfriends came and went, but otherwise everything stayed much the same. My father's remarriage was the cause of one of the few occasions when my mother's carapace of capable, busy divorcee came a little unglued.

I caught her sitting on the sofa with a photograph album opened on her lap, a tissue pressed against her nose. My parents' wedding photos, my mother choosing to marry in a white mini-skirt, my father in flares, his hair long, his smile gauche.

'Don't torment yourself,' I said, squeezing her shoulder.

She shook her head. 'I can't help it. It *was* a lovely day. We were so happy, we really were.'

What could I say? Nothing lasts for ever, nothing is set in stone? No point. To mourn is necessary. I left her alone with her pictures, her memories, having already decided not to attend my father's wedding. My mother wouldn't have objected if I'd gone; my reason for refusing the invitation had more to do with a feeling that I no longer had a part to play in my father's life. I wished him well, I wished him and his bride every possible happiness, but I had no stake in his future. If I'd ever married, I daresay he would have turned up, given me away, performed his role with good grace but not, I felt, with any great emotion.

'I do think you ought to go,' my mother later told me. 'I don't want him to think you're snubbing him, or that I've turned you against him.'

'He won't think any of those things. I'll send a card and a present.'

He sent me a letter expressing disappointment that I wouldn't be with him on his "special day". His fiancée, he said, was keen to meet me, particularly since she'd read and admired my book. I did, then, feel a little guilty, a little mean-spirited, and sent a reply requesting copies of some of the wedding pictures if he could manage it.

He brought the photos with him when we next met up in England, but he didn't bring his new wife. 'Miriam sends her best wishes,' he told me.

'She's very pretty.' She was, though I would have said so even if she hadn't been.

'Clever, too. She really *would* like to meet you. It's a pity she couldn't get time off work otherwise she'd be with me now.'

I never did meet her. Every Christmas she dutifully signed the card my father sent me and always he'd enclose a recent photo of the two of them taken in some sunny location, my father's arm around the waist of his petite wife. I never showed them to my mother, whose card was signed solely by my father.

No one could have accused my father of failing in his duties to his first family. He was generous, insisting on providing me with a monthly allowance like a Victorian patriarch. I don't know how much money he gave my mother, but it must have been more than ample. He sent frequent, impersonal postcards and responded point by point to everything I wrote in my occasional letters to him.

His new wife had two teenage children, broad-shouldered boys whose interests inclined towards anything sporty. I suppose, if pressed, I would say I was grateful my father hadn't married someone young enough to bear his children. How I would have dealt with that I can't imagine. As it was, the only additions to their family came in the form of cats and dogs, the wellbeing of which my father reported in minute detail.

'He's living the good life now,' my mother would say with a wistful sigh. 'In all those years we were married, he never took me abroad. Now he swans all over the place with that woman of his.'

"That woman" – a deliberately reductive phrase, for my mother knew my stepmother's name as well as I did; had even commented on it, wondering if she were Jewish. And of course I never thought of her as my "stepmother", a meaningless word in the circumstances.

'But we're all right, aren't we?' Mother would add brightly. 'We've nothing to complain about.'

As the years passed, though, she found things to complain about. Every time I brought home a new boyfriend, I could see her mentally writing out the wedding invitations and choosing a hat. My marriage – to just about anyone – would have gone some way to making up for the disappointment of being the mother of a writer who wouldn't write. The closer I got to thirty, the more nervy she became.

'It's not a joke,' she snapped when I told her I was in no hurry. 'By the time you get to your age, most of the suitable men are already taken.'

She assumed I wanted children. I wasted a great deal of energy trying to persuade her not all women yearned to be mothers. I also thought it was a bit rich, this insistence that I find a husband before all the men ran out, since I was her only child and hadn't come along until she was thirty-five, by which time she'd been married for ten years. Perhaps she worried I might share whatever complications had compromised her own fertility.

'It's the modern way, I suppose,' she said, 'but I don't understand it. If you had a proper career, of course, that would be different. I don't think you know *what* you want.'

What I wanted was probably less relevant than what I needed, which was a kick up the backside. Money still trickled in from sales of my book, I didn't have to worry about a mortgage or bills, I could get steady work of an undemanding nature, therefore I took the path of least resistance and coasted through life, perpetually in neutral. Looked at objectively, it was a pretty disgraceful way to live. I could hardly blame my mother for losing patience with me.

My career as a writer wasn't completely in abeyance. I managed to win a few minor prizes in competitions with my short stories, a form that suited me better than the long haul of the novel. Each cheque gave me a frayed rope to cling to, something to convince me I had some talent of my own. But what might Madeleine have produced had she lived? Had she deprived the world of a stunning body of work? Or would *The Song of the Air* have been her only novel? An emotionally fragile girl, could she have coped with fame? These useless questions gnawed at me, made me feel as guilty as if I'd killed her myself.

All right, I'd stolen her book, but it had done nothing except blight my life. Or so I thought in my darkest moments, immediately acknowledging this as a gutless shifting of responsibility. Most of the mistakes I'd made hadn't been so hideous that I couldn't set them right, but to own up to having claimed authorship for a book I hadn't written – that I couldn't do. And if I couldn't do that, nothing else I did seemed to make much sense. A reputation, a life, built on a lie.

And writers are a snarly, spiteful bunch – witness the brickbats hurled at authors found to have puffed their own novels in on-line reviews, and the vindictiveness of writers who've had their novels shredded by critics. A splinter of ice is one thing, a pen sharpened to a murderous point quite another. Owning up to what I'd done was not an option. The bile that would have flown in my direction didn't bear thinking about. And who, really, could have blamed them? I would have been presented as a kind of vampire. There would have been no room for nuance, for the mundane aspects of the story, and anything I said in my defence would have carried the craven stink of someone making excuses for shoddy behaviour.

The older I got, the harder it became to shake myself free from the past. My contact with my father lessened, and by the time I was thirty-two it was rare for him to visit more than once a year. Miriam had health issues (he was vague on the details) that necessitated him being at home as much as possible, and if he wasn't as overt as my mother in querying my lack of direction, he was clearly puzzled by my disinclination to write more novels or find a satisfying job.

And then, when I was thirty-four, my mother fell ill. Since she was only sixty-nine, I wasn't at first greatly concerned. Nor did the doctors seem able to pinpoint precisely what was wrong. With each week that passed, she became more and more frail. She had no appetite, her weight dropping rapidly from a healthy ten stone to just under seven. She fought tooth and nail against being admitted into hospital ("Once they get you in those places you never come out again, not once you get to my age"). I didn't want to force her, but neither could I stand to see her slumped in the armchair from which she could barely force herself to move, her head lolling, an untouched cup of tea on the table beside her.

She put on a brave face when she was finally admitted, flirting with a paramedic, casting aspersions on the three other ladies on her ward.

'They look a right barrel of laughs, I must say,' she whispered to me as I arranged her belongings in the locker beside her bed. 'If they snore I shall discharge myself, I don't care what the doctors say.'

She grumbled about the pressure socks the nurses insisted she wear, about the heat, about the nurses' uniforms, and about anything else she could think of. I bought her a newspaper to read and she grumbled about that, too.

'No wonder the NHS is in such a mess,' she said. 'They dump you in here when they don't know what else to do with you, but you're lucky if you see a doctor for more than a couple of minutes a day. You wonder what they *do* with their time, don't you?'

'I'm sure they know what they're doing.'

'I shall be so bored in here.'

Bored and fretful she was, her complaints endless. I visited as often as I could – as often as I could bear. I would be irritable with her, then screwed up with guilt when I left. After each visit I had as little appetite as she did, my supper often consisting of a bag of crisps and a glass of vodka. Did either of us suspect she'd been right to fear that she would never leave hospital? We always spoke of the future; of how long it was likely to be before they released her, of what we'd do when she got home. I believed she would come home; planned little treats for her, resolved to be a more considerate daughter and companion.

Her death came without warning. People said she was

lucky – better the swift demise than lingering helplessness – but I couldn't see it like that. Swept away by my own guilt, I felt sure I should have respected her wish to stay out of hospital. Being there might have prolonged her life, but she'd been unhappy. I should have tried harder – we could have afforded to hire a nurse to come in, I could have become her carer.

'You did what you thought was best,' my father told me. He'd come over for the funeral, awkwardly moving around the house he'd once shared with us.

'I did what was easiest,' I said.

'Most people do. Don't fall into the trap of wallowing in your own torment.' He wandered into the kitchen. 'Where do you keep the teabags these days?' he called.

'Top cupboard next to the sink. And I do try not to dwell on it, but I can't help feeling I let her down – that I didn't do enough.'

'No one knows what "enough" is, that's the problem. As much as I love Miriam, I sometimes lack patience with her and it's partly out of fear, because I want her to be entirely healthy and can't bear the thought that one day I might lose her.'

I walked into the kitchen so that I could speak to him above the noise of the boiling kettle. 'I'm sorry. I didn't realise things were that bad.'

'Oh, well, she'll probably outlive me in the end, but your mother dying does bring all those negative feelings to the surface.'

'I never thought.'

He handed a mug of tea to me. 'Will you stay on here or sell it and buy something smaller?'

'Oh God, I never thought.'

186

'It's yours to do with as you wish. I shan't insist on having my share of the proceeds.'

I winced.

'Yes, I know, but there's no point being sentimental about it. This house was always going to be yours eventually.'

We had an evening to kill before the funeral the next day, after which my father would fly back to France. I didn't want him to feel obliged to talk to me, about the past or anything else, but when I switched on the TV, every programme was too near the bone: divorce, death, arguments, more death.

'Have you still got the Mahjong?' Dad asked.

I had, and we managed a couple of games before we both decided, just after ten, that enough was enough and we might as well call it a day. He slept in the spare room and I hoped he got more sleep than I did. But it was nice to know he was there in the house I would always think of as my mother's, never mine.

The funeral itself was a mercifully brief affair, religious in that cold, buttoned-up English way. The coffin slid behind the crematorium curtains to the strains of Elgar's 'Nimrod'. My father's hand gripped mine, but I didn't dare look at him. Very different, of course, from Madeleine's funeral in a packed-to-the-gills church. The Andersons didn't turn up for my mother's funeral and I wasn't sure if I was annoyed or relieved. It didn't really matter.

I'd let it be known that anyone who wanted could come back to the house afterwards for tea and sandwiches, that awful British version of the Irish wake, and a couple of neighbours popped in briefly to drink a hurried cup of tea in an atmosphere of flabby embarrassment, my father providing the conversation that I simply couldn't muster.

'A lot of sandwiches left over,' he commented, when the last person had scurried away with an audible sigh of relief.

'I'll have some of them for my tea. Take the ham ones to eat on the plane if you want.'

He shook his head. 'Too depressing.'

'Yes, I know. You can almost imagine there's a whiff of embalming fluid about them.'

He squeezed my arm. 'Grit your teeth, Gabby. The first few days are bound to be the worst. And let me know what you want to do about the house and we'll try to get it sorted as painlessly as possible.'

He was a nice man, my father. If his kindness presented itself in a rather disinterested way, that probably suited me better than excessive emotion. His parting words: 'Call me if you need me. I mean it.' And I would have, but he was right. After a few days of teeth-gritting and fielding well-meaning comments of the "How are you getting on?" variety I began to relax a little; could even admit to myself without too much of a pang that it was a relief not to have to pay any more visits to that over-bright, over-heated hospital ward.

My mother had died at a relatively young age, but her death didn't leave me with the same gaping hole of despair Madeleine's had. I was answerable only to myself from now on, responsible for no one else's happiness. Perhaps I revelled just a little too much in the freedom that brought, but there were also many days when I gazed blankly at the walls, bewildered by a sudden sharp access of grief, an impotent desire to return to some innocent state of grace – to childhood, where my parents always had the power to make everything right again.

CHAPTER SEVENTEEN

I had been too easily persuaded by Simon into writing my confession, and for the basest of reasons. If I could be completely honest with him, make him understand me, wouldn't he forgive me? But that wasn't entirely true, either. It was his love I wanted to earn; to convince him that I was worthy of him. To confess was to render myself vulnerable; to strip myself bare for him.

In any case, once Simon had moved on, I could burn what I had written.

'Tell me you're feeling better for getting it off your chest.' Sprawled on the sofa, glass of red wine in his hand.

I poured myself some wine. 'I dislike reliving the past. What point does it serve?'

'Maybe none.' He lifted a leg, rested his foot on the edge of the table, toes curling to keep his grip. 'You could say no.'

Did women ever say no to him? There are men like that, of course, with a charm that's invisible to most people, but capable of reducing the susceptible ones to abject slavery, abject misery. Was Lord Alfred Douglas such a man? Oscar Wilde helpless, his wit and talent useless in protecting him against his beloved Bosie. Is it beauty, simply, that is sufficient to blind the besotted victim to the fatal flaws in the loved one's character?

'I'm not a blackmailer,' Simon added softly. 'I don't want you to hate me. I never wanted that.'

'But I'm not the person you thought I was. You feel cheated.'

His mouth broke into a grin that was entirely without affection. 'You've no idea how I feel about you.' Then, as an afterthought, though his tone was stiff, 'I forgot to say, that bloke rang while you were out. Russell. He said he'd phone again later.'

'Did he say anything else?' Whom had he believed Simon to be?

'Not much. Maybe I should have said I was your toy-boy and that you couldn't come to the phone because I'd tied you to the bed.'

'I'm glad you didn't.'

'Why? You don't care what he thinks.'

'True, but what's the point of winding him up?'

'Because he's a dick and because it might get him to stop ringing. I think you want him to keep ringing, don't you? That way you know he still cares about you.'

'Not at all,' I said.

'Don't believe you.'

'That's up to you.'

'If he stopped ringing it'd be like he was dumping you all over again, wouldn't it? Just like Madeleine did. Maybe that's why you've let me stay so long, because you know everyone leaves you in the end.'

When Russell phoned again, it was to inform me that he and Michelle were getting divorced.

'I'm sorry,' I said. It seemed he wasn't in the mood to rant and I could almost pity him.

'I really wanted it to work out,' he said. 'I'm guessing you're still not keen on the idea of us meeting up?'

'No. I'm sorry your marriage has broken down, but we could never be friends – you must see that, surely?'

'Remember Paris?'

'Yes, I remember Paris.'

'I'll never forget it now. The city of lovers, what a joke!'

'Stop projecting your guilt on to me. It doesn't wash any more.'

A long, long pause. 'God, you've become hard,' he muttered.

'Better than being a pushover. What does it matter to you what I've become, anyway?'

Simon mouthed at me to put the phone down.

'Russell, seriously, don't phone again. If you do, I'll get my number changed.'

'I just want our relationship to have meant something, otherwise splitting up with Michelle seems so stupid, so pointless.'

'If it ever meant something it no longer does, not to me. Goodbye, Russell.'

I'd failed to find the phrase that would deal the devastating blow, the unequivocal striking-through of any connection between us.

'I'll buy you a caller display unit,' Simon said, 'then you'll know when he's calling and you won't have to answer. They're only a few quid.'

'That simple,' I murmured.

'Why waste time and energy speaking to him unless you get a kick out of it?'

Did I? Did I actually want to drag my ex-lover around with me? Maybe I enjoyed sparring with him, with a

191

vindictiveness that sprang from the fact that he had no emotional hold over me.

'Are you going to carry on letting him dick you around or are you going to tell him where to go?'

'Simon—'

'Does he mean more to you than I do?'

'It's hardly the same thing.'

'You need to choose. Him or me.'

'He's nothing to me.' *And I'm nothing to you...*

'Prove it, then. Wouldn't you do it, for me?'

His beautiful, beautiful eyes. *Yes, Simon, I'd do anything for you.*

'And if I don't?'

A surly shrug. 'None of my business. But you'll let him worm his way back into your life, I know you will. You're not strong enough to resist, and he's even weaker than you are.'

'Why do you have to be so nasty?'

'It's for your own good. That's what my stepmother always used to say when she was being a bitch. Is Russell so important that you can't give him up?'

'I've given him up.'

'He wants you back, but only so that he can fuck you over again. Don't argue, I know it's true.'

'I wasn't going to argue.'

'Promise, then. Promise me you won't speak to him ever again.'

In an odd way this seemed more significant than the confession I was writing. Paper could be burned, but I believed promises mattered; that one didn't go back on them no matter what.

'Promise,' he repeated, taking my hands in his. The

touch of his skin was enough to make me agree to anything he asked. He was being unreasonable, taking far too much on himself. My thoughts, my actions. He was taking me over, body and soul, and I was too weak, too besotted, to resist.

'I won't speak to him again, I promise.'

'Good. Once you've written out everything that happened, and written Russell out of your life, you'll feel better. Everything will be okay then, I swear it.' He bent to kiss my cheek, his fingers in my hair, tugging just enough to hurt. 'Trust me.'

Trust me: I'm a doctor, a priest, your friend. Trust me, when I'm jabbing the needle in your arm; when I'm pressing a rosary into your hand; when I'm slipping Rohypnol into your drink... My father advised me never to trust anyone, but my father was immune to the charm of beautiful men.

It was Mr Latham who informed me that he'd been speaking to the head librarian at our nearest library who ran the local book group.

'Quite popular, these things, aren't they? Rather a good idea, I think.'

Did he imagine I might want to join? That if I couldn't find a comfortable place in church, I might pray with the other worshippers at the altar of literature and thereby find spiritual sustenance?

'I mention it,' he added, 'because Mrs Evans wondered if you might be persuaded to give a little talk to the group – nothing too strenuous, just an informal chat about how you came to write your novel, the perils and pitfalls of publishing, that sort of thing.'

'Me!' I squeaked. 'But it was all so long ago.'

'I gather Mrs Evans is something of a fan. You might get some book sales out of it if nothing else.'

When I told Simon about this conversation, he hooted with laughter.

'Will you do it?'

'How can I? It couldn't be anything other than hideous.'

'It might inspire you to write a sequel.'

'Very funny.'

'Well, you *have* published stuff, haven't you?'

'Not like that; not like *her*.'

A painful silence. 'No, not like her.'

At least I was prepared for the email from Viv Evans: a brief message simply requesting that we meet to talk over her proposal. I sent her a few suitable dates and times, and she responded with an invitation for coffee and biscuits at her house.

The directions to Viv's house, a couple of miles away, written on a postcard Blu-Tacked to the steering wheel, I returned Simon's cheery wave without enthusiasm and set out on a Tuesday morning.

Viv stood waiting for me at her front door, immediately recognisable in a patchwork velvet skirt and red fleece, her legs bare, sensible Birkenstock sandals on her broad feet. Her greying hair was pinned up in such a fashion that it would only require a few twigs to persuade a passing starling it had found a readymade nest.

'I love bright colours, don't you?' she said, showing me into her front room, not waiting for me to respond before adding, 'I hope you're not allergic to cats? We've got three of the brutes.'

'No, I own a cat.'

'You're a cat person? Excellent! In that case I'm sure we shall get on.'

It seemed a rather tenuous basis for future friendship, but I daresay she was just doing her bit to put me at ease.

She wheeled in a trolley. On dainty china plates there were chocolate digestives, wafers, Viennese whirls, Jammie Dodgers and goodness knows what else. And a china teapot and a couple of Clarice Cliff-style mugs.

'Your love of colour extends to the crockery, I see.'

'It's my dream to own a complete set of genuine Clarice Cliff tableware, but it's far beyond my purse, alas.'

'And you'd always worry about damaging it, wouldn't you?'

'Oh, I shouldn't let *that* worry me. These things are meant to be used. What's the odd chip between friends?'

A hearty woman, not the type I generally got along with. People like her tended to interpret diffidence and reserve as moodiness, out of which one should be forced to snap.

'Now.' She sat down, feet planted a good yard apart, and slapped her knees. 'Help yourself to tea – I know I said coffee, but I think tea is nicer with biscuits, don't you? – and grab a plate. Take whatever you fancy, don't bother asking first, and don't forget to sign my book before you go.'

'Thank you,' I managed to say, feeling as if I'd been battered by a hurricane.

'First things first. Dicky Latham did warn you that I was going to contact you, didn't he?'

Dicky? Of course he must have a first name, but I couldn't believe he allowed anyone to address him by that ridiculous diminutive. My surprise must have showed.

'I don't call him that to his face, of course. Means well, but a bit of an old woman, don't you think? Anyway, I'm guessing you wouldn't be here unless you were basically amenable to addressing our little group.'

'I've never actually done anything of that kind before and it's such a long time since the book was published—'

'Oh, *that* doesn't matter. We still read Dickens, don't we? Jane Austen? Eliot? Doesn't matter that they haven't produced any new stuff for centuries.' She chuckled, gently nudging the trolley towards me with her foot.

I grabbed a few biscuits. 'I'm hardly in the same league,' I protested.

'It will be a great treat for us to have a living author to quiz. We're readers rather than writers, but one or two of us enjoy a little wordsmithery of our own.'

I tried not to wince, disguising my distaste with a firm bite into a Jammie Dodger.

'We meet on Thursday evenings, seven till nine. Is that okay for you?'

I nodded.

'And if you want to bring along that handsome young man you live with, do feel free.'

'My...? Oh! You mean Simon? He's not my young man, he's just the lodger.'

'Really? How disappointing! Well, bring him along anyway. Does he like books?'

'He's studying literature at university.' Or was. Or might not have been, for all I knew.

'Even better!'

I wouldn't let him come. I wouldn't tell him Viv had suggested it, and I'd tell her on the night that he'd come down with a virus.

'What sort of books do you choose for the group reads?'

'We stick to novels – anything with a bit of meat to it, if you know what I mean.'

'And the members, what are they like? Just, you know, so I can gauge how to pitch what I say.'

'We're a varied bunch. Meeting in the evening means we don't limit ourselves to the retired and the unemployed. We've got one young lad in his early twenties – long hair, headband, bit of an arty type – but you don't have to worry about us being old fuddy-duddies. We read *Fingersmith* a while back and we've tackled a Jeanette Winterson, so we're pretty broad-minded.'

'Yes, I see. Well, that's very heartening.'

'The group has been going for less than a year and we've only had one member drop out, and that was due to poor health.' She brushed crumbs from her skirt on to the floor with an expansive couldn't-care-less gesture. 'You know, there are so many things I want to ask you, but I shall be very disciplined and save up my questions for when you speak to the whole group.'

'Do you— Are you a writer yourself?'

'Oh, the odd duff poem – jingling birthday card rhymes, the occasional short story. For personal amusement, nothing more.'

'Where are your cats?' Only one indication of the presence of cats: a little plastic ball with holes in it and a bell inside.

'Bette's upstairs – she's an indoor cat, deaf as a post. The other two are out, murdering the local wildlife. The corpses aren't so bad – it's when they bring things back that are mangled but still alive. One is forced to finish

197

them off for their own sake, but my God, it's awful!'

On this gruesome note she apparently decided our tête-à-tête was at an end, stretching out an arm to grab a book from the shelf behind her, which she then presented to me to sign.

'Is there any special message you'd like?'

'Could you dedicate it to Tom and Viv? Tom's my hubby – he's a fan, too. Such a lovely thing, a signed copy. I can't *wait* to show you off to the group!'

Viv's first, predictable statement: 'You've not brought your young man with you. Shy, is he?'

'Stomach bug,' I said. Viv's disappointment was so palpable I wondered if the invitation had been issued solely so that she and the others could gawp at Simon. 'And he's not my young man, as I'm sure I mentioned. He lodges with me, that's all.'

'Oh, yes.' So much invested in those two words. A knowing wink, a nudge-nudge, an I-believe-you-thousands-wouldn't.

Unsure of the etiquette, I'd brought along a copy of my book, but felt it would have been not quite the done thing to bring along books to sell. I'd also brought a bottle of wine for Viv, though I wasn't sure why – it wasn't a dinner party, after all, and I'd be lucky to get more than tea and biscuits.

'My dear, you shouldn't have! And I shouldn't say that, because it's rude, so I'll simply say thank you *so* much.' She kissed me on the cheek, the powdery smell of her skin making me recoil.

Taking hold of my wrist, she led me into a room that seemed to have shrunk in size now it was filled with people

– perhaps only ten or eleven, but enough to make a crowd.

'No point going through everyone's names, you'll never remember them all.'

I noted the arty young man with the headband, immediately marking him down as pretentious and book-snobby, and I decided the man with a genial grin and a paunch must be Tom (I was right). For the first half hour or so, very little was required of me as the book club members discussed the previous month's group read, *A Room with a View*. My opinion was sought.

'It's a long time since I read it,' I said. 'It's a little... well, it's good, of course, but it does feel rather dated in the way that *Maurice*, say, doesn't.' I was winging it, the only image of the story fixed in my mind taken from the film: Helena Bonham Carter and Julian Sands kissing in a cornfield. *Was* it a cornfield?

'I think it has to be ultimately frustrating for the modern reader,' a woman of seventy or so volunteered. 'Lucy is presented as gaining freedom by the end of the novel, but it's only the freedom to marry a man. She doesn't have to marry awful wormy Cecil, but there's nothing else she can do – according to Forster – except marry. It seems like a bad joke, doesn't it, to those of us living when women have so many more options open to them?'

I smiled, feeling a strong and immediate liking for this tiny woman with a cap of white hair and what looked like carpet slippers on her feet. She looked me in the eye.

'You should have written more books. Why didn't you?'

Taken aback, I gazed imploringly at Viv, who immediately swung to the rescue, reminding the little bird-like woman that they must stick to the programme.

'Gabrielle will be more than happy to answer questions later on.'

'So *bossy*.'

'Now, now, Lisel – we don't want to risk running out of time, do we?'

Lisel rolled her eyes. She caught me smirking and winked at me. She would likely give me a hard time during the Q and A, yet I rather looked forward to it.

They carried on discussing *A Room with a View*, but no one's comments struck me as being as perceptive as those of Lisel, who felt Lucy should have married Cecil.

'At least she could have despised him cleanly,' she said. 'And then she could have gone off and had nice affairs with whomever she fancied. Romantic love is so terribly over-rated.'

I wanted to talk to her, to ask about her life. Extraordinary as it sounds, I felt she might have been the one person who could understand what I'd done.

At a nod from Viv I stumbled through an ad hoc (and necessarily invented) explanation of how I'd come to write *The Song of the Air*, how I'd sent it off without expecting anyone to publish it, and how it felt at once magnificent and anti-climactic when I finally held the book in my hands.

'But why no more?' Lisel asked. 'The book seems to be written by someone who had so much more to say. Why didn't you say it?'

I stared at her blankly. She was the English teacher and I was the could-do-better kid who hadn't done her homework. Worse, I was the kid who'd cribbed someone else's homework and hadn't bothered to disguise the fact.

'I couldn't,' I finally managed to say. 'I didn't know how.'

200

'Too much too soon, was it?' Viv suggested.

'No, it wasn't that. Everyone wanted me to repeat the trick, but I'd forgotten how to do it. And the longer I went on not writing, the more confidence I lost until no one cared any more anyway.' I was on the verge of tears, stumbling so close to the truth, but far enough away that what I said made no sense.

'Well, it's a damn shame, whatever the reason,' Lisel said.

When we adjourned for tea and biscuits, Lisel drew me over to one side. She spoke quietly, and as she was five foot nothing I had to stoop to hear her.

'My dear, I'm sorry if I was harsh with you. I did wonder if there was perhaps some personal reason why you didn't write another novel and I'm sorry if I put my foot in it.'

'There is a reason, but it's one I can't share with anyone, much as I'd like to.'

She nodded sagely. 'I thought as much. Do forgive me for being clumsy.'

'Please – there's no need – and it was worth coming to hear your critique of *A Room with a View*. You put into words the thing that has always nagged me about that book.'

'Poor, dear Lucy,' she sighed. 'Well, some women aren't fit for much more than marriage, but if Lucy was such a woman then she didn't deserve to have a book written about her. Isabel Archer is another one – *Portrait of a Lady*? Loathsome book! I can just imagine horrible Henry James chortling with pleasure as he pushed Isabel into Gilbert's arms.'

'Well... different times, of course.'

201

'No excuse,' Lisel snapped. 'I've told Viv that if she ever picks a novel by Henry James for us to read, I shall boycott the group.'

'Did you by any chance used to be a teacher?'

She grinned. 'For my sins. Head of English at a private girls' school. The Henry Hill Hickman School, in Reabrook, where I live. Do you know it?'

'Yes.' I knew of the school and I knew the village, little more than a hamlet, five or so miles south of Morevale.

'Do I remind you of some hideous old baggage who put you off Shakespeare for life?'

'Only in a superficial way. My English teacher used to bowdlerise Shakespeare, for which I never forgave her.'

'Quite right of you. Shakespeare without the bawdy is like – oh – chips without salt, or cappuccino without the chocolate sprinkles. Are you glad you came tonight or has it been hellish, on the whole?'

'Both,' I said. 'I'm not sure I'd want to come again, put it like that.'

'Fair enough. But if you ever fancy a chat—' She ripped a sheet of paper from the pad Viv kept next to the telephone and wrote down her address and phone number. 'I don't do email, I don't Skype, and I don't like people phoning me after nine in the evening. And always ring first – I dislike people turning up unexpectedly.'

I wanted to be like Lisel, the kind of person who set out her terms so there could be no confusion, no ambiguity.

'Are you married?' I asked, noticing that she wore no wedding ring.

'Was *your* English teacher married?'

I shook my head. 'The rumour was that her fiancé had died in a tragic accident.'

She gave a strange, enigmatic smile. 'We all have our little secrets, don't we? Perhaps I'll discover yours. And perhaps you'll discover mine, who knows?'

The remainder of the evening passed pleasantly enough. No one quizzed me too thoroughly about the book, and whenever someone asked a question that sailed a little too close to turbulent waters I'd look at Lisel, whose imperceptible nod and small smile gave me courage.

At the end of the meeting Viv led a ragged round of applause to thank me for coming and I was presented with a small box of artisan chocolates.

'I'm afraid we can't pay you in actual money,' Viv said, 'but these are rather lovely, don't you think?'

A heart-shaped box with a red bow tied around it diagonally. Not entirely appropriate, and rather too reminiscent of the fancy chocolates Russell used to buy for me.

'We should have bought you a bottle of good single malt whisky,' Lisel said as we walked back to our cars. 'Typical of Viv to go for something so ridiculous.'

'Why typical?'

'No imagination. Well, at least you can eat the chocolates, which is more than you could a bunch of flowers.' She unlocked the door of her car, a dusty black Golf. 'Goodnight, my dear. I'm glad we met.'

I presented the box of chocolates to Simon when I returned home. He raised an eyebrow. 'My fee for addressing the book group,' I said.

'So how did it go?' His voice was hard.

'It was fine. I met a very interesting elderly lady.'

'An interesting old lady and a romantic box of choco-lates. Does it get any better than that?'

'They were all perfectly nice people.'

'I'm sure they were. Most people are, at first. I expect you thought I was nice when you first met me, didn't you?'

'Aren't you?'

'You've no idea.'

How much damage could he do? He knew too much and it was entirely my fault that he did. Subconsciously, perhaps, I'd wanted to tell someone, had felt it was time the truth came out. Simon was not the person I should have told. I had no excuse for my behaviour, which was predicated on my hopeless greed for him. I adored him and I loathed him. Hated him; loved him.

'No,' I said, 'I have no idea.'

'Like most people, I can be kind when it suits me. Generous, even. Shall I kiss you?'

'Don't.'

'No? Isn't that what you want? How long is it since Russell buggered off? Six months? A long time to be without anyone.'

'You're not as wonderful as you think you are. A pretty face will only get you so far in life.'

'You don't really believe that, do you? It's the beau-tiful people who will inherit the earth, not the kind ones.' His vindictive gaze on the heart-shaped box which sat there like a reproach. 'Aren't you afraid of the future? Don't you ever worry that Russell was your last shot?'

'My last shot at what? Love?'

'Wouldn't you risk everything for love? Even your life?

Wouldn't you?' He reached out to touch me, his hand travelling from my neck to my breasts, lingering there, his expression blank. 'Aren't you?' I felt his thumb press against my nipple and couldn't repress a sharp intake of breath.

He smiled, his eyes glittering with contempt. 'Your life,' he whispered.

CHAPTER EIGHTEEN

The end was in sight. I had written a scrupulously accurate account of everything that occurred from the time Madeleine went to university to her death. How Simon chose to interpret the facts was up to him. Only one piece of information really mattered: I hadn't written the book. In publishing it under my own name I had followed Madeleine's wishes as I interpreted them, but the reading public – *had* I cheated them? The book would be the same no matter whose name was on the front cover.

Why had I gone through with this? For one reason and one reason only. And now that it was nearly done, I had to face up to the fact that Simon could renege on a promise that had been unspoken, implied. Of course he would renege! He'd got what he wanted, had proved the extent of his power over me. He knew as well as I did why I'd gone along with this nonsense.

I loathed what I saw in the mirror Simon had held up to me. The fact that I recognised my flaws meant nothing. I was old enough to know better yet I was behaving with as little sense as I'd had when I was sixteen. Was I really still that girl? Simon was right – I should have moved away. I should have grown up, but I hadn't.

'Why do you care so much?' I asked him. 'What is Madeleine to you?'

'The truth is important, isn't it?' he said. 'Look, you're tired. Why don't I fix us some delicious drinks? Pink grapefruit juice mixed with lemonade. I could add a dash of vodka, but it's a bit early in the day.'

'*Much* too early.' He made the drinks with vodka and sat next to me. 'So, you want to know why I'm so keen for you to write down the story of *The Song of the Air*.'

'You said something about truth.'

'Yes, but a particular kind of truth. Fiction is a bunch of lies about people who don't exist, right? But even a made up story has to convince the reader. It has to feel as if it's real.'

'Yes—'

'Maybe I think it's important that people understand where the line is between real reality and fictional reality. Once you've dealt with actual reality, it will give you freedom.'

'Freedom to do what, though?'

He looked me in the eye. 'To write your own books.'

'Madeleine had the talent. All I had was ambition.'

'Sometimes that's all you need. If you want something badly enough.'

'But I'm not sure I do want it, not any more.'

'That's my point!' He leaned towards me, the ice jangling wildly in his glass. 'I want you to get that desire back.'

'But what does it matter? Even if I did write a book, I can't reinvent myself. *The Song of the Air* exists – anything I write will be compared with that.'

'Only by other people.'

I laughed. 'Yes – by publishers, readers, critics – all the people who matter!'

'But with the length of time that's elapsed since the book was published, it would be like starting over.'

It was possible. I thought of Jean Rhys – all those novels in the 1930s about flaky women on their uppers, and then *Wide Sargasso Sea* in the '60s, completely different from anything she'd written before.

'All you have to do is be a bit mysterious about why you stopped writing after the first novel,' he added. 'People expect writers to be weird and arty with all kinds of personal demons. You'd get away with it.'

The phrase made me shiver. Did I want to "get away with it"? Was that what I'd been doing all these years? Except, of course, getting away with it hadn't taken me very far. *The Song of the Air* had thrown a loop around my neck. The smallest attempt to fight free simply tightened it, preventing me from doing anything worthwhile.

'And you – how would you react if I wrote and published a book? Would you be there beside me with your hand held out for the cheque?'

'For agreeing not to sell my story to the press, you mean?'

'Well, the literary press. I doubt *The Sun* would be interested.'

He took a sip of lemonade. 'It's true I was disappointed when I found out you hadn't written the book. But you've suffered for it, haven't you?'

His hand, cold from the lemonade glass, placed lightly on top of mine.

'Don't patronise me,' I snapped.

His hand squeezed mine with the gentlest of pressure.

'I'm not after sympathy – God knows, I brought it all on myself – but all that damn book brought me was guilt and a kind of awful blankness.'

'Then you've learned a valuable lesson, haven't you?'

Something in his eyes gave me pause. I felt he'd said one thing but meant something quite different. He hadn't, after all, promised that he wouldn't reveal my confession to anyone. I couldn't begin to imagine how knowing the truth would affect Madeleine's parents. What I'd done would seem to them truly despicable. They would go to the press if Simon didn't, and from the perspective of grieving parents it would doubtless make a good human interest story.

'Are you really writing a novel,' I asked, 'or was that just a blind?' Another lie, another element in the strange game he was playing with me.

He stretched out his legs, crossing them at the ankle, the glass of lemonade resting on his crotch. 'Once I'd got it all plotted out I lost interest. If I can't write something that's perfect, I'd rather not bother.'

'So what will you do?'

'Go back to uni, knuckle down, try to get a job. I'll probably end up teaching – what else do you do with an English degree?'

'You seem prepared to give up very easily.'

'On writing? I liked the fantasy. You know, like Ernest Hemingway – bumming around Paris, swigging whiskey from the bottle, occasionally crouching over a typewriter to churn out some muscular prose.'

'I'm surprised you're a fan of his.'

'I'm not, particularly. I can be any kind of writer I want, can't I? Unlike you, lumbered with Madeleine's book. You couldn't write anything else without having that story in the back of your mind. You'd feel obliged to mimic her style. Unless, of course, you decided to set the record straight.'

'You know I can't do that. I'm not prepared to do that.'

'You should think about it. Don't her parents have a right to know?'

'But you said—'

'I did, didn't I? I can't help wishing you had the guts to tell them the truth. I'd love to see the looks on their faces.'

I shivered. What he would relish was my disgrace, my complete humiliation.

After lunch, Simon made another attempt on his novel. 'This was supposed to be my all-or-nothing, now-or-never crack at being a writer, wasn't it?' he said. 'I'm not a quitter.'

I didn't know what he was. There were times when it seemed he genuinely cared about me, or at least about my writing. At other times he was cruel, taunting me, meting out the punishment I felt I deserved. He was slippery, mercurial. I couldn't read him. I made excuses for him because he was young; because I preferred to see the best in people. Because I wanted him. Because that always got in the way of everything else, no matter how hard I tried to see him objectively.

I read for a while, but the non-muscular prose of Virginia Woolf was too rarefied to suit my agitated mood. I located the scrap of paper on which Lisel had written her contact details and rang her.

'Gabrielle, how nice to hear from you.'

I wasn't sure what to say. I couldn't very well invite myself round to her house, which was what I wanted.

'Are you busy?' she asked. 'Silly question – you'd hardly have rung me if you were.'

'I very much wanted to speak to you again.'

'Why don't you come round? You can try one of the frangipane slices I baked this morning. Posh Bakewell tarts without the icing, really, but they turned out quite well.'

'Only if you're sure.'

'If I didn't want you to come, I would say so. I might have concocted a plausible excuse, but I've made it a rule, now that my time is my own, never to do anything I don't want to do.'

'Is that possible?'

She chuckled. 'Not always. But more often than you might imagine.'

When I told Simon where I was going, he rolled his eyes.

'Jesus. Lavender and mothballs. She'll probably want to talk about the war and how plucky everyone was during the Blitz.'

I ignored him.

The interior of Lisel's house was surprisingly modern.

'I dislike this trend for eulogising old things simply because they're old,' she said. 'If it's very old we call it antique; if it's within living memory, it's vintage or retro. It's a little fetishistic if you ask me.' She presented her frangipane slices on a plain white plate. 'Do you like old things, Gabrielle?'

'I'm afraid I do.'

'You're young. I suppose they seem quaint to you. They remind me too much of my stuffy childhood. Tell me what you think of the cake.'

'It's lovely.'

'Baking is something else that has become fetishised. What's the phrase? Food porn! My, my—' She shook her head, stirring tea in a brown china pot. 'In my day—' She chuckled again. 'That dates me, doesn't it? And it's an awful phrase. As if "my day" has been and gone. As if I were already six feet under.'

She was the kind of older person I liked best – sharp, interested in life, more invested in the present than in the past.

'We ought to have got to know each other before this, Gabrielle. I admired your novel enormously.'

I couldn't hide a wince.

She smiled. 'Perhaps you don't care to be reminded of it?'

'No, not really. I was a different person then.'

'Well, of course you were! Do you hate the book very much?'

Here was an opportunity to unburden myself. And she might understand. But wasn't it too big a gamble?

'I think I understand,' she continued. 'A big success relatively early followed by – excuse me for speaking bluntly – nothing. It must have been galling, the expectation that you should write something equally brilliant, if not more so.'

No. She had no inkling. I couldn't disabuse her.

'Something like that,' I muttered.

'Tell me... The young man who lives with you – Simon, isn't it? Viv mentioned him in that coy manner of hers that sits rather oddly with her bullish physical presence. Excuse my candour, but I prefer to call a spade a spade.'

'She believes Simon and I are lovers.'

Lisel poured out the tea. 'Would you like to be?'

There's a fine line between candour and rudeness.

Instead of answering, I said, 'At the book group, you mentioned something about having little secrets and wondering if I'd discover yours. A deliberately enigmatic statement?'

A little shrug of her thin shoulders. 'Silly of me. You'd been speaking about your English teacher, the one whose fiancé was tragically killed.'

'You think that was untrue?'

She held up a hand. 'My dear! The young are so callous. Perhaps it was true about the fiancé. Many women would feel unable to get over such a loss. But if you and your classmates had thought she might be a lesbian, for instance, would you have been kind to her?'

'No. Different these days, of course, people are a bit more civilised. I'm ashamed to say we would have taken the piss without mercy.'

'Precisely. And that's the reason why so many people keep secrets – not because they're ashamed, but because they can't be bothered to deal with idiots. And who can blame them?'

'Your secret, then?'

'And *yours*?'

I shook my head.

Lisel grinned and passed me another frangipane slice. 'Some secrets are better shared, but most are better kept.'

'Now aren't you guilty of being coy?'

'Perhaps. But I feel no great need to unburden myself, and frankly I'm more interested in you.'

'In me, or in my relationship with Simon?'

'Oh, my dear, I couldn't care less what you do or don't get up to with him. I lost interest in that sort of nonsense a very long time ago. You seemed uncomfortable at the book group, very guarded when you answered our questions. I don't think anyone asked anything particularly intrusive.'

'No, they didn't. I just didn't know how to answer them.'

'It *is* a brilliant book. Viv's ordered extra copies for the library. You must be pleased it's still in print.'

'I thought that part of my life was over and done with. I rarely thought about it until I met Simon.'

Her smile suggested encouragement and a barely-suppressed curiosity. I kept her waiting. Whatever she wanted to know, she would have to ask.

'Shall I make more tea?' she said finally. 'Or would you prefer coffee? Only instant, I'm afraid, but a decent one.'

'Coffee would be nice.'

While I waited, I browsed her bookshelves – a thing the bookish always do in other people's houses.

'And what is your verdict?' asked Lisel, returning with two mugs of coffee. 'Do they pass muster?'

I looked up and smiled. 'Of course.'

'There are more in the attic. The ones down here are those I am likely to re-read. I suppose I ought to get rid of books I know I'll never read again, but one becomes oddly attached to them.'

Her collection was an exemplary mixture of nineteenth century and modern classics and more recent literary fiction, much of which I recognised from Booker longlists.

'You want to know about Simon, don't you? Where he came from, what he's doing here?'

'I've no intention of pressing you for information. I admit to a certain curiosity about him, which I suppose is inevitable in a retired old schoolmarm like me with too much time on her hands.'

'I expect he'll be gone soon. It'll be odd, having to adjust to life without him – without him being there. Back to solitary meals and—' I took a deep breath, 'back to pleasing myself.'

'A double-edged sword, that. Pleasant to be able to do exactly as one wishes, but some things are better shared.'

I nodded, not trusting myself to speak.

'You'll miss him,' Lisel stated. 'Perhaps you and I might have the odd meal together? I sense you're not the type who needs someone around all the time, and neither am I. And I could hardly be an adequate substitute for a good-looking young man.'

'Thank you,' I mumbled, taking refuge in the coffee, which was probably less bitter than it seemed to me at that moment.

'And *don't* thank me, please! I haven't the gift for being able to receive thanks with any kind of grace. If I offer something it's because I want to, not because I want my ego stroked.'

'I hope I'm like you when I'm older.'

'You can say plain old, I shan't take umbrage. But I wouldn't recommend it. I've been called eccentric, even wise, but frankly that's poppycock. I've simply learned that it's nearly always best to speak plainly if it's possible to do so without causing pain.' She winked. 'Saves a lot of time, that's all. I'm neither kind nor generous, so please don't imagine I am.'

'Would you like to meet Simon?'

'No, I don't believe I would. Clearly he means a great deal to you, but I rarely find the young interesting. They haven't done enough or seen enough or read enough. If you are, as I suspect, in love with him, you would want me to find him extraordinary, and it's highly unlikely I would.'

She was more entertaining than Viv, her conversation more piquant, yet I suspected Lisel would not be the sort of person one could depend upon in an emergency. Viv would be the one on hand with sympathy and a blanket. Did that make Viv the better person? Did it make Lisel more heartless or simply more honest?

Idle thoughts, of no great consequence except that I envied people who had a best friend: someone on whom they could rely, someone they'd known since childhood with whom they'd shared all the major traumas of adulthood. Would Madeleine and I have remained best friends if she'd lived? For several years before her death I'd felt her slipping away, and I'd never understood the nature of the demons that had hooked their claws into her skin.

'What are you thinking?' Lisel said.

'Hm? Oh, I was thinking about someone I used to know. A friend. She died young.'

'Ah, yes – Maddie Anderson.'

'You knew her?'

'Not really. I met her and her parents when they came to the school to enquire about bursaries and scholarships. Maddie would have been thirteen or so at the time. I remember when your book came out and noticing that you dedicated it to her. I thought about introducing myself to you – I very much wanted to congratulate you on having written such a fine book at a young age.'

'Why didn't you?'

'Oh, I expect I was concerned that you'd be gauche and inarticulate – writers sometimes are, they make up for it on paper – and it would have taken some of the shine off the book if I'd discovered its author to be an irritating person. It's a pity,' she added, setting down her mug on a glass coaster, 'that our paths have never crossed before. Perhaps it was for the best.'

'Yes – perhaps.'

'We must keep in touch, if you'd like to.'

'Yes, I would.' We might even become friends – a serious, grown-up friendship that would be enriching but also strangely unsatisfactory. But that would be my fault, my notions of what friendship should be stuck in a groove: friends shared nail polish, moaned about homework, swooned over boys. It was high time I grew up, stopped wanting things I couldn't have. I needed to learn to accept my lot along with the bulk of humanity for whom life is, on the whole, a series of small disappointments and niggardly compromises.

CHAPTER NINETEEN

It was done. My full confession, circa five thousand words, signed and dated. I handed it to Simon, asked that he read it while I was out at work, adding that I didn't want to have any kind of discussion about it. Everything I had to say on the subject was set out unambiguously on the pages he held in his hands.

'All right,' he said, 'it's a deal. And when you get home, we'll lock it in your wall safe.'

The safe in question was a fairly cheap model, purchased after a spate of burglaries in the village and now home to the few bits of valuable jewellery I owned. I'm sure an expert could have opened it in moments, but professional cracksmen tended to target mansions, not the kind of place I lived in.

I wasn't sure Simon could be relied upon not to open a post mortem on the document, but really there was little I could usefully add. All the salient facts were there. I'd omitted nothing relevant, even the things it most pained me to admit. I would have defied any lawyer to quibble with it. I had stated the facts plainly, scrupulously shying away from interpreting or manipulating them.

When I returned home, I found the table laid with a fresh gingham cloth. Two plates, a quiche, lots of salad.

He grinned, a tea towel tucked into the waistband of his jeans, oven gloves draped over his shoulder.

'I wanted to do something nice for you. I know it must have been tough to write all that stuff, and you needn't have done it. You could have told me to fuck off, but you didn't.' He placed glasses and napkins on the table. 'I didn't mention this before, but I bought a bottle of champagne – we can have that tonight.'

And now, of course, I wanted to know what his reaction had been when he read my confession. Did he think less badly of me? Did he understand? Was I, indeed, forgiven? The lunch spread suggested this.

'There's also a fruit salad thing for dessert. And I bought some elderflower cordial.'

'You *have* been busy.'

He sat opposite me and grabbed my hands. 'I know I've been a pain in the arse and I'm sorry. I know you don't want to talk about it, but I just want to say – reading what you wrote, and how honest you were – it made me understand what you'd been through, how it all happened.'

'You don't despise me?'

'I didn't understand the full picture, because it's not clear-cut, is it? I mean, it's definitely one of those grey areas, ethically speaking. I was wrong to go off at the deep end with you. Can you forgive me?'

That was all I'd wanted. His forgiveness. His affection.

'In my heart I knew it was a mistake to pretend the book was mine. I thought I was doing what Madeleine wanted, but maybe that wasn't what mattered most. At the time I thought it was.'

'You did what you thought was right. Let's eat.'

'Yes. But *did* I do what I thought was right, or was

219

that an excuse?' I held out my plate for Simon to heap it with salad.

'No point beating yourself up about it.' He cut the quiche into four equal segments and offered one of them to me.

'Thanks. I'm guessing you didn't actually make the quiche.'

'I heated it up. That counts, doesn't it?'

'I suppose so. You might have burnt it, after all.'

'I reckon there's one more thing you need to do before you can move on properly.'

'Oh? And what might that be?'

'You should visit her grave.'

I froze. How did he know I'd never been back there since the funeral? It was, perhaps, a reasonable supposition. A few times I'd even bought flowers intending to place them on her grave, but something always held me back. Once or twice I'd got as far as the cemetery gates, on one occasion roughly thrusting my bouquet into the arms of a shocked woman in black whose grief can't have been helped by my bizarre gesture.

'I never go there,' I told Simon. 'I couldn't. I can't.'

'Never?'

I shook my head. 'The funeral was bad enough.'

'Yet you like cemeteries.'

'Not when they contain the mortal remains of my dearest friend. That makes a huge difference.'

'What are you afraid of?'

'I'm not afraid. I can't bear it, that's all.'

'Too sad?'

'Too final.'

'Think about it. I really, truly admire you for writing

220

everything down. You've spent most of your life running away from stuff instead of dealing with it. You put up with Russell because it seemed better than being alone. You probably put up with me for the same reason. How will you ever move on if you can't face up to the past, especially the shitty stuff?'

'I know she's dead. Going to see her grave won't make her any less dead.'

'You can never look her in the eye and explain how you feel. Visiting her grave is the nearest you can get. Why can't you do that?'

One day I would have to go there, face the demons, face the ghosts. It might even help to have Simon with me. What did I fear? Breaking down. The sight of fresh flowers laid on the grave by Madeleine's parents. The inscription on the headstone, the wording of which I couldn't remember and didn't want to know.

Simon witnessed my placing of the written confession in the safe. It was a mere gesture, after all. Once he'd moved out I would destroy it. He relied too heavily upon whatever integrity I had and the burden of guilt I'd carried with me for over twenty years.

We spent the rest of the day reading and, in Simon's case, writing. He worked in half-hour bursts, reporting regularly when he came down to make coffee.

'It's going well, then?'

'I don't want to tempt fate, but I reckon I've got a handle on it now. Couldn't you try to write a book, one that was truly yours?'

'But I have nothing to say – nothing at all.'

He leaned against the sink, one foot resting on top of the other. 'You could write a book about Madeleine.'

'A novel? No, Simon. No.'

'Just a thought.'

Sometimes I felt he was even more obsessed with Madeleine's memory than I was. But he was young enough to be captivated rather than repelled by the morbid romance of her death, all that potential and promise wilfully expunged, the stones of expectation heavy in her pockets as she dragged herself beneath the water.

'Besides, if I did that I'd still be shackled to the past, wouldn't I? I thought the whole point was for me to free myself from Madeleine and move forward.'

'Writers use their past in their fiction, don't they?'

'Some more than others. There's a difference between drawing upon it and using it wholesale.'

He turned to face the sink and rinse out his cup. 'Like I said, it was just a thought,' he mumbled.

Had I hurt his feelings? Why was he so bothered? His interest in my life was something I still couldn't fathom. I had long ceased, in his eyes, to be the writer he thought I was.

'I know you mean well,' I said, 'and that you're only trying to help. I'm sorry if I sounded brusque.'

'Doesn't matter. I'd better get back to the writing, hadn't I, else I'll be no better than you.'

He swept past me after he'd uttered this comment. In time he'd learn that insults are more effective when delivered with subtlety.

Simon emerged from his room at around six, when I was about to start cooking. 'What's for dinner? I'll cook if you tell me what to make.'

What sort of person would he be in ten years' time, I

wondered, once he'd lost that raw quality that was a measure of his youth and also part of his charm? At least I hoped he would lose it. Qualities that are endearing in a young person are far less appealing in people old enough to know better. I often wondered what sort of woman Madeleine might have become and if we'd have liked each other. Would she have married, had children? Would she have written other, greater, novels and swung right out of my orbit, my jealousy poisoning the well? The pointlessness of such questions didn't prevent me from asking them.

I handed Simon a recipe book, a Post-it note marking the relevant page. If he wanted to cook, let him cook.

Ice cream and champagne. The ice cream exquisite. Vanilla, in a sexual context, means plain, no frills; the Lidl of sex. I've always thought this unfair. A really good vanilla ice cream, made with cream, sugar, free-range eggs and Bourbon vanilla pods, is surely proof that excellence can always be achieved if one uses the finest ingredients.

The champagne was equally good, a Veuve Clicquot that couldn't have cost much less than fifty quid.

'It's good, isn't it?' Simon said. *Simon says put your hands on your head. Simon says...*

I nodded.

He caught my hand in his, turned it over, kissed the inside of my wrist, the pulse point.

Here we go again...

'More champers?' I asked.

His mouth still pressed against my skin, he shook his head.

Pleasure; tenderness; a sense of awe. This body – his body, my body, our body. The softness and warmth of his skin, the smell of it, a smell I wish I could capture. I need to analyse it, so that I can remake it when he's gone. Sweat, lemons. Tangy, sweet.

The weight of his body on mine. The warmth of his breath against my ear. The rhythmic movements of love, skin against skin, my fingers in his hair. Our mouths opening as wide as they would go. The taste of him. His tongue flicking inside my mouth. The gentle nip of his teeth. A list, a catalogue. Impossible to describe an experience at once mundane – easy as eating, as breathing – and extraordinary, unique, unexpected. A gift. Tears.

'Simon—' I want to say his name over and over, like a prayer.

Never leave me.

But of course he will.

I glance up at his face. He's a million miles away, his head tipped back, the Adam's apple prominent. And I am merely stunned – stunned with love for him. Love I cannot, must not, speak.

I love you, I mouth, then dip my head, my cheek resting against his belly. This love has no use, it's irrelevant. It won't be long before he leaves me. He'll return to uni, find himself a lovely girl with skin as apricot-soft as his. Will he be kind, or will he tell her about me, smiling when he sees her little moue of disgust?

'How could you?' she might ask. And he'll shrug, reach for her, lose himself in her arms.

A little death, a sour taste; bruised fruit.

CHAPTER TWENTY

'Are you ready?'

'As I'll ever be.'

Sheer folly. All these years I'd avoided visiting Madeleine's grave. Had my mother chosen to be buried rather than cremated, I suppose I should have had to pass through those high metal gates, and likely the other mourners would have attributed any nervous reaction to understandable grief for my mother's demise. A big black hat might have hidden my tears, the deathly paleness of my face.

'I bet it won't be as bad as you think,' Simon said. 'And afterwards we'll have afternoon tea in that quaint little café. Scones with jam and cream. You'd like that, wouldn't you?'

'Yes,' I whispered. 'Yes, of course.'

'Shall we go, then?'

The cemetery was not a large one. Situated roughly half a mile from the church, it had been constructed to take the overflow as the village expanded and the small grave-yard abutting the church was no longer adequate. A heavy padlock hung from the gate. For a moment I thought the gates were locked. Simon pushed and they parted.

He turned to me with a weak smile. 'You don't get out of it that easily.'

'Let's get it over with.'

Few of the graves dated from before the twentieth century, the headstones a mixture of plain white marble and polished black granite. No lichen-encrusted monuments, no weeping angels, the older headstones were equally plain, recognisable by virtue of being made from stone, weathered by time, the inscriptions harder to read.

A dirt path ran from the gates. Graves either side, and in the middle a group of three or four spreading yew trees. I knew precisely where Madeleine's grave was, but I stood in the middle of that path, my eyes fixed on the trees, as if I'd suddenly and irrevocably lost my bearings.

'Gabs?' Simon's hand cupping my elbow. 'You haven't forgotten where she is, have you?'

'No, of course not.'

'Come on, then. Take me to her.'

I looked at him. 'Why do you care so much? About Madeleine?'

He shrugged. 'She matters to you, therefore she matters to me.'

I'd shown him photos of Madeleine and he'd pored over the pictures, murmuring about how pretty she'd been. Did he have some necrophiliac interest in her? But that was absurd! No, just a common or garden fascination with a beautiful, gifted girl who'd died too young – the same kind of glamour that pulls visitors towards the grave of Jim Morrison in Père Lachaise.

My hands and knees trembled as we approached Madeleine's last resting place. The first thing I noticed was the bouquet of fresh flowers. Her parents, of course, would come here regularly; would feel it a terrible dereliction of duty if they failed to keep her grave looking pristine. I imagined her mother on her knees, plucking each weed from between the green glass chippings. There was a proper grave vase for the flowers, Madeleine's name inscribed upon it in gold, a far cry from the dirt-clouded jam jars that served as flower holders on some of the graves.

Simon crouched next to the headstone. Something in his manner – the slow, deliberate tracing of each letter with his fingers – made me freeze.

'Simon?'

I wanted to reach out to him, touch him; wanted him to reassure me that the prickling of my scalp and the nausea rising to my throat were the result of my own emotions rather than a reaction to his.

'Simon!'

Still crouching, he looked up at me. No tenderness in his expression, no pity. He opened his hand. Dangling from it, a chain with a gold locket. Hers. Madeleine's. Was he a thief on top of everything else?

'Where the hell did you get that?'

The pendant swung gently to and fro. 'You recognise it, don't you?'

My first thought was that, whatever happened, we mustn't bicker beside her grave. But he'd brought me here for a reason, one that had nothing to do with helping me come to terms with Madeleine's death. This was all about him. Him and her. I'd always suspected his interest in Madeleine was excessive, but had shut my eyes and ears to the possibility of there being some back-story about which I knew nothing. A connection as complicated as the one I had with her.

'Did you ever wonder where she went, that year she dropped out of uni?' Simon spoke softly, but it was the softness of a tiger stalking its prey on silken paws, waiting for the perfect moment to strike.

The succession of postcards. Foreign postage stamps. But no details, no substance.

'You must have wondered, surely?' he insisted.

'She was travelling. Sorting her head out.' Even at the time I'd known there was more to it than that. But did I really want to know?

'She didn't even need a passport,' he said. 'She hardly ever left one room for months. For as long as it took.'

'What are you talking about? I can show you the postcards, for God's sake.' The postcards were real, the postmarks genuine, the handwriting hers.

'And I can show you a birth certificate.'

'What? Whose?'

'Look at me, Gabrielle. Look at my face. Look properly.'

Didn't I know every perfect inch of it?

'We all resemble somebody,' he said.

The penny dropping and still – *still* – a stubborn refusal to believe what was being revealed to me.

'No... No, it can't be that!'

Simon nodded, satisfied. He'd made his kill.

'I was born,' he said. He sat on the kerb that enclosed her grave. 'I was born,' he repeated, gazing at the headstone.

My stomach lurched. Everything now made complete, terrible sense. What on earth had I done in telling him I'd passed off Madeleine's novel as my own? Had he known all along that I wasn't the author? Either way it wasn't lost on me that I'd confessed to the one person who would, with some justification, wish me to suffer for what I'd done. Madeleine's parents had no appreciation for literature, might have looked at me blankly had I explained to them about her book. If they'd read it, they wouldn't have understood it. But Simon – her son – did understand. He would never forgive me.

'Aren't you going to say something?' he said. 'Don't you want to know how it was managed?'

I couldn't speak.

'My father was a university lecturer,' he continued. 'His wife... I doubt she was happy about it, but... In any case, I've never heard the full story. Versions, that's all. I never called her Mum – she didn't want me to. She was just Sophie. An inoffensive woman, weak and timid. A lot like you, in fact.'

'I think we should talk about this somewhere else.'

He shook his head. 'This is where it must be.'

'So many lies—' Mine as well as his. I was no better.

'Dad gave me the locket on my eighteenth birthday. He said Madeleine sent it to him shortly before she died. Sophie didn't even know he had it. She went mental. She was all right most of the time, but sometimes she'd lose it. She was never violent or anything, she'd just get into these terrible rages when she'd spew out all these resentments she normally kept locked up. She thought I was a nasty piece of work. She knew how much I despised her.'

There was nothing I could say. Nothing I wanted to say. I wondered why he'd waited so long to reveal his identity to me. He didn't seem triumphant; he was no moustache-twirling villain standing over the prone body of the helpless female victim, even if that's more or less how I felt.

'I knew about you, of course. My dad didn't have many photos of Madeleine and I guess her parents still have most of them, but there was one photo she'd kept pinned to a board in her room at uni: a picture of her with you. Dad let me have it. I never met her parents, by the way. They don't know I exist and I'd prefer they didn't.' He shrugged. 'Awkward for everyone. Too much explaining. I'm not sentimental.'

No, he certainly wasn't that.

'When did you find out about the book?' I asked.

'Quite recently. I thought the book was yours – admired it, genuinely – but then my dad asked if I wanted to go through some of Madeleine's stuff she'd left with him. He said he'd never had the heart to go through it and I guess that was true, because if he'd found the manuscript, he'd have realised immediately what it was and what it meant.'

'What manuscript?'

'The first book she wrote. Before *The Song of the Air*. It's badly typed, some of the pages are torn, a couple are missing altogether. She dedicated it to you. That's when I started thinking, but even then, even when I wrote you that first letter, I thought maybe some fluke had produced two exceptional writers who just happened to be best friends.'

'And then I confessed to you.'

'Yeah. I didn't expect that. I wanted to meet you to find out about Madeleine. I had to get to know you first, make you trust me.'

'You're looking at me as if you hate me.'

He shrugged, his gaze sliding to the gold locket. 'You stole her book. You watched her die.'

'She abandoned you.'

He shot me a murderous look. 'She would have come back for me if she'd lived. I know she would. When she could have afforded to support me.'

He'd deluded himself and that was entirely under-standable. Madeleine should have confided in me – I would have helped her, done whatever I could. Had she trusted me so little? To keep from me something like that, yet to give her book to me – it made no sense.

'I knew her,' I said. 'You didn't.'

He stood. 'Maybe it's true she let you have *The Song of the Air*, but that's only because she wasn't thinking straight. She didn't know what she was doing. I don't think she cared about anything by then.'

'Not even you?'

'If she cared so much about *you*, why didn't she tell you about me? You watched her die, knowing the book would be yours to do with as you wanted.'

'It wasn't like that.'

'You didn't save her. You could have.' He took several paces towards me. I backed away. 'Why didn't you?'

I had no answer. It had happened so suddenly – I really had tried...

Excuses.

All those years I'd been haunted by Madeleine's death and now I was confronted with the full extent of my guilt, my failure. She'd wanted to die and I'd let her.

'I can't swim,' I murmured. 'I was out of my depth. I didn't want to die. She did.'

Would he hit me? Spit in my face? Kill me? I sank to the ground, too sad to cry, too hurt by everything I'd done; by everything I hadn't done.

231

'And after all that you still fancy me, don't you? Of course you do. You want me to fuck you.' A statement, not a question. For I did; of course I did.

And what happened next might seem incredible – grotesque. And it was.

He yanked me up by one arm, dragged me over to the stand of yew trees. Pushed me against a tree. Unbuckled his belt. Unzipped his jeans. He was hard. I was his.

'You want it, don't you?' he said, his cock pressed against my pubic bone.

'Yes,' I whispered. 'Yes!'

He pulled down my jeans and fucked me. No preliminaries, no tenderness, simply the act of penetration. And, my God, I wanted him so much! The vicar himself might have walked along the path at that moment and I wouldn't have cared. Simon, inside me, was all I wanted. Despite everything.

And after he'd come, and the little shudders that followed, he zipped himself up again as if nothing had happened.

Tears fell from my eyes. He took pity on me, I suppose, for with some show of gentleness he helped me put my clothes straight. Then he pulled me to him and kissed me hard on the mouth. A kiss that felt more like a punch.

Bewildered, I followed him back to Madeleine's grave, as I would have followed him anywhere. And, in my shame, the bleakness I felt was occasioned by the knowledge that what he'd given me over by the yew trees was a parting gift. Russell had given me Paris, Madeleine her novel. Simon gave me a fuck.

I brushed my tears away, wondering what on earth would happen now. It had been ridiculous to imagine

Simon had ever wanted me. I'd never fooled myself into believing that he loved me or that we had any kind of future together.

But that wasn't true, was it? Each fleeting kiss, each touch of his hand had persuaded me he felt something for me. Not love, not that, but some measure of affection, of need.

'What do we do now?' I asked.

His eyes opened wide. 'I promised you afternoon tea, didn't I?'

The idea was so absurd, I laughed. 'What? Are you mad?'

'Aren't we both a bit mad?'

So that's what we did. Simon and I sat opposite each other. A red and white checked cloth on the table; a plate of scones, pots of jam and clotted cream in front of us.

Simon lifted the tea pot. 'Shall I be mother?'

I nodded. Words seemed beyond me.

'Well. This is surreal, isn't it?' Simon said, pushing a cup towards me.

'It's horrible,' I managed to whisper. I'd looked forward to this little treat, expecting to eat my scone in a happy glow of accomplishment and relief.

'I expect you'd like to know what Madeleine's first book is like. Personally I think it's even finer than *The Song of the Air*. It deals with some of the same themes: the fear of and longing for abandonment; ideas of personal liberty and how far you can take that.'

He was quite the critic. Clearly he knew Madeleine's work inside out. Better than I did, for he had the precious first book, the one I'd never dreamed existed.

'It's called *The Flight of Birds*,' he said. 'There are a

couple of characters who turn up in the next book. I wonder if she planned to write a trilogy? You wonder where it came from, don't you, all that talent?'

I gazed at him dumbly. The playground bully, enjoying himself at my expense.

'It's odd she never mentioned it when she gave the second book to you. Doesn't seem likely it could have slipped her mind. But I guess she wasn't thinking straight, was she? Hardly knew what she was doing.'

In his eyes I was no better than a thief and a murderer. I'd let her die; I'd stolen her book. He couldn't stop riffing on those two fixed ideas.

'Would we have got on, do you think, me and Madeleine?' he asked, spreading a split scone with jam and cream. 'Am I the sort of person she liked? What were her boyfriends like?'

'All sorts,' I mumbled, adding, 'She wasn't fussy.'

He pursed his lips. 'That's not very nice. Did you ever share blokes?'

'Share?' *What did he mean?*

'Yeah – you know – swap guys between you.'

'No. That's a disgusting thing to suggest.'

But just once, we had.

'Bet you did. Bet you always wanted everything *she* had.'

One evening, both of us tipsy, round at the house of Madeleine's boyfriend, the older brother of one of her friends, rugby player shoulders and film-star looks. I'd hooked up with his mate as a favour to Madeleine.

Up in the boy's bedroom, the lights out. Madeleine and her bloke got the bed, but when we were all done she tapped me on the shoulder, whispered into my ear. Then Madeleine and I simply changed places.

234

When the lights went on again I hated everyone in that room, myself most of all. Madeleine seemed not to care; it didn't mean anything to her. Men – sex – never did matter much to her. Or so it appeared. What did I know about her at all?

'She had everything she wanted,' I said. 'Why would she throw all that away? I'll never understand.'

'So would she have liked me, d'you reckon?'

'As her son, or as her lover?'

'Is that a bitchy thing to say or just honest?'

'What does either of us know about honesty, Simon?' *Or love, either*.

'Aren't you going to have a scone? They're pretty good.'

'I'm not hungry. And to answer your question, I doubt Madeleine would have cared one way or the other about you. I don't think she cared about anyone.'

'I thought you loved her.'

'I don't know any more. I admired her, envied her, would have loved her if she'd let me. I thought I knew her best, but even if that's true I'm not sure it's worth much.'

Having demolished one half of his scone, he stared lugubriously at the other as if it had wilfully defeated him.

'I ought to be your son, not hers. We're more alike.'

'How would you know what Madeleine was like? You can't tell from a few photos.'

'And the stuff my dad's told me. He wasn't in love with her, he told me that. And he was pretty pissed off when she told him she was pregnant.' He looked up, a bemused expression on his face. 'I don't think he liked her very much. Mind you, I don't think he likes Sophie much, either. Maybe he's just rubbish at picking women.'

'I thought you idolised Madeleine. Isn't that the plot you've chosen? Talented, perfect, vulnerable young woman, life and reputation ripped apart by heartless friend – me, that is.'

He took the gold locket from his pocket and placed it on the table between us. 'I wanted everything to be simple. I wanted to *make* everything simple, so I can understand it.'

'That's not how we understand things. It's not about making things simple, it's about appreciating the complexities.' The sound of me trying to let myself off the hook – did he hear it? Is that why he sneered? Did he sneer?

'When I wrote you that first letter—' his hands on the table, his fingertips almost touching mine, 'all I thought about was learning what Madeleine was like. That's all, just that.'

'I know. You said.'

'I didn't turn up intending to cause havoc in your life,' he added.

But you did – you did!

'Fact is,' he continued, 'I don't know what to think about any of it – about her, about you. About that fucking book.'

The book. It always came back to that. Two books, now. If they'd never existed...

'Simon... I don't know what you want, I don't know what you're going to do. I'm not even sure I care.'

We both stared at the golden locket. Madeleine's presence between us, as it always would be. As it must.

236

CHAPTER TWENTY-ONE

Somehow we got through the rest of the day, but I couldn't face the prospect of sharing another meal with Simon. In the event, neither of us was hungry. We grazed on nuts, crisps, biscuits, all washed down with lots of wine.

'You have to go,' I said.

'I know. But we need to talk first. We need to discuss what we're going to do with Madeleine's first book.'

'There's nothing to talk about. You've won, haven't you?'

'Don't be like that,' he said, as if I were the unreasonable one. 'There are a number of options. We could destroy it, but I don't believe you want that any more than I do. It needs to be published.'

As Simon described it, the book was closely related in style and theme to *The Song of the Air*, and there were those recurring characters who couldn't be explained away if the book were published as anything other than a novel by Gabrielle Price.

I wished Madeleine had destroyed it. Or else given it to me. Why hadn't she? Why did I get the second book but not the first?

'You can't expect someone in her mental state to have made sensible decisions,' Simon said when I put this to him. 'She didn't think it through. Isn't that obvious?'

We sat together in my living room, our backs resting against the sofa, knees drawn up, the inevitable bottle of red wine between us. Glasses half full; half empty.

'If we publish it in her name, I'll have to come clean about the other book. That, too, is obvious.'

'I know.' His knee kept bumping against mine, a sensation at once intimate and irritating, but I didn't shift away.

'Well? Is that what you want? Is that what you're proposing to do?'

If that's what he planned, I could hardly prevent him. The book was in his possession and he could prove he was Madeleine's son. The book rightfully belonged to him as her heir. I could never prove she'd given *The Song of the Air* to me.

'What's to stop me from saying you copied elements from my book and that Madeleine had nothing to do with either of them?' I said.

'The typescript has written corrections and notes on it. In her handwriting. Easy enough to check, I should think. Her parents will have kept stuff with her writing on, won't they? Mother's Day cards, that sort of thing.'

'Go on, then. What are you going to do?'

'It's a tough one.' His bland tone and expression were maddening. 'You can read it, if you want,' he said. 'I brought it with me.'

'Then... You must have known all along that I didn't write *The Song of the Air*.'

'Like I said, I thought you might have collaborated. Honestly, that's what I thought, knowing you'd been friends and grown up together and everything.'

So the book was in my house. There, within reach. Or

so he said. Could I believe a single thing he told me? He sprinkled his speech with words like "honestly" and "truth", but they were just words, without weight or meaning.

'I could give it to her parents, couldn't I?' he said. 'I wonder what they'd think? I wonder what they'd do?'

'For God's sake, Simon. Put me out of my misery.'

I sensed he was building up to something and enjoying the journey, enjoying my fear and apprehension. I wasn't wrong.

'I've taken your confession,' he said. 'You'd written down the safe code on that notepad by the phone. I mailed it to myself at my parents' address.'

'You're lying.'

'Easy enough to check, isn't it?'

He was right. I had nothing left with which to bargain. The horse had bolted. I changed the safe code anyway. Stupid of me to have written down the original one, which I thought I'd cleverly disguised as a telephone number among many other genuine ones.

'It was insurance,' he said. 'I knew you'd destroy it as soon as I'd gone. Anyone would.'

I could hardly bear to look at his smug face, but I forced myself to do so.

'What have you done to me?'

'Now you know what it feels like. You betrayed your best friend, now I've betrayed you. You knew I wasn't to be trusted, didn't you? You never really did, but you didn't care as long as I was here. You wanted me. You couldn't figure out what I wanted from you and I gave you just enough to make you believe I wanted to fuck you. Enough to keep you hoping I could be Chéri to your Léa.'

'He loved her!' I said. Ridiculous. They were fictional characters, the strings pulled by Colette – forty-seven when the first *Chéri* novel was published – a writer who understood how devastating it is when a beautiful woman must come to terms with her ageing body.

'Yes. But when Chéri meets Léa again after his marriage, he realises how much she's aged. Fat, old, repulsive. A woman who knows she's lost her appeal; a man so disillusioned he sees no escape except a bullet through the brain.' He mimed the action of shooting himself in the head.

I'd been in my early twenties when I first read the two *Chéri* novels. Even then, protected by youth, I'd found them depressing; even then already mourning the inevitable process of ageing, the misery of seeing my breasts sag, my skin wrinkle, my waist disappear. Bad enough at the best of times, so much worse when the disintegrating body is being scrutinised by a young, pitiless man.

My relationship with Simon was based on lies, misunderstandings, games. And I was no better, allowing myself to fall for his gorgeous face. What qualities did he possess beyond the physical that attracted me? Not enough.

'There's nothing you can reproach me with,' he said. 'Whatever I've done, you've done worse. Anyway, you put up with awful Russell for long enough, didn't you, however badly he treated you?'

'Russell was a sordid mistake. But that's no excuse; I knew what I was getting in to. I didn't even have the saving grace of being in love with him.'

'Why, then?'

'I thought I needed someone.'

240

'Was he any good in bed?' He shifted closer to me. 'Better than me?' He put the glasses and the wine bottle on the table and sat astride me. 'What was I like?' I noted his use of the past tense and what that implied. 'Was I good? Did you like me being inside you?'

I shook my head. 'You don't need me to tell you.'

He laughed and got up to take the glasses into the kitchen.

I remembered Madeleine telling me she wanted to learn the violin. She had no particular ear for music, but that wasn't the point. She'd heard about some guy whose girlfriend played the violin for him, naked. This image appealed to Madeleine. She was used to being looked at by men, but what she wanted was to stand naked in a room and play such beautiful music, the man with her would simply shut his eyes, moved by the sounds she made. That's what she wrote about – the freedom to be found once we lose the body and only sounds and thoughts remain.

She told me – playfully but, I think, seriously – that I was boring for choosing *Dracula* as the most erotic book I'd ever read. More curious than I about transgressive sex, she read *The Story of O* and wanted an owl mask. She said love was worth nothing unless it killed you. Love, for her, was something to be feared, not celebrated.

'And anyway,' she said, 'it probably doesn't exist. Not the kind of love that's written about in novels. Grand romances, eternal passions.'

'Too wearing,' I joked.

'You can't love someone that much without wanting to die,' she said.

I didn't understand then, and I didn't understand now. What I felt for Simon raided the borders of sexual obsession, but I'd experienced similar feelings before – that adolescent desperation for someone; the sense that if you lose them, life itself will become meaningless. Was that what Madeleine had felt for Simon's father? Or was it the loss of her child that destroyed her? But hadn't she given him up willingly? Whenever we talked about love we meant romantic love, sexual love. Any other kind was beyond our understanding and largely irrelevant.

The Song of the Air dealt obliquely with love in suggesting that true freedom could be found only in renouncing the lusts of the flesh. Whenever anyone asked me about that aspect of the novel I fudged the issue, distancing myself from the book's narrator, insisting that this idea was intended to be metaphorical rather than taken at face value.

'We find ourselves only by first losing ourselves,' was the line I took. Madeleine had given me the novel, but not the key to interpreting it.

If I wanted to lose my body, it was only so that I should not have to watch its gradual disintegration.

'What are you thinking?' Simon murmured, sauntering back into the room and sitting far away from me.

'Everything. Nothing. Love. Death.'

Revenge.

He said the manuscript of Madeleine's first book was in the house. He'd taken my written confession, why shouldn't I have her book in return? Surely that's what Madeleine would have wanted.

'I want to read the book,' I said.

'Maybe later. I only have the original, you see, and I

couldn't trust you with it. You must see how unwise that would be.'

'You know I would never destroy it. You know how I feel about books being burned.'

'This one's different, though, isn't it? It's the one thing that stands between you and... And what? Ruin, really. It would crush you, wouldn't it, for the world to know what you'd done? It might even kill you.'

He was right. There was only one thing to be done. I scrambled from the floor and rushed up the stairs. I would fight him to the death for the manuscript if necessary. I couldn't allow him to ruin my life. That book was mine! Simon had never even known Madeleine. She hadn't wanted him.

I opened drawers and threw them on the floor. I tipped out clothes, books, everything I could lay my hands on. I didn't care what damage I did.

'It's under the typewriter.' Simon stood in the doorway. I glared at him, picked up the typewriter, flung it onto the floor. He winced but made no move to stop me from grabbing the manuscript tied with string, the title and Madeleine's name on the cover page in her handwriting. I clutched it against my chest.

'You couldn't destroy it, could you? Not a book. Not *her* book.'

Stalemate. To destroy it unread was impossible, I simply couldn't bring myself to do that. But it was mine now and it must stay that way. I walked towards the door. Simon didn't move.

'You'll have to get past me,' he said. 'I won't let you.'

I pushed him. He was slim and wiry, stronger than he looked, but I took him by surprise. We scuffled on the landing, ridiculous and undignified, but I refused to let him beat me. The manuscript held up in front of me like a shield, I shoved him backwards. He lost his footing, tumbled down the stairs. He groaned, so I knew he was conscious. I stepped over him, ran through the house, then realised I had nowhere to hide the manuscript. Was my only option to destroy it?

I ran back to check on Simon. I could see his chest rising and falling, but he wasn't moving. I'd have to risk putting the papers in my safe and trust that his talents didn't include safe cracking.

He called out my name.

'I'm sorry,' I said, walking back to him.

'No you're not. You might have killed me.'

'Don't over-dramatise. Let me have a look.'

He had a small graze over his right eye and a bump on his forehead that would likely come out in a fine bruise.

'Will you let me put some antiseptic on it?'

He gave me a murderous look but nodded.

It was odd how little thought I had given to the surely bizarre fact that I had slept with the son of my best friend. If she'd lived – if she'd reclaimed Simon as a baby – it was likely he would have grown up thinking of me as a kind of aunt; a sender of generous birthday presents, someone he was forced to be polite to for his mother's sake. I felt rather like his mother as I dabbed his grazed forehead with a cotton wool ball soaked in TCP. For once, I felt in control.

'Would Madeleine have made a good mother, do you think?' he asked.

'How can I possibly say? She never had so much as a goldfish to look after.'

'She wasn't the nurturing type, was she? I bet not, anyway.'

'No, not really.'

'Sophie told me I should be grateful, because Madeleine could have chosen to flush me down the lav. She actually used those words, can you believe it? *She* wished Madeleine had got rid of me. I wish I'd been adopted. My dad's had other affairs since Madeleine; we all know about them. Sophie knows. I hear her crying sometimes and I just sit there, thinking what a stupid bitch she is. Why does she stay with him?'

'She probably doesn't know what else to do with herself. Some women don't. My mum went through a phase of reading *Spare Rib* magazine, but she would have done better to find herself a part-time job.'

The magazine had arrived through the post with a band of brown paper around it. For six months or so my mother read each copy from cover to cover, mildly raging against men, against injustice, against South Africa and anything else she thought worth complaining about. My father gently took the piss, asking if she'd bought some dungarees yet and if she wanted him to address her as "sister". It was the only time my mother showed any streak of rebellion. I never found out what brought it on and sometimes wished she could have gone the whole hog, painting peace signs on the windows and picketing outside patriarchal institutions.

'Maybe she had an affair,' Simon suggested after I'd explained what *Spare Rib* was. 'With a communist who wanted to raise her consciousness.'

'Not very likely.'

'An affair with a woman, then? A tempestuous Sapphic romance?'

Also unlikely.

'Have you ever done it with a woman? You and Madeleine?'

'Shut up, Simon.'

'I'll leave,' he said. 'Go back to my parents.'

'Yes. Good.' It was time he went. The sooner he left, the sooner I could start trying to repair the damage he'd done.

He thought of me as Léa. A woman on the brink of defeat. The fictional Léa's victory over the passing years was also the conquest of love. An acceptance of her defeat would, I felt, have been a braver ending.

CHAPTER TWENTY-TWO

More reliable than an alarm clock, Pushkin could be depended upon to wake me at seven-thirty every morning. I'd no need to get up that early, but my mother's example had taught me that lingering in bed was the thin end of the wedge. One slovenly habit would surely lead to others. Besides, cat ownership precluded the temptation to laze in bed. Pushkin, a typically insistent cat, would miaow, attack my toes and push her nose against my face until I consented to get up and attend to her needs.

I couldn't hear Simon moving around and he clearly hadn't fed the cat, so where was he? Had he left without saying goodbye? I slipped my dressing gown on. Pushkin – purring, tail erect – rubbed against my legs, triumphant at having achieved her goal. I followed her downstairs and into the kitchen. When I picked up her food bowl to clean it, I glanced through the window and saw Simon. Dressed in hoodie and jeans, he was staring down at a small bonfire. My first thought was to rush out and tell him to put it out: the smoke would annoy the neighbours. But then I froze. What was he burning? What was he *doing*?

Pushkin head-butted my leg.

'All right, all right,' I muttered, slopping her breakfast into the bowl.

I went outside to speak to Simon. 'I hope you've got a good explanation for this,' I said. 'No one around here has a barbecue at this time of year, let alone...'

My voice trailed away to nothing. I saw what he was burning. Pages of typescript.

'You didn't think I'd be stupid enough to leave her book lying around in my room and direct you straight to it, did you? What you've got in your safe is a bunch of blank pages under the cover sheet. Never thought to check what you had in your hands, did you? Too eager to get it away from me.'

Madeleine's novel. The one I'd never had the chance to read.

'It's a bonfire of the vanities,' he said, staring at me with smoke-reddened eyes, feeding the fire page by page. 'I was right not to trust you, wasn't I?'

I'd wished the book hadn't existed, but I couldn't bear to see it being burnt. And this was the only copy of Madeleine's first novel in existence.

'But why?'

'Isn't it obvious? She never wanted either of us. You were the boring friend who kept hanging round. I was the kid she should have flushed down the bog. The only person she knew how to love was herself. I'm destroying her book just like she wanted to destroy me.'

'She was depressed, she couldn't cope. If she'd lived—'

'But she didn't, did she? You made sure of that! Aren't you going to try and save it?' he asked. 'Don't you fancy grubbing around in the ashes to rescue what you can? Go on!' He grabbed hold of me, forced me on to my knees, pressing me close to the flames.

'You're mad!' I said, struggling uselessly against his

firm grip, wincing as another typewritten sheet turned black, friable, unreadable.

'You should be pleased. You're safe now.'

'You're doing this for me, then?'

'Don't be stupid, of course not. I still have your confession, remember?'

I winced again. Maybe he *was* mad, some faulty wiring in his brain: a chemical imbalance, the same kind of thing that had driven Madeleine into the icy water that closed around her like a fist.

'I don't understand,' I said. 'Anything would have been better than this.'

'Even your shame? How would you have stood it? You know you wouldn't. You'd rather have killed me than have anyone else know what you'd done. Isn't that true?'

'If you were really so worried about me getting my greedy hands on it, you didn't need to let me know of its existence. Why destroy it? It makes no sense!'

He crouched beside me, prodding the last of the pages with a stick. 'Why does anything have to make sense? Life doesn't, not for most people. *You* grew up with loving, devoted parents. All I had was a cold father and a woman who resented my existence.'

'Plenty of people put up with worse.'

He glared at me. 'And what comfort is *that* supposed to be? Madeleine would never have come back for me, I know that. She was heartless, like all writers. They like bad things to happen because it gives them something to write about.'

'That's not true. She wasn't like that.' Unfeeling at times, too wrapped up in her own concerns, but not heartless. 'She was complicated.'

'And I'm simple. Simple Simon. That's what my dad used to call me. I'd have only been any use to him if I'd been some kind of child prodigy. It used to hurt. I didn't realise until I was in my twenties that it was all about him – *his* failures, *his* not being clever enough. He really minded that he wasn't a great professor at Oxford or Cambridge. I should've dropped out altogether, told him to stick his precious education up his tight arse.'

'But you did okay,' I said.

'Okay? Is *this* okay?' He plunged his hands into the still-hot bonfire, gathering handfuls of blackened scraps of paper, scattering them over himself.

'Stop it, Simon – stop it!'

'Why? Do I frighten you? Is this the kind of behaviour you don't understand? Is this why you let Madeleine drown?'

'Why do *you* care? She didn't love either of us.'

'Life is so shit,' he said, rocking back on his heels, weeping. 'People always let you down.'

I was merely the latest in a long line.

He wiped tears away with soot-blackened hands, leaving streaks around his eyes and on his cheeks.

'Come inside,' I said. 'You can clean your face – I'll make you a cup of coffee.'

He allowed me to lift him to his feet. Before we went inside, I stamped out the last smouldering sticks and bits of paper. Just to make sure, as soon as I'd got Simon seated at the kitchen table I filled the kettle with cold water and poured it over the remains of the bonfire.

I passed him a box of tissues and he made a few indifferent passes against his face with one.

'When are you leaving?' I asked.

He shrugged. 'Do you mind? Will you cry when I go? Did you fantasise about us being writers together with me servicing you at regular intervals? Was that how our life together would have looked, to you?'

'I always knew you had another life to go back to.'

'Yeah. What a life!'

'Go back to uni. You might as well.'

'Not creative writing. I'm sick of writers – sick of words.'

'Sick of me.'

'When I came down this morning and started that bonfire, I rehearsed all these things I was going to say to you, to hurt you. To make you cry. It would have been so easy.'

He still could. He still might. He'd done harm, but once he'd gone my life would revert to the way it had been. Dull, eventless days; each day the same as the previous one, as the next one. Unless, of course, Simon chose to mail a copy of my confession to Madeleine's parents. How could I learn to live with that possibility hanging over me?

I made coffee and set a mug in front of Simon.

'Do you hate me?' he asked.

'You made no promises.'

The manner in which he sat – hunched forward, hands around his mug – reminded me of the first time we met, that awkward conversation in the café. Right from the start he hadn't played a straight bat and I'd taken insufficient care to guard against the dangers he represented. The moment I first saw him I had wanted him, needed to keep him near me for as long as I could.

'What will you do, after I've gone?' he asked.

'Maybe I'll write a book.'

251

'You could always marry the nice vicar,' Simon said.

'I don't think atheists make very good vicars' wives.'

'Don't see why not.'

It riled me that he could, even in fun, propose so restricted a future for me. The terrible thing was that I could see myself in the role, planted in Mr Latham's kitchen wearing jeans and a checked shirt, doling out tea and sympathy to parishioners who would inevitably look upon me as the vicar's deputy – a spiritual triage. My own beliefs would remain unexamined, for I would simply be the handmaiden, the conduit.

'Anyway,' I said, 'Mr Latham isn't the marrying type. Even if he were, it wouldn't work. It would be cowardly and I'm sick of being a coward.'

He reached out and touched his fingertips to mine. 'Will you miss me, after I've gone?' he said softly. 'Will you reach for me in bed when you're half asleep, and shed a tear when you realise I'm not there?'

I pushed his hand away. 'Don't.'

A slow, sweet smile spread across his face. 'I know the answer anyway.'

I narrowed my eyes. 'Is that the best you can do? Do you not understand what a soft target is?'

He shrugged. He was a mess. Messed up by his parents, the ones who were present but useless and the one who'd turned her back on him.

'It was all a power trip for you, wasn't it? Isn't that what this whole insane month has been about? You didn't care whether or not I started writing again; you didn't care about me except as someone you could manipulate.'

'I did care,' he said. 'I thought I did, anyway. I just wanted to know the truth. I wanted someone to be

252

honest with me. I wanted to hate you. You were like those women my dad screwed. I thought you were, anyway.'

'Why did you care what your dad did? You weren't sorry for Sophie, were you? You despised her.'

'They're all as bad as each other. People fucking with other people. All my life I've had to put up with my dad belittling me, Sophie bitching about Madeleine. It was like I was the punch bag for everything they thought had gone wrong with their lives. My dad—'

'What? What about your dad?'

'He's a selfish bastard. He wanted Madeleine to get rid of me just like Sophie did. No one was ever straight with me, except when it suited them; when they wanted to use me as a stick to beat someone else with. That's what it was like.' He gripped my hands, his eyes pleading with me to believe him, to take his side.

'I know,' I said. 'You wouldn't have understood Madeleine any more than I did. She was unknowable. I think you're the same.'

'Do you?' He shook his head. 'You only confessed by accident. If we hadn't argued, you never would have told me. And when you did, I saw how I could hurt you, make you pay.'

'No, Simon, you knew long before then how you could hurt me. You knew exactly how I felt about you, didn't you? My weakness, as you saw it.'

He shrugged, couldn't look me in the eye. 'I saw you were basically a decent person. That's why it all fell apart. The bad guy act – it's not who I am, I swear it. If you'd been straight with me from the start, I would have been straight with you.'

I doubted that. Cajoling me into writing my confession had been a form of punishment. He'd wanted someone else to feel what it was like to be battered, as he had been, by people with their own confused agendas.

The one thing, the only thing I wanted to know was whether or not Simon had had any feelings for me at all. It was of no relevance to his future or mine, but it mattered. How could I ask him? How could I trust him to tell me the truth?

'Shall we keep in touch?' he asked.

'What on earth for?' The clean break would hurt, but it was better in the long run.

'Not even the occasional postcard?' *His mother's son.*

'Can't stop you, can I? You know my address.' The odd postcard, perhaps, but in time he'd move on, forget about me, and I would never contact him.

'What will you do with my so-called confession?' I asked.

'So-called?'

'You've destroyed the only real evidence that Madeleine wrote *The Song of the Air*. My confession was nothing more than a work of fiction you composed yourself from scraps of information, then forced me to sign. You resented growing up without your mother. In some twisted way you held me accountable and dreamed up a bizarre plot to suit your fantasies. You made me write it down. I was a victim of gaslighting. That's all I need to say. No one knew Madeleine could write, but everyone knew I did.'

He hung his head. 'I got out of my depth, lost sight of everything except my own anger and pain.' Tears in his eyes. So young, so damaged. I was tougher than he'd ever be.

I reached out to stroke his hair. Sobbing, he let me take him in my arms. We clung together. I held him as if I were trying to stop him falling apart.

Mechanically I performed my duties for Mr Latham. A man of routines, he might well have appreciated having a wife who could provide a buffer between himself and the more emotionally needy of his parishioners. An unfair thought. He was well-liked, approachable, and participated in village activities with good grace and humour.

'I think we're in for a storm,' he said when I took his lunch in to the study.

The rain began to fall while I was in the kitchen cutting up a lasagne into single portions for freezing. Mr Latham asked if I'd like to get home before the weather worsened. I felt safer in his kitchen, where I knew what was expected of me and where I knew myself to be useful.

'At least take a break. Have a cup of coffee. You do far more than I pay you for.'

He switched on the kettle. 'Well, I should like one, so you might as well join me.'

Small acts of kindness always had the power to move me. I gazed at the rain slashing against the window. Angry tears sprang to my eyes. Too much like pathetic fallacy.

'Gabrielle – you're crying.'

'Am I?' I tore off a sheet of kitchen towel and scrubbed my eyes. 'I'm terribly sorry.'

He drew out a chair and invited me to sit down. 'Coffee won't be two ticks,' he said.

'Really, there's no need, I'm perfectly all right.' I didn't want to be one of his emotionally needy parishioners, burdening him with problems any normal woman would have shared with a female friend over a bottle of Cabernet and a chick flick.

'You're upset. I've no wish to pry, but I'm equally reluctant not to attempt to help in whatever way I can.'

'You're very kind,' I mumbled. 'Kinder than I deserve. I dislike being the type of woman who can't control her emotions. It's undignified.' *At my age*, I might have added. A young woman sobbing elicits natural pity in most people. Embarrassment is the more likely reaction to a weeping middle-aged woman, the assumption being that she's either menopausal or drunk.

'Dignity doesn't enter into it,' he said. 'Is there anything at all I can do?'

Wipe away my sins? Make Simon love me? Marry me?

'No, really, there's nothing. I've got myself into a bit of a pickle, that's all. It's not serious.'

'Serious enough that you should weep over it. And, as you said yourself, you're not a woman whose emotions often betray her. One can't always be stoical.'

'I couldn't explain if I wanted to. It's a tangle – a mess. I've allowed life to pass me by. No, it's worse than that: I've deliberately passed it by. I haven't made enough of an effort.'

No guts, no glory.

He handed me a cup of coffee. 'Take your time. I'd like to sit with you for a while, if I may. You don't have to talk if you don't want to.'

He sat opposite me, his own mug in front of him. The table was otherwise bare, and I couldn't help thinking we looked like a study for a Victorian genre painting with a subtle moral message, although what that message might have been, I couldn't decide.

'Simon will be leaving soon,' I said.

Mr Latham's nod, his murmured, 'Ah', suggested he properly read the significance of that statement. 'No doubt you'll miss him.'

'I've always thought myself a self-contained person, not the type who needs other people around.'

'Perhaps you might consider getting more involved in village life? There's always plenty going on.'

'I know. But that's not really what I want.'

'Then perhaps you ought to think about looking for a more satisfying job. Not that I want to lose you, but you're wasted on a dull old stick like me. Or is that not what you're looking for, either?'

'I'm not sure. I think I might try to write a book.'

'I'm sure everyone would be pleased to see your name in print again.'

'The first book,' I said, choosing my words carefully, 'was the product of youthful folly. It was written by a person who no longer exists.'

'You feel you are no longer the same person?'

'I never *was* that person.' I looked him in the eye, daring him to probe, to ask the pertinent questions.

'Surely... Is this something you really want me to know?'

I shrugged. 'Does it matter any more? The book was written by a ghost.'

'Ah... I see.'

Did he? Or was he taking the comfortable route of misinterpreting my words? My own fault for being elliptical.

No guts...

I gave him a rough summary of events, omitting Simon's role in the story.

'That is indeed quite startling. Naturally you will expect me to advise you to come clean about your – deception, I think we might reasonably call it?'

'I suppose.'

'I wonder if any good can be achieved from owning up at this late stage?'

'What I did was wrong. That, I think, is clear. But the only people I could be said to have harmed are the Andersons, who don't care about literature.'

'And yourself,' he murmured. 'I think you are the person who has been most harmed.'

'Don't, please, tempt me into self-pity.'

'Indeed I'm not trying to do any such thing. I'm trying to view the situation objectively. A great deal of time has passed since the book was published. Sleeping dogs are sometimes better left undisturbed, are they not?'

'You don't think it's cowardly?'

'I ask only what *good* would be achieved from confessing.'

He patted my hand and I felt comforted, almost blessed. He'd told me what I wanted to hear, yet I felt oddly disappointed.

Mr Latham gave me an uncharacteristically roguish smile. 'You wanted me to tell you to blazon it from the rooftops so that you might enjoy your sufferings.'

I started a little, my mug listing slightly to one side. 'Not to be forgiven? Isn't that what Christianity teaches – forgive those who do wrong, or words to that effect?'

'People, I'm afraid, can be terribly unforgiving. I think

of myself as a pragmatic Christian, if that doesn't sound impossibly wishy-washy. Barbara Pym, you know,' he added in an apparent non-sequitur. 'I hired you largely because you admire her novels. I know you to be a good person, a Christian in the broadest sense of the word. I want no further harm to befall you.'

I'd misjudged the man, thought him aloof, a cold fish, timid. He would never make a churchgoer out of me; but an ally, a friend... it did at least seem possible.

'I think the rain is easing off,' he said. 'Looks like we won't get a storm after all.'

'No. No storm.' For a while, at least.

CHAPTER TWENTY-THREE

The next day, Simon packed his bags. My skin clammy, teeth gritted, I couldn't trust myself to speak without betraying my emotions. His face expressionless, he seemed equally disinclined to engage in small talk, and the time for anything more was over. This, then, was it; the day after which I would have to find a way to negotiate a life that had been tossed around, upended, splintered.

Pushkin on my lap, I stroked her fur, my eyes constantly straying to the clock. Simon intended to catch the ten-fifteen train. Just under an hour to kill until it was time for me to accompany him to the station. Those awkward few moments after he'd found his seat and before the train departed. The last feeble wave, the awful tug of watching the train pull away, and then silence, returning home to a house that would feel subtly but horribly different. I would talk too much to the cat, trying to fill the spaces, knowing the exercise to be a futile one.

Eventually I would get used to Simon's absence. I would find the courage to enter his room, confront the fact that no traces of him remained. I toyed with the idea of advertising for a lodger, but it wouldn't do. Better to learn to cope without him than seek desperately for some kind of replacement, however unsatisfactory.

I heard the soft thud of his rucksack hitting the carpet

near the front door and braced myself. Pushkin jumped from my lap and trotted over to greet him. He knelt down to stroke her. Don't say goodbye to her, I pleaded silently; say nothing, nothing at all.

Coffee. I would make coffee. Must keep busy. Perform each task slowly, carefully, concentrate on the moment.

'Coffee?' I shouted through to Simon, my voice shrill.

'Might as well.'

The last time I would ever make him a cup of coffee...

That was not the sentimental road I needed to be travelling down.

'Biscuit?'

'Sure. Why not?'

Another glance at the clock when I took the coffee in to the living room. Still fifty minutes to get through.

'Well, it's been—'

'Don't.'

'Okay.' He grabbed a biscuit from the plate. 'So we'll sit here in silence, shall we?'

'I'm sorry. But you must realise... This is difficult for me.'

'Me, too. You know how tempting it is to stay here? I know I couldn't – it would be hopeless – it wouldn't do you any good, would it?'

'What's *that* supposed to mean?' I snapped.

He shrugged. 'We need to get on with our real lives. I mean – none of this has been quite real, has it?'

'Where do your parents really believe you to be?'

'Told them I was going to Wales with a mate. It's not like they care.'

And then we did sit there in silence, drinking coffee neither of us particularly wanted, uncomfortable as two

261

strangers forced to share a table in a restaurant. This was worse than waiting to go in to the dentist, or into an examination hall, for there would be no resolution, no freedom from pain, no sense of accomplishment. Maybe if we walked very slowly to the station... But I doubted that would help. We must simply bear them, these long minutes, conscious this was the last time we would sit together in my house. Never again would we recite Baudelaire over too much red wine. Never again would I hear him banging out useless words on the typewriter. Never again...

'Shall we get out of here?' I said, unable to bear the thoughts that wouldn't stop. 'Take the long route to the station?'

'Okay.'

Take the mugs into the kitchen. Rinse them. Put the uneaten biscuits back in the tin. Make sure the back door's locked. Don't think. Don't think...

Cruel sun. Where was the rain now I wanted it to fall?

'Nice day,' Simon said without enthusiasm.

I didn't care about warmth, sunshine, the birds in the trees. Those things weren't for me; they offered no comfort, no consolation. The sun was too harsh, the birds too loud.

All the things we said. All the things we never said...

'Are you going in to work today?'

'No. When you – I phoned Mr Latham. Explained. He said to take the day off.'

'Thoughtful of him.'

'He's a good man.' *And you, Simon, you're not, but that isn't enough to prevent me from wanting you, even now. Still. Always.*

'A friend?'

'Maybe. I'd like to think so. I could do with one.'

We reached the train station with ten minutes to spare. Here, at least, was somewhere that suited my mood. I've often wondered if stations in other parts of the world are as bleak as the British variety. Soot-blackened bricks, Victorian wrought iron, chipped paint on the wooden benches. Morevale being a branch line, the station didn't even boast a refreshment room.

'You'll have to buy your ticket on the train,' I said.

'I know.'

I kept my eyes on the pigeons without which no train station is complete and read every word of the two posters in front of me, one advertising a romantic novel set in war-torn Budapest, the other a "God needs you" Christian poster (*Seven days without prayer makes one weak*).

Clever, I thought; then, no, silly.

The next train to arrive would be Simon's.

Big metal bitch come to take him away...

'Here,' he said, handing me a torn scrap of paper. 'It's my home address. Just in case I've left anything behind.'

I shook my head. If he'd left anything behind, that was too bad.

He stuffed it into my jacket pocket. 'Just take it,' he muttered. 'Otherwise I'll keep posting cards to you with it on.'

'You didn't bring much. What could you possibly have left behind?'

Me. You're leaving me.

I heard the rumble in the distance, getting closer. I stood, Simon did likewise, hiking his rucksack on to his shoulder. The grating noise of the train coming to a halt. The insistent beep indicating the doors were open. I looked away from Simon.

'Go on, then,' I said. 'You can get in now.'

'Yeah...'

I stepped away from him, couldn't bear it if he tried to give me a goodbye kiss.

'Go on, then!' I repeated. 'They don't give you much time to get on.'

He pressed the button, boarded, found a seat, dumped his rucksack on the table.

I shouldn't have come. Too awful.

Simon gazing out of the window at me, his face blank.

The train began to move.

Away, for ever and ever...

My timid wave. No answering one from him. My arm dropping to my side. Such desolation.

Everything was the same as it had been before. The sleepy station, the pigeons, the posters. I picked up a sweet wrapper, deposited it in a bin. Now what? Return home to a house that was far too quiet. Dry and put away the mug Simon had drunk his coffee from. Feed Pushkin. Find something to occupy myself until it was time to – to do what, though? Make another cup of coffee?

Not yet. I couldn't face all that just yet.

In a daze, I walked away from the station, the sun glaring down on me, everything too bright, hurtful.

'My dear, are you all right?' Viv caught hold of my arm.

'What?'

'You were walking a little unsteadily. Migraine, is it?'

'Yes... yes, that's it. The sun—'

'Would a cup of tea help? Nice and refreshing. My treat.'

I allowed her to steer me into the nearest café. A sympathetic face. Someone to talk to. A friend.

She ordered a pot of tea for two. 'Coffee's all well and good, but it doesn't quench your thirst, does it?'

'No; no, it doesn't.'

'Get a lot of migraines, do you? Codeine's the only stuff that works for me. Not that my GP approves. Thinks I'll get addicted to the stuff. Get them to find a cure, then, I tell him.' She paused, frowned, shook her head slightly. In a softer tone of voice, she added, 'You're very out of sorts, aren't you?'

I nodded, my hand pressed against my right temple, though I had no headache.

'Is it just migraine, or something else?'

I clutched a paper napkin in my left hand, afraid I might start to cry. I wasn't all right and couldn't pretend I was. I shook my head, not trusting myself to speak.

The waitress brought over our order.

'I'll let it stand for a while,' Viv said. 'Unless you particularly like weak tea?'

Another shake of my head. I had a pain in my throat from keeping my tears in check.

'I'd like to say I'm not the type to pry,' Viv said quietly, 'but I probably am. Except I really *don't* want to pry, but I *am* concerned. I'm aware we don't know each other very well, and I probably feel I know you better than I do because of your book. Though it's a mistake, isn't it, to read autobiography into fiction?'

I nodded.

'Hard to resist, of course. And I know you're a quiet

265

person, and probably a lot thinner-skinned than an old loudmouth like me.' She chuckled and gave the pot a stir. 'Shall I pour? It's roughly the right colour now.'

'Thanks,' I managed to say.

'Now. I saw you walking from the direction of the train station. You don't have any bags or parcels with you, so I'm assuming you were seeing someone off. Bit of a *Brief Encounter* moment, was it?'

I managed to smile, not because she'd read the situation more or less correctly, but because of the absurdity of the thing. *Brief Encounter* was a film I'd seen only once, but I recalled the clipped accents, the repressed passions, the noble, uncomprehending husband.

'Something along those lines.'

'Will he be coming back, do you think?'

I shook my head and added a dash of milk to my tea. 'I doubt I shall ever see him again. I expect it's for the best.'

'That's neither here nor there, is it? You might not think it, but I'm a very emotional person myself. Gets on my husband's wick, but I don't think being all stiff upper lipped about things is helpful. I don't say we should carry on like the Italians or the Greeks, but I'm sure bottling things up is unhealthy. You've never been married, have you?'

'No.'

'Do you mind?'

'Perhaps, when I was younger. When there was still a chance I might meet someone suitable, have children. But I haven't really minded for a long time, not until I met Simon. And even then... I knew there was no future in it. I accepted that, or thought I did.'

'You get used to having someone around the place, don't you? It's the company as much as anything.'

'It's not even that. Not company for the sake of it. I'm not sure I even liked him very much.'

'Oh, I see. Well – being in love with someone – that's another thing altogether. That's something that just has to run its course.'

'But what if it doesn't? What if I feel this way for the rest of my life? I couldn't bear it!'

Viv patted my hand and topped up my tea. 'We've all been there, lovey. It *does* pass, and even if it doesn't, you learn to live with it.' She opened her eyes wide. 'What other choice is there? I know everything is harder as we get older – not as easy to bounce back – but we also have the wisdom of experience. We *know* that no one ever died of a broken heart.' She took a sip of tea. 'Play some sad records. Have a bottle of wine and a good old weep. It'll do you the power of good, I promise.'

She said the right things, the sensible things, but I was too desolate to be convinced.

'Shall I come back with you?' she offered. 'Just so you have someone there with you. Help you tidy up, if necessary. Remove the traces.' Hearty, reassuring, just the sort of person I needed. But wasn't it cowardly to need someone? And was that thought the result of misplaced pride?

'We can pick up a bottle of wine and some chocolate on the way, if you like,' she said. 'Look, I don't want to force myself where I'm not wanted, and I'll probably get on your nerves very quickly, but if I can be any help, I'm more than willing.'

I accepted, putting myself in her hands. She chose a

bottle of wine and a box of chocolates ("Cheap and cheerful – quantity's more important than quality in this instance, I feel") and escorted me home. While I tided up downstairs, I told her which room had been Simon's and gave her a carrier bag in which to throw anything he might have left behind.

'There wasn't much,' she reported, sweeping past me to put the bag in the bin. 'Are you all right? Not too harrowed?'

I shook my head, though I still felt dreadful.

'Worse in the evening, perhaps.'

'I'll be fine. Honestly.' Suddenly I knew I couldn't stand to have her in the house with me, as if we were holding a wake. I wanted to be on my own, to get used to how the house felt without Simon in it. Viv would want to fill the house with sounds – TV, music, her own voice endlessly chattering. She meant well, but she was right – she *would* get on my nerves, and we didn't have the kind of relationship that would have enabled us to sit around in pyjamas getting tipsy and laughing at the stupidity of life.

'Well, if you're sure... Remember, I'm only a phone call away.'

'I will. And thank you. You've been an absolute brick.'

She smiled sadly. 'I wish I could do more. I wish I didn't feel so useless.'

'You're not. I'm not very good at accepting help. I think I need to be alone for a while. Get used to it, you know?'

'Yes, I understand,' she said with a sigh. 'You're not an easy person to get to know. I'm gregarious, but you're not. But I mean it, about phoning me if you need someone, for anything at all – a chat, whatever. Well, I'll love you and leave you.'

Viv deserved better than my aloofness, but it was too late for me to start relying on other people. I supposed it was possible to make new friends at my age, but inevitably I would compare any friendship with the fraught relationship I'd had with Madeleine. I wasn't sure it was possible to have a true friendship with someone who didn't understand the complicated bond that had existed, that still existed, between Madeleine and me.

I felt more comfortable with Mr Latham. When I told him that Simon had gone and it was unlikely I would ever see him again, his first comment was to wonder whether or not Simon would ever write his thesis on Mary Webb.

'I'm sorry,' he added, 'I daresay that's fairly low on your list of concerns. You will miss him.'

'I will.'

And that was that – no tea, no sympathy, no advice. But when I removed my striped tabard prior to leaving for the day, he came to speak to me.

'I'm sorry I wasn't very forthcoming about Simon,' he said. 'One hardly knows what to say in the circum- stances—'

'Nothing would help,' I told him, folding my tabard. 'I saw Viv Evans after I saw him off. She was very kind.'

He winced. 'I suppose she's the sort of person... That is, she means well. A little overpowering sometimes.'

'I was quite happy to be overpowered,' I said with a smile. 'But now I just need to be very quiet for a while. Even if I hadn't... Even if I hadn't loved him, it would still take me a while to adjust, having got used to having someone else around the house. Someone to talk to other than the cat.'

Because he frowned, I added, 'I don't mean to sound self-pitying. I'm really not. I can take quite a lot on the chin. It's just... Oh, I don't know. I just don't know what the *point* of it all is.'

He still looked concerned.

'Ignore me,' I said. 'Too wrapped up in my own nonsense, that's all. Too aware that it *is* nonsense. Maybe I just need someone to tell me to get over myself.'

He smiled. 'Isn't that what the young people say? They can be brutal. There's nothing wrong in admitting we can't always cope with everything life throws at us.'

'I shall be perfectly all right again in a few days. Weeks, possibly, but I'll get there.' I spoke brightly, afraid of imposing too much, taking advantage of my employer. If he were a doctor, I wouldn't trouble him with my aches and pains. I had no right, especially as I didn't believe in the God Mr Latham served.

'Well... Be kind to yourself, won't you?' he said. 'You're allowed to grieve, you know.'

'Yes – yes, I will – thank you. I'll be off now.' I hurried away before the tears started, back to my silent house. I threw open the windows so I could hear something, anything: birdsong, the squeals of children; a distant revving engine. Ordinary noises; proof that the world still turned, and I was along for the ride. I'd cook something comforting for dinner and I'd allow myself a small glass of wine. Then I'd read some old favourite novel, telling myself this was the sort of thing I liked doing, that small pleasures were like seed pearls, worth treasuring. I liked my home, I liked my job; I'd never had to struggle to make ends meet. Everything I wanted was under my roof.

Except Simon. Except him.

CHAPTER TWENTY-FOUR

I opened the safe, expecting to find the blank pages masquerading as a typescript. Nothing could have prepared me for the shock of discovering the safe to be empty except for my poor pieces of jewellery. For a long time I simply stared, unable to believe what I was seeing – or rather, not seeing. I felt all around the cavity as if the papers could possibly have slipped into some crevice I hadn't known was there, my fingernails scraping against metal as it dawned on me what he'd done.

I cursed myself for assuming Simon wouldn't be able to crack the code. I'd made it memorable for my own sake, but the numbers were those Simon must have smiled over as he pressed the buttons on the keypad. The date on which we had first met.

I understood what he'd done. He hadn't burned Madeleine's novel at all. He'd burned something, but the pages must have come from the bin in his room. Her novel had remained in the safe where I put it after I'd snatched it from his room. He'd won. He had my confession, which might not have meant much on its own, but with the manuscript of Madeleine's first book he had everything he needed to crush me if he chose to do so. I groaned at my foolishness and the horror of knowing I'd never be free of him. I'd wanted him to stay with me for ever, and now I wished I'd never met him.

After I finished work at the vicarage, I rang Viv and asked if she'd like to come round for coffee. I didn't want to rely on anyone, but I knew I'd kept myself too distant, unwilling to get involved with the concerns of other people, disinclined to share anything of my life.

Viv turned up with an apple cake she'd baked herself. 'Too much cinnamon, but tell me what you think.'

'It's very nice,' I said, taking an exploratory bite. 'Very moist.'

'Oh, good. Now, call me an interfering old such-and-such, but I was chatting in the library to Lisel the other day – you remember her? Sharp old lady, astonishingly well-read. Anyway, your name cropped up when we were discussing the book group. I'd very much like to broaden its scope and set up a sister group for writers and would-be writers – workshops, readings, library-based initiatives. Someone like you, with your background, would be a valuable asset to us.'

I wanted to back away, resist any attempt to involve me, and I was sure this was simply a ruse she'd cooked up to "take me out of myself". It smacked of good intentions and I was surprised Lisel would be party to anything so crass.

'It's thoughtful of you to ask—'

Viv shook her head. 'Don't think I'm asking out of the kindness of my heart. There aren't enough young people in the library, and I fear if we're not careful we'll be closed down as no longer viable, along with too many other libraries. If I can show the powers-that-be we have a vibrant reading and writing community, we might get a stay of execution. But I can't make that happen on my own. So how about it?'

I remained dubious. What she said was doubtless true – libraries, like post offices, were a dying breed. The timing, though, was a little suspect.

'I know what you're thinking,' she said, blithe and to the point. 'You think I'm giving you this opportunity because I feel sorry for you, because I think it might mend your broken heart. And maybe it will, but frankly my priority is my job – which I love, by the way, and I've no desire to trek into Shrewsbury every day, *if* they offer me a role there – and you're the nearest thing we've got to an actual proper writer. The only other writers I know are authors of books on local history, all fine and dandy, but it doesn't get anyone's juices flowing, does it? Not like *your* remarkable story.'

I wasn't sure if she meant the book was remarkable or my own personal story.

'I'm thinking about writing another book,' I said. 'I might not have much time for extra-curricular activities. Not that I'm saying no, but I would like some time to think about it.'

'But you *will* think about it, won't you?'

'Yes, I promise. And it was good of you to ask.'

She shrugged and passed me another slice of apple cake. 'We need all the help we can get, frankly. It's no longer enough for a library simply to offer books for people to borrow. We have to become multi-media experiences or accept our inevitable death.' She heaved a dramatic sigh. 'Too many books, not enough readers, that's the problem. We need to catch 'em young and keep 'em. Anyway, how are you bearing up?

273

'So-so,' I said. Could I believe everything Simon had told me about his father's coldness and Sophie's rages? Perhaps he'd exaggerated, but to what purpose? I hoped he *had* exaggerated, for his sake. As much as I loathed the distress he'd brought into my life, I hated to think of him growing up knowing he was unwanted and resented by the people who should have protected and comforted him.

I realised Viv was gazing at me expectantly. 'I'm sorry – I missed what you said.'

'You looked as if you were miles away. Thinking about this book you're going to write, I expect.'

'Yes; that was it. I'm afraid writers do tend to wool-gather.'

Perhaps, I thought, I might write a book about Simon, about his life as I imagined it panning out. Perhaps a tempestuous and impossible romance with a faded aristocratic beauty who might threaten to kill herself when he announced he intended to leave her, and then... Well, there were many possible routes he could take. But how would I weave in his backstory? I should have to invent one for him in case the book was ever published and he picked up a copy and recognised himself. It might amuse him, but it might not, depending on the path he actually took.

But I could never publish it, could I? Easy to imagine Simon gleefully contacting the publisher, demanding an interview, self-righteously brandishing my confession before presenting them with the *coup de grâce*: Madeleine's first novel. A son cheated out of his rightful inheritance. A writer who'd been denied her place in the canon.

'My dear, you really are very abstracted today!'

'I'm terribly sorry,' I said with a shake of my head. 'I'm having one of those days when memories won't leave me alone.'

'Ah.' A knowing look. 'I've always thought "Better to have loved and lost than never loved at all" a foolish saying. It's something you don't realise until it's too late – until you've already had your heart broken.'

Hard to imagine Viv with a broken heart; she seemed too practical, too resilient. Too insensitive, even, though that was unfair. What did I know about the workings of her heart? As little as she knew about mine. Garrulous though she was, I hardly knew her, and very likely never would. I had my secrets and I daresay she had hers. There's no reason why we should unburden ourselves to everyone who shows a kindly interest in us. She thought me aloof, but my reserve was my protection. It prevented me from revealing too much: things no one needed to know.

'You *will* get over it,' she added. 'One simply has to.'

Brisk, rational, her sympathy would extend only so far. At some point I was expected to pull myself together, put the past behind me, or else be accused of self-indulgence. I would have agreed with her had Simon been nothing more than a fling, a genuine brief encounter.

Viv stood and stretched with her hands in the small of her back. 'Do try not to dwell too much, you'll only upset yourself. I'll leave you the rest of the cake, if you'd like it – No, don't argue, I'm quite sure. I made it for you.'

An act of kindness that made me regret every snarky thing I'd thought about her. I tried not to be too effusive in my thanks in case she thought me strange, but I wanted to hug her.

She gave me a kindly smile. 'You look done in. You've been through the wringer and I've been impatient. Forgive me, dear, won't you?'

'Nothing to forgive,' I said. 'You've been a tower of strength. I don't know what I'd have done without you.'

Clichés, but I meant them. With Viv's help, maybe I'd learn how to do the friendship thing.

'Call me whenever you want,' she said as she let herself out. The friendship model Madeleine had left me with wouldn't do any more. The intensity of teenage relationships can't be replicated in middle age, and that's probably just as well. I accepted that between Madeleine's death and Simon's arrival, I'd effectively absented myself from life, drifting from one dysfunctional relationship to another. Afraid of falling in love, afraid of not falling in love; afraid of making a friend who meant as much to me as Madeleine had done. The risk of loss and rejection.

I wasn't going to be afraid any more. Pain, I decided, was preferable to numbness. To feel *something* is better than to feel nothing at all, else how do we even know we're alive?

Simon sent postcards. I ripped them up. He sent me a letter from Venice, but made no mention of the papers he'd taken from my safe, instead confining himself to gossipy stuff, telling me he was "getting friendly" with an American lady of a certain age with money to burn. This claim I took with a generous pinch of salt. He had charm, yes, but of a limited kind. Still too wet behind the ears, surely, to appeal to an American sophisticate. But who knew? He might not even be in Venice at all.

Madeleine had faked a long succession of postcards apparently sent from all over Europe.

I miss you, he wrote. *Does that sound crazy? It does to me. I've thought about coming back. My dad and Sophie barely even noticed I'd been away. All they said was that they were glad I'd finally come to my senses. Nothing has really changed between us. At least in books you get a proper ending, but life just goes on. Don't you think life ought to come with a built-in satnav? Venice is beautiful – all those pastel-pink scabrous palaces – but it stinks like hell.*

At the bottom of the card he wrote his home address in block capitals. *Write to me sometimes*, he added.

No, Simon. No. Not even to beg.

I half-hoped he would ditch the American lady for an aristocratic Venetian and enjoy a life of ruined luxury. His golden, boyish looks might appeal to an Italian princess in the autumn of her years. Lacking parents who were willing to support and guide him, he might simply drift through life, though more elegantly than I had done. With time and experience he might hone his charms, make them work for him. Equally, he might choose to do the sensible thing: return to university, throw in his lot with the world of academia.

A part of me still refused to believe that Simon was Madeleine's son. But how else could he have known about her, stumbled upon her manuscript? The dates added up and Madeleine had vanished from sight for months. Whoever he was, Simon existed, and he'd blown a hole in my life almost as large as the one Madeleine had created.

If I told Viv that Simon was Madeleine's son, if she knew... But of course she mustn't know, and I must therefore dissemble, and bear the pain occasioned each time a postcard arrived with its brief, pointless message, its brutal reminder that his life was going on without me. I would never be allowed to forget him. I couldn't put the past behind me; he wouldn't let me.

How ironic, now that I'd been placed in a position where I could never seek a publisher no matter how brilliant a book I wrote, that the need to write burned more fiercely than it ever had.

When another postcard arrived from Simon, I pinned it to the cork pin board above my computer.

Venice, I typed, *city of masks and glass and murky water. Of palaces and ducats and pickpockets who pluck heart-shaped rubies from empty pockets. Of young men with beautiful faces who quote Shakespeare to ladies in the early autumn of their years, making them sing, making their branches erupt with one final freakish blossoming of love...*

I helped myself to lemonade. Lisel had invited me to her house for a meal and she'd slipped off to the kitchen to fetch more bread.

'I shall be seventy-six in less than two months' time,' she said when she returned. 'Such a nuisance, getting older. I can't bear it when people tell me I'm wonderful for my age, as if I were a pocket calculator.'

'It's meant as a compliment, I'm sure.'

'Oh, certainly, which is why I always smile graciously. What else can one do? Viv keeps dropping hints about some birthday surprise she and the other members of the book group have planned for me, and I'm sure it will be awful. I'm already dreading it, even though I'm terribly grateful at the same time.'

Perhaps it would be nothing worse than a few balloons and a cake loaded with too many candles. To say that Viv meant well was to damn her with faint praise, and really she deserved more credit for her kindnesses.

'Viv tells me you're writing again,' she said. 'That *is* good news.' Perhaps sensing from my dipped head that I didn't care to pursue this subject, she added, 'And how are Viv's big ideas for putting Morevale on the literary map coming along?'

'Oh, I doubt her ambitions are anything like as grand as that. She wants to keep her job, that's all. She's certainly very enthusiastic.'

Lisel frowned. 'Don't let her boss you into doing anything you don't want to do. It's far more important you get your book written.'

'Oh, I shan't let her boss me, although the book probably won't come to anything.'

She leaned back in her chair. We'd enjoyed an informal meal of vegetable lasagne and salad. 'Shall we have our dessert in the conservatory? I'll put some coffee on.'

I took a seat at the glass-topped rattan table. Dessert turned out to be a fruit pavlova topped with slices of kiwi fruit and drizzled with passion fruit pulp.

'Home-made, for what it's worth,' Lisel said, placing her cardigan over the arm of her chair. 'I like good food, but no dish is worth spending more than an hour in the kitchen to prepare.'

I gazed out at the garden, which she assured me would be a riot of hollyhocks, lavender, buddleia and rhododendron in the summer. A winding path led to a small wooden structure at the bottom of the garden, which I supposed one might describe as a mini summerhouse, just large enough to contain one padded seat.

'The daffodils will soon be out,' Lisel said, following my eye. 'I like to sit out here even in bad weather. It reassures me.' After a pause, she added, 'So why did you start writing again?'

I spooned up some of my dessert, thinking what a pity it was that passion fruit were so fiddly and each fruit held so little.

'Simon,' I said.

'Clearly you don't want to elaborate, and there's no reason why you should.'

'It would take far too long to explain. I'm not even sure I *could* explain in any way that made sense.'

'Secrets—'

'We all have them. As you said yourself. And yes, I have secrets, but I no longer feel any great urge to share them. I did speak to the vicar. I think that helped.'

Lisel smiled. 'Cheaper than a psychiatrist, at any rate. Pleasant man, isn't he? Oh, dear, that does sound mealy-mouthed!'

'Pleasant being a euphemism for what, exactly?'

She leaned back, pursing her lips, fingers tapping the armrests of her seat. 'Timid, perhaps. One can't dislike him, but I'm not sure there's much backbone there. Perhaps he has hidden strengths. I wonder why he never married. Couldn't find the right type, do you think?'

'Type?'

'Competent, no-nonsense, self-effacing. Or am I being unfair?'

'I don't know. Simon... Well, he once made a silly

suggestion that I should marry Mr Latham myself.'

Lisel raised her eyebrows. 'What an appalling prospect! Or is it? I've never fancied the idea of marriage.'

'I often wonder if Madeleine would have married if she'd lived.'

'A great pity what happened to her. Such a tragic waste of a young life for the sake of a few moments' inattention.'

'It wasn't an accident. She killed herself.'

'What did she want to go and do a thing like that for?' Lisel shivered and draped her cardigan around her shoulders. 'Her parents expected too much from her, of course,' Lisel continued, dropping a plastic cover over the shattered remains of the fruit pavlova. 'All that boasting about Maddie being brilliant; all the remarkable things the girl was going to do with her life.'

'What sort of things?' Had they had any inkling, then, that Madeleine was writing a book?

Lisel chuckled. 'I'm basing my judgements on one conversation I had with them when Maddie was thirteen. Even then they were talking about her future as an academic and the brilliant marriage she would make to some eminent professor or other. It was all pie in the sky.'

Was that all? As vague as that? I couldn't help but feel relieved.

'I can't have exchanged more than a handful of words with them after they decided ours wasn't the right school for their precious daughter, by which they probably meant the fees were too high, even with a scholarship.'

'They rarely spoke to me after she died. I think they blamed me, thought I should have done more to help her.'

'Goodness me, what could you have done? You weren't responsible for her actions. No one was.'

281

'I knew she was unhappy, depressed even.'

'And? If you'd spoken to her parents, would they have paid any attention?'

'Probably not. But – I was there, you see, when she drowned.' *A problem shared...* 'I shouldn't have mentioned it.'

'Well, there's no point telling me half a story.'

'I followed her. I saw her step into the water, I saw her go under... I tried to reach her, but I can't swim. I was useless. Worse than useless. I would have done better to run for help instead of thinking there was any point in following her into the water.'

'It doesn't take many minutes to drown. You were young and frightened. Unless you pushed her into the water yourself, which I assume you didn't, then you shouldn't torment yourself with these thoughts. What possible *good* can it do?'

'None, of course. But maybe there's a part of me that wanted her to drown.'

'Quite possibly, if you saw her as a rival – however unconsciously.'

'I always suspected her parents knew that, and that was why they turned against me.'

'Far more likely they simply resented you for being alive when their daughter wasn't.'

'So... If you had reason to believe someone intended to take their own life—'

Lisel raised her eyebrows. 'I'd let them get on with it. I'm sorry if that sounds callous. Oh, in reality I suppose I would try to help – tell them to speak to their doctor or priest, depending on their inclinations. None of us is a saint. We can't *save* other people in some Christ-like fashion, however much we'd like to. As I heard someone say on the radio yesterday, the past is a statement, the future a question. We all have the occasional dark night of the soul about things we could have done better, but dwelling on them is fruitless.'

'What's done is done?'

'Well, isn't it? Your guilt, shame, whatever you want to call it, won't make a damn bit of difference to Maddie or to her parents.'

'You think I'm wallowing?'

'Yes, I think you are. Would you prefer to go back inside?'

'I'd like to stay here for a little longer.'

Lisel took her time fetching the coffee; deliberately, I assumed, to give me time to compose myself. All these years I'd lived with Madeleine's ghost hovering over my shoulder. My best friend. But she wasn't. I'd hung on to that fiction for too long, unwilling to concede that we had grown apart; that we'd remained friends out of habit and perhaps, in her case, a sense of obligation. Giving her manuscript to me had not been an act of love, but rather a parting gift after she'd shucked off everything else, having decided not to stick around. She'd already given away her son and I would never know the circumstances in which that had happened; could only conjecture, and clearly there was nothing to be gained from that.

Lisel gently squeezed my shoulder. 'All right now?'

I nodded, taking the tray from her.

'If she hadn't died—'

'But she did. Why didn't *you* go to university, Gabrielle?'

'I wasn't clever enough. A plodder.'

'Let me guess – Maddie was a straight-A student, seemed to produce good work without any effort?'

I nodded.

'Do you ever wonder what happens to these child prodigies that occasionally make the news? Children who can read fluently when they can barely walk, solve complicated algebraic equations while they're strapped in a high chair? At some point most of them level off, the academic gap between them and their peers narrows. Perhaps it never completely disappears, but it becomes far less spectacular.'

'Madeleine wasn't like that. Just very bright, very gifted.'

'I daresay, but perhaps she peaked too soon, while you might have peaked – academically speaking – at university. It might have been good for you to get away from her – properly away, I mean, rather than being separated because *she* chose to leave.'

'Did you ever have a best friend, Lisel? Someone you thought you'd do anything for?

'Not since I was about eleven, and only then because I went to a boarding school, where friendships tend to be quite intense. I grew out of any tendency to hero-worship when I overheard my favourite teacher moaning to a colleague about how much she loathed her job and the brats she was obliged to teach.'

'That's a bit different, though, isn't it? An adult – someone in a position of responsibility; someone you didn't really *know*.'

'Even so, it made me realise – and I was only a child, remember, still very innocent in the ways of the world – that people might say one thing but mean something else. We place a lot of value on whether a person is trust-worthy or not, but is it really the most important thing? Would you rather be liked or trusted?'

'I'd be happy with either.'

'And Madeleine – did you trust *her*?'

'With what? My secrets? My life?'

'Just generally. You see, I wonder if you saw things in Maddie that weren't there. Because she died – young, tragically – that makes it difficult for anyone to criticise her without sounding heartless. But it doesn't mean her life meant any less.'

Had I, in fact, hung on to a poetic stereotype – the golden girl, the beautiful corpse?

'I suppose, if I'm honest, I often disliked her in the last few years. I think I got on her nerves. I felt like the poor relation. She chose not to entrust me with her biggest secret, which I discovered only quite recently. But she must have had her reasons.'

'Let go of her. She was as flawed as the rest of us. Don't be like the pitiful pet dog who refuses to leave its master's grave, pining away through misplaced faithful-ness.'

I smiled. 'I was never her slave.'

'Not in fact, perhaps, but wouldn't you have done anything she'd asked of you? If she said that you, and no one else, were the person she needed?'

'But she never did.'

'So add rejected suitor to list of roles you need to relinquish.'

'You ought to be a psychologist,' I teased.

'Good lord, no! I think it's a shame when people become so mired in the past they forget to live in the present. I don't think that's quite what you've done, but it irritates me that you speak about yourself so humbly when you compare yourself with Maddie.'

I'd heard it said that in any relationship there is the lover and the one who is loved. Perhaps there is always one partner who loves just a little bit more, and of course that had been me with Madeleine. We were both only children, neither of us particularly spoilt or indulged by our parents, our upbringing identical in most respects. She wasn't bossy and I hadn't been unusually shy. Somehow, though, we had slipped into our roles, with me mentally walking two paces behind her, proud to have such a beautiful, clever friend.

'I'm getting cold,' Lisel said. 'I think it's time we went inside.'

I carried the tray into the kitchen. Lisel made more coffee and showed me a few snapshots of herself when she was younger. I was particularly taken by a photograph of her standing next to a powder-blue Mini, posing with one hand on the car door as if to open it, get in and drive away, her eyes hidden behind huge sunglasses, legs encased in knee-high white plastic boots of the type fashionable then.

'My brother's car, not mine,' she said. 'I was terribly jealous – I had to catch a bus to work while he whizzed off in his snazzy Mini. He died a few months after this photo was taken – a climbing accident. I asked my father if I could have the car since it was of no further use to Nick. He was never a violent man, rarely lost his temper, but he slapped my face.'

Gently she laid the palm of her hand against her cheek, as if she could still feel the sting of that slap.

286

'He sold the car,' she continued. 'We never discussed the matter, but I don't think we ever quite forgave each other. Nick was another of those golden people, like Maddie. When memories are the only things that remain of someone, it's only the good ones we want to preserve.'

'He was your only sibling?'

'Yes. We were close – I admired him – but there have been times, since his death, when I've come close to hating him – for dying, for leaving our parents with me as poor compensation.'

'But you got over it? Learned to live with it?'

'One must. The remark I made about the car was insensitive, but it wasn't my fault he'd died; not my fault if my parents wished – as I'm sure they sometimes did, for they were only human, too – that I had died instead of Nick.' She gave a gentle laugh. 'Don't look so shocked, my dear. They were kind, loving people, but grief isn't reasonable. I daresay Maddie's parents wished you had been dragged lifeless from that river instead of their daughter, *and* felt soul-crushingly guilty for thinking such a thing.'

When I got home I poured myself a glass of whisky, something I rarely drank. In my mind I kept seeing that picture of the powder-blue Mini, Lisel posing next to it in her fashionable Sixties clothes, faking ownership of something that could never be hers.

CHAPTER TWENTY-FIVE

'It's nice to see you so busy,' Mr Latham said. 'The work-shops and so forth.'

I'd decided there was no point in being half-hearted. I'd allowed myself to get caught up in Viv's enthusiasm, and the fact that my novel was progressing well made me feel I had some justification in describing myself as a writer.

Viv had coached me in the rudiments of how to run a workshop. The hardest part was finding a tactful way to tell someone their work had little merit. One always had to find a few constructive things to say, and for most people that seemed to be enough. My credentials – my status as a published author – were usually sufficient to give my advice some weight. And the ambitions of most of my students didn't rise far above getting a poem in the Poets' Corner section of the local free paper. Thus I tried to tailor my advice to suit their modest ambitions, querying a clumsy rhyme, a faulty scansion. I was almost as delighted as they were when they pitched up for workshop sessions brandishing a copy of a freebie news-paper or parish magazine in which their work had been included.

'Do you have any budding geniuses?' Mr Latham asked, polishing his glasses with a cotton handkerchief.

'A couple who like to think they are.' One obnoxious young man in particular, who had no time for any writer apart from Chuck Palahniuk and never forgave me for telling him he wouldn't get anywhere unless he was prepared to read more widely.

I felt rather embarrassed that I'd ever entertained a fanciful notion of marrying Mr Latham. Timid, Lisel had called him. Kind-hearted, well-meaning, but I couldn't help wondering if he was as wary of becoming too closely involved with God as he was with people. God, I supposed, asked rather less of him than human beings with their complicated, disruptive emotions. Arm's length and no further.

'You certainly seem a lot more cheerful,' he said, replacing his glasses, making finicky adjustments that would have annoyed any wife. He sounded relieved. Our relationship could return to how it had been before – polite, amicable, but with that perceptible distance between us. I felt certain he would never marry, although he might have been the type to make a late, reckless marriage to a widow a little older than himself with a colourful wardrobe and a forceful personality. I almost felt like warning him of the dangers posed by this mythical potential bride. Wrong of me to ascribe unworldliness to him simply because he was a vicar. No reason, either, to suppose he wouldn't welcome the embraces of a jolly widow with – as the phrase goes – no side to her.

'It's good fun on the whole,' I said. 'I never knew there were so many aspiring writers around here.'

For most of them it was simply a hobby, on a par with knitting or baking. For others, writing functioned as therapy – they used poetry and fiction to make sense of their feelings, their difficulties, their grief. At first I'd been hard pressed to know what to say when someone shared with me a poem or short story about their miscarriage, their redundancy, their irritable bowel. But they didn't want to create great art from their misfortunes, simply work out their feelings and make their mark. Writing gave them a voice, even if their work was only to be shared with me and the other students in the workshop. Indeed, I made it a condition of membership that students didn't discuss other people's work with outsiders. What happened in Vegas stayed in Vegas.

Many of the students asked me for reading recommendations and I tried to tailor these to their individual tastes and styles.

'You're a big hit,' Viv had told me. 'I'm getting all sorts of interesting requests at the library for books you've recommended.'

I dared not ask if anyone had requested *The Song of the Air*. I rather hoped not. Occasionally someone would mention it during a workshop session and I would refer to it lightly as juvenilia, something that existed independently of me and which I no longer recognised as my own work.

'If you write about your own life,' one student asked me, 'but change the facts, make it different in significant ways, is that cheating? Is it still fiction?'

I told her that we all make fictions of our lives to some extent. In everyday life this would be called lying. In the context of fictional writing, it becomes a transformative act. Reasonable, allowable. We touched on the subject of libel and I explained how outraged some of Sylvia Plath's relatives and friends had been when they recognised their fictional selves in *The Bell Jar*.

'But were they right to be offended? And didn't their complaints simply draw attention to correspondences most people would otherwise not have seen?'

'I'd be a bit annoyed if someone put me in a book,' the questioner said. 'But if they'd changed all the names and it was about stuff only me and the writer would know about, I don't see that it matters much.'

Viv told me after one workshop session that I was a "natural" and would have taken to academic life "like a duck to water". She asked me if I'd consider studying for a degree with the Open University and perhaps go in for teacher training.

'If I were fifteen years younger, maybe,' I told her. 'I don't really see the point now. I'd spend too much time regretting all the years I wasted when I could have been – I don't know – a lecturer or whatever. Besides, I think I'm of more use in the workshops. I like the mix of ages and abilities. Though I do feel a bit of a fraud – I'm not qualified to do what I'm doing.'

It was all something of a lark, really, and since I wasn't paid, I felt under no obligation to be brilliant. No homework to set, no targets to meet. I had no formal job description, thus I was free more or less to make it up as I went along, suiting the sessions to the needs of the students. I kept the sessions going long after they were supposed to finish because I enjoyed them, and because my students wanted me to do so.

Lisel scoffed when I fed her the "bit of a lark" line.

'You can say that if you like,' she said, 'but it's clear

you're dedicated to your students – albeit in a disinter-ested way, which is how it should be.'

'You're not going to suggest I start training to be a teacher, are you, like Viv keeps doing?'

'Wouldn't dream of it. If what you're doing is enough for you, then stick to that. Save your ambition for your novel. It's going well, is it?'

'Yes, I think so. Hard to tell until I get to the editing stage. But I'm not sure I mind if no one wants to publish it – I'll have written it, that's the main thing.'

She poured me another glass of ginger wine. We met often, our friendship growing gradually, quietly. The kind of friendship I suspected I would never have had with Madeleine. Lisel and I never imposed upon each other, and if we broached painful subjects it was with tolerance and honesty. Lisel could be blunt, but she was never boorish.

I'd once dreamed of living with Madeleine, a sort of idyllic *Ladies of Llangollen* existence, quite apart from the world. Only now did I see how ridiculous this notion was, even as a fantasy. Two women, whether or not they're lovers, can live together perfectly happily, but Madeleine wasn't the type to rub along with anyone. She wouldn't have been content with such a tranquil, cow-like exis-tence. I would have smothered her; she would have diminished me even further.

Lisel was more self-assured than I, less interested in what anyone thought of her, and I doubt she would have encouraged my friendship if she hadn't enjoyed my company. Perhaps I'd fooled myself into believing that a friendship wasn't worth the name unless it had the intensity of glowing, molten glass.

Simon's room was now my study. It no longer mattered that the room reminded me so much of him – he was at the heart of the story I was writing. This wasn't therapy, a working out of my feelings; nothing so crude as that. My story was about an imaginary Simon, and the more I wrote, the less of the real Simon I recognised in the character taking shape on the page.

On a table next to my desk were piled several reams of paper. Good quality, eighty-gram paper. Blank pages no longer frightened me. They represented possibilities, stories to be told. I'd also pinned a photograph of myself with Madeleine on to the cork board: a picture taken when we were both about fourteen on a trip to Warwick Castle with her parents. Cheesy grins for the camera, Madeleine's arm draped around my shoulders, her head resting against mine. A photograph I'd always loved, but it showed nothing more than a brief moment in time. Seconds later Madeleine had been moaning that her feet hurt, her mum reproving her for wearing strappy sandals instead of sensible trainers like mine.

I worked on my novel until I'd written my thousand words. With a bit of luck I'd write another thousand when I got home from work. I took my coffee cup downstairs and swilled it out; I rarely drank the whole mug. My story would distract me and the coffee would sit forgotten on the table, a greyish skin forming on the top.

The parcel had arrived while I was at work. The "Sorry you were out" card gave no indication of the sender or the nature of the parcel's contents. I hadn't ordered anything; I was expecting nothing.

I was no wiser when I presented myself at the sorting office with my ID. My address had been typed on a sheet of white paper and taped to the parcel. No return address. The postmark claimed the parcel had been posted in Leeds, which meant nothing to me.

I carried the parcel to my car and opened it there and then. Clipped to a stack of papers was a handwritten note, in Simon's hand.

I couldn't destroy it. How could I? Nazis and religious maniacs burn books. It took me a few goes to work out the code, but it's the date on which we first met, isn't it? It's all here, everything I took from you, including your confession. I just wanted to frighten you, have that power over you. But you already know that, don't you? It was my own story I burnt on that bonfire, the rotten words that clumped together and wouldn't fly. Do with her book whatever you want, just don't burn it. I don't understand all the stuff that went on between you and M, but if this book belongs to anyone, it belongs to you – not morally, not ethically, just because it does. Maybe we'll meet again some day? You probably hope we don't. I hope you can think of me fondly and I hope you wish me luck. Maybe one day I'll write a book. Maybe I tried too soon, before I had something to say. Don't worry about me (you won't, why should you?). But don't forget me.

He showed his youth in this message, but there was something there, hints that he might be a writer one day. And what to make of the substance of this long paragraph? Sentimental nonsense, though I did wince when

I read the line *It was my own story I burnt*. Was I reading too much into that phrase? Surely I was.

He would expect me to publish Madeleine's book as my own – wouldn't he? But I wasn't sure if I could bear to read it, let alone pass it off as mine. In any case, I'd no intention of doing so. What, then, to do with it? Another gift I didn't want. Another novel that should never have been written.

I could make no decision until I'd read it, of course.

I turned to the first page.

A few words, scribbled symbols, nothing that made sense.

I turned to the next page. A drawing of a bird sandwiched between two dense but apparently unconnected paragraphs.

Another page. More scribbles and some gnomic phrases repeated three times. Ciphers? A coded message?

Simon had told me this book was even finer than *The Song of the Air*, but this was no novel at all. The notes on many of the pages were written in Madeleine's hand, but taken as a whole it was little more than a disconnected accumulation of phrases, ideas, intricate sequences of symbols, sketches and word pictures.

What, if anything, did it mean?

Was this a joke? Whose? Hers, or Simon's?

I turned to the final page.

It was blank. Not even a page number.

I turned to a random page about a third of the way through the typescript with one paragraph written in the middle of it.

Birds follow a particular pattern of flight, I read. *They do what they must do. (Not all birds fly. Not all birds sing.) A world without birds would be a worse one. No birds sing, they say, near the sites where concentration camps once infected the land. Birds know. But how can they? Have you ever wanted to fly? I did, when I was a child. If I just tried hard enough... now I prefer the water to the air. To swim. To sink. Dragging weeds. Down there where no birds sing.*

The whole paragraph had thick black lines driven through it. Was this an experimental novel, a work in progress, or...

If you tell me your secret, I'll tell you mine. And what will you choose to reveal? And why? And do you think I will believe you? Because I won't. Because I don't know the difference between truth and fiction. I tell lies all the time. We all do. We do it because it makes life easier to bear.

I shook my head, allowing the pages to drift to the floor in any old order. I had nothing more to fear from either Madeleine or Simon. And even as my shoulders slumped with relief, I felt my eyes welling with tears. Elusive to the last, my Madeleine: the girl no one would ever be able to pin down, whose life no one had figured out.

I would never have visited the swimming baths if it hadn't been for Viv. She had some loopy idea it would be good for me, that it would help me to relax. I told her I couldn't swim and she insisted it was about time I learned.

'You've got a cossie, haven't you?'

'Yes,' I said. I hadn't, but I feared she would offer to lend me one of hers if I said no. I bought the plainest black costume I could find, the sort we'd worn for school swimming lessons, our school having had the dubious luxury of its own outdoor pool.

A plain rubber cap. Goggles.

My hackles rose the moment we entered the sports complex. The stink of chlorine, the damp tiles, the cramped changing rooms. Too many women gathered in one place, brushing their hair, wet feet slapping against the tiles, carrying on conversations as they changed.

'All set, then?'

Viv strode ahead of me. I tried to keep my unkind eyes from the cellulite on her thighs. I doubted I looked much better.

'You'd better stay in the shallow end,' she said. 'You don't mind if I go and have a dive, do you?'

'No, of course not. I'll just paddle around until I feel more confident.'

'That's the spirit.' She pointed to the kickboards and noodles, swimming aids that had replaced the oblong foam floats I remembered from childhood. 'Help yourself.'

A lifeguard grinned at me and asked which one I'd like. I chose a kickboard and settled myself on the edge of the pool, watching Viv waddle towards the diving boards.

Cautiously I twisted and eased myself into the water. My feet firmly on the bottom of the pool, I remembered my father's impatience when he brought me here as a child. A strong swimmer himself, he insisted on taking me to the baths every Sunday morning. It took me a long time to stop resenting those early mornings, on a day when I could have lazed in bed till ten, coming home with my hair still damp, my eyes pink and stinging.

I lurched forward, arms in front of me, trying to forget that Sunday morning when Dad encouraged me to swim beyond the shallow end. How I'd panicked, thrashing in the water as manically as a shark with the scent of blood in its nostrils. Why hadn't he come to my aid? Why did he simply watch as my head went under, again and again, until I was certain I was about to die?

I wondered what expression had been on his face as he gazed at me. Terror? A sense that he'd gone too far? Or perhaps determination, that I must see this through, just like the time when he took his hand from the bike I was riding without stabilisers for the first time. The horror when I realised he'd let go. The sheer joy of hurtling across the field, just me and the bike. I'd done it! I could do it!

I was heading towards the deep end, but I was no longer frightened. My limbs understood what they needed to do; it was just me and the water. I imagined my father's face relaxing, tender pride replacing anxiety. He'd always known the right time to let go.

The kickboard forgotten, I turned under the water and powered back the way I'd come. The lifeguard was speaking to a teenage girl. I could see the glint of a pierced navel every time my head turned in their direction.

Behind me I heard a loud splash and turned back to see Viv spluttering in the water after her dive, choking and laughing at the same time. My hands felt for the side of the pool. Viv would be astonished when she saw the progress I'd made.

ACKNOWLEDGEMENTS

I would like to thank everyone who has encouraged me to keep writing over the past few years. Their support and friendship means a great deal. In particular I would like to thank Chris Wyles, who has cheerfully read everything I've thrown at her and who has a real talent for spotting when a story is working and when it isn't.

I would also like to thank Jennie Rawlings for the beautiful cover concept. Also copy editor Alison Jack and typesetter Leigh Forbes.

Most of all I would like to thank Louise for believing in the book and for all her hard work and perceptive suggestions, without which this book wouldn't be nearly as good as it is.

LWB INTERVIEWS HELEN KITSON...

When did you decide to become a writer?

I think it's fair to say that writing chose me. As soon as I learned to read and discovered the magic of stories, I began making up my own stories in my head. In *Maddie*, Gabrielle recounts a memory of a teacher being impressed with one of Gabrielle's poems. '*In later years I used to tell journalists that was the moment I knew I wanted to be a writer.*' In reality the poem was a prayer, but apart from that the memory is my own, and the teacher in question (lovely Mrs Marsden) did much to inspire my lifelong love of words. I went through phases of wanting to be a solicitor, a vet, even (absurdly, given how clumsy I am) a ballet dancer, but writing was the one constant throughout everything.

What kind of books do you enjoy reading?

I read more fiction than anything else, and my tastes are quite broad. I read a great deal of 19th and early 20th century fiction and I have a particular fondness for the Persephone and Virago Modern Classics series. I also enjoy crime fiction and historical fiction, but really I'm open to anything that's well-written and has something to say. I enjoy books that challenge me, but there are also many authors I return to time and time again because I know they won't let me down.

Apart from writing, what are your passions?

Art is a major passion and I'm studying for a Master's degree in art history, which is proving a brilliant experience that has changed the way I look at artworks in galleries and museums. I'm also very interested in the history of photography, with a particular fondness for the work of Julia Margaret Cameron and Cindy Sherman. Learning how to take better photographs is high up on my "to do" list. Most of my major interests are quite random and include making soup and visiting cemeteries!

How did you conceive *The Last Words of Madeleine Anderson*?

I had an idea buzzing around in my head that wouldn't leave me alone. I wanted to explore the idea of a "one hit wonder" writer and delve into the possible reasons why someone who'd written a great book would suddenly stop writing. Everything else grew from that one idea, and what initially began as a simple idea ended up being quite complicated as I fleshed out Gabrielle and dug into her psyche.

Do you have a favourite among your characters?

It would have to be Lisel, the wiser, older friend I wish I had! I think she makes a good foil for Gabrielle's naivety. I really like writing older characters who prove that you're not done with life just because you've hit a certain age. Lisel has regrets, but she's comfortable in her own skin. She is sharp, curious about people and the world, enjoys living life on her own terms and she doesn't need anyone else to make her life complete.

Can you tell us anything about book 2?
I would if I knew what it was going to be! I have so many ideas bubbling away at any one time, and I also need to rewrite each story multiple times until it becomes clear what the story is really about and what I want to say.

Who are your favourite writers, and why?
I have dozens of favourites! Daphne du Maurier for superb storytelling. Helen Dunmore for lyrical, compelling writing. Barbara Comyns for her strange, surreal novels that couldn't have been written by anyone else. Others are favourites simply because they're woven into the fabric of my life and my writing and resonate with me on a personal level (Barbara Pym, Anita Brookner, Jean Rhys).

What are the highlights so far of being a published author?
The best bit is when you get to hold your own book in your hands. It's such a special moment. Because I'd already been around the block a few times as a published poet, I don't think I had unrealistic expectations. I knew the world wouldn't change overnight. For me it's been more of a series of quiet triumphs rather than explosive highs, and I'm fine with that.

And what are the lows?
The whole process has been a real eye-opener into the publishing world and how it operates. It's frustrating knowing the hoops indie publishers have to jump through compared with the big publishers. It is what it is, so there's no point moaning about it, but it does seem unfair when there are so many great indie authors and publishers out there struggling to be heard.

Do you have any advice for readers who are also writers?

Be the kind of writer whose books you'd want to read, and tell the stories you need to tell rather than the ones you think you should write or to fit in with whatever happens to be popular at any given moment. There's no one right way to be a writer or a single career trajectory, and there's no secret formula for writing a good book.

ALSO FROM
LOUISE WALTERS BOOKS

Louise Walters Books is the home of intelligent, provocative, beautifully written works of fiction. We are proud of our impressive list of authors and titles. We publish in most genres, but all our titles have one aspect in common: they are brilliantly written.

Further information about all our books and authors can be found on our website:

louisewaltersbooks.co.uk

FALLIBLE JUSTICE

Laura Laakso

*"I am running through the wilderness and the
wilderness runs through me."*

IN OLD LONDON, where
paranormal races co-exist
with ordinary humans,
criminal verdicts delivered
by the all-seeing Heralds of
Justice are infallible. After
a man is declared guilty of
murder and sentenced to
death, his daughter turns to
private investigator Yannia
Wilde to do the impossible
and prove the Heralds
wrong.

Yannia has escaped a
restrictive life in the Wild Folk conclave where she was
raised, but her origins mark her as an outsider in the city.
Those origins lend her the sensory abilities of all of nature. Yet Yannia is lonely and struggling to adapt to life
in the city. The case could be the break she needs. She

enlists the help of her only friend, a Bird Shaman named Karrion, and together they accept the challenge of proving a guilty man innocent.

So begins a breathless race against time and against all conceivable odds. Can Yannia and Karrion save a man who has been judged infallibly guilty?

This is fantasy at its most literary, thrilling best, and the first title in Laura's paranormal crime series Wilde Investigations. There is a wonderfully human element to Laura's writing, and her work is fantasy for readers who don't like fantasy (or think they don't!) and perfect, of course, for those who do.

Available in paperback, ebook, and audio.

ECHO MURDER

Laura Laakso

"I'm part of every bird I meet, and they are all within me."

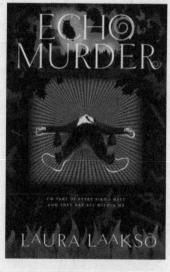

YANNIA WILDE RETURNS to
the Wild Folk conclave
where she grew up, and to
the deathbed of her father,
the conclave's Elderman.
She is soon drawn back
into the Wild Folk way of
life and into a turbulent
relationship with Dearon,
to whom she is betrothed.

Back in London, unas-
suming office worker Tim
Wedgebury is surprised
when police appear on his
doorstep with a story about how he was stabbed in the
West End. His body disappeared before the paramedics'
eyes. Given that Tim is alive and well, the police chalk
the first death up to a Mage prank. But when Tim "dies"
a second time, Detective Inspector Jamie Manning calls
Yannia and, torn between returning to the life she has
built in Old London and remaining loyal to the conclave

and to Dearon, she strikes a compromise with the Elderman that allows her to return temporarily to the city.

There she sets about solving the mystery of Tim's many deaths with the help of her apprentice, Karrion. They come to realise that with every death, more of the echo becomes reality, and Yannia and Karrion find themselves in increasing danger as they try to save Tim. Who is the echo murderer? What sinister game are they playing? And what do they truly want?

The second of Laura Laakso's Wilde Investigations series reveals more of her wonderful characters and their complexities and struggles, both personal and professional. The crucial human element that sets Laura's work apart really comes to the fore in this fabulous sequel.

Available in paperback, ebook, and audio.

DON'T THINK A SINGLE THOUGHT
Diana Cambridge

"Hello? Hello? Emma, is that you?
Emma! It's only me... Hello? Are you there, Emma?"

1960S NEW YORK: Emma Bowden seems to have it all - a glamorous Manhattan apartment, a loving husband, a successful writing career. But while on vacation at the Hamptons, a child drowns in the sea, and suspicion falls on Emma. As her picture-perfect life spirals out of control, old wounds resurface, dark secrets are revealed, and that persistent voice in Emma's head that won't leave her  alone threatens to destroy all that Emma has worked for... Taut, mesmerising and atmospheric, *Don't Think a Single Thought* is a novel of dreams and nightmares, joy and despair, love and hate. It lays bare a marriage, and a woman, and examines the decisions – and mistakes – which shape all of our lives.

311

Diana Cambridge's debut novel is beautifully written, and tackles big themes in few words. Sophisticated and refreshingly short, this is the perfect holiday or handbag book.

Published in paperback, ebook, and audio.

THE NASEBY HORSES
Dominic Brownlow

'I only know Charlotte is not dead. I feel it within me,
her heartbeat the echo of my own. She is with me still.
She is near. I have to save her,
for that is all in life I have ever been required to do.'

SEVENTEEN-YEAR-OLD Simon's sister Charlotte is missing. The lonely Fenland village the family recently moved to from London is odd, silent, and mysterious. Simon is epileptic and his seizures are increasing in severity, but when he discovers the local curse of the Naseby Horses, he is convinced it has something to do with Charlotte's disappearance. Despite resistance from the villagers,  the police, and his own family, Simon is determined to uncover the truth behind the curse, and rescue his sister.

Under the oppressive Fenland skies and in the heat of a relentless June, Simon's bond with Charlotte is fierce, all-consuming, and unbreakable; but can he save his adored sister? And does she want to be saved?

313

Drawing on philosophy, science, and the natural world, *The Naseby Horses* is a moving exploration of the bond between a brother and his sister; of love; and of the meaning of life itself.

Literary, but gripping and readable, this was the first Louise Walters Books hardback.

Published in hardback, paperback and ebook